G000075121

OUT OF THE BLUE

M.M. HARROLD

RED DOG
UK

Published by RED DOG PRESS 2022

Copyright © M.M.Harrold 2022

M.M. Harrold has asserted his right under the Copyright, Designs
and Patents Act, 1988 to be identified as the author of this work

This book is sold subject to the condition that it shall not by way of
trade or otherwise, be lent, resold, hired out, or otherwise circulated
without the publisher's prior consent in any form of binding or
cover other than that in which it is published and without a similar
condition including this condition being imposed on the
subsequent purchaser

First Edition

Hardback ISBN 978-1-915433-04-6
Paperback ISBN 978-1-915433-02-2
Ebook ISBN 978-1-915433-03-9

www.reddogpress.co.uk

To Sarah and Diego: my heart, and my home.

Blue

A primary color commonly associated with law enforcement; "the thin blue line"

The Blues

A melancholy music originating in the Deep South and deriving primarily from work songs and spirituals

PART I

THE NORTH MISSISSIPPI
HILL COUNTRY

1.

2008

AMANDA SMITH KILLED her husband in a state park at the stroke of midnight. A man she never saw heard the shots and called the law. Amanda stood frozen, her eyes locked on the prone body. She'd expected at least a twitch or two. Nothing. No movement. The sirens grew louder as blood pooled in the hard clay. She dropped the gun when brown-clad Sheriff's Deputies ordered her to. Flashlights lit up a face without tears. Neither Deputy knew her. Or the dead man at her feet. As she was handcuffed and folded into the back of a patrol car, she remained stoic. The Ford's blue lights whipped across the base of the tree line and reflected against the shallow dew from an unexpected downpour hours earlier.

The recently-deceased had been a hard-shell Baptist minister, the lead pastor of a church in Shaw, a small town thirty miles from Forrest Springs in the far corner of Slate County, Mississippi. A charismatic ambassador for Christ to a few; a cult leader to most. Newly ordained as a murder suspect herself, Amanda broke her silence as she was escorted into a cramped office. In a soft voice, she politely requested a phone call. The handcuffs were removed. She was led to a pale green desk phone, one step up from a rotary. Amanda dialed a lawyer's number from memory. Cherry Winter's law office on Main Street was closed. The call was forwarded.

A cell phone chirped in a white brick Tudor several blocks from the town square. The lawyer stirred from a restless sleep, opened the phone, and heard a woman she'd never met speaking in a robotic voice. Groggy, she glanced at the green block numbers glowing from the clock next to her bed. 2:06 a.m.

"I'm in jail. They say I killed my husband," snapped her awake.

The lawyer rallied quickly, not yet knowing who "they" was.

"Who is *they*?" Cherry asked.

"Forrest Springs police Sheriff's arrested me, but they brought me here."

"I'm on my way, don't say a word to anyone until I get there," she said as her feet hit the floor. "Anyone," she repeated and hung up. She stood and walked in the dark to her closet, flipped a light switch and squinted as the light from an exposed bulb assaulted her eyes. Her first murder case in three years; the last one really didn't count. News cameras were unlikely in Forrest Springs at any time, unfortunately, especially in the early hours of a Saturday morning. But Cherry still left her house in an oatmeal linen suit. She swiped on pale lip gloss as she walked out to the driveway barefoot, her Tori Burch flats were in her SUV. She caught green lights down Main Street and pulled into a visitor spot at the police precinct eighteen minutes after her new client's call. She walked in. There wasn't a cop in the place that didn't know her, and she was waved past the counter to a back office.

Detective Sam Browning sat across from Amanda Smith in a drab, windowless interview room. Two Styrofoam cups of lukewarm water and a plastic pitcher sat between them. Browning leaned back in his chair and chewed on an unlit cigar. He wore a short-sleeve shirt with a garish paisley tie. He pulled the cigar from his mouth as she opened the door and walked in. A younger man in a creased uniform stood with his back to the wall behind Browning. The younger man spoke first.

"Counselor, don't you hate it when a murderer rousts you from your bed at two a.m.? Hope it didn't wake up one of those perps of yours sleeping next to you."

Seven years earlier, Cherry had dated a former dope client for a couple of months. A Black former dope client. The white cops—and most of the Black ones—never let her forget it. And likely never would.

Browning looked over his shoulder, his jaw tightening, the cigar flattening. The younger man stared at him for a moment and then left.

I read about the murder the next day. I'd cut and cleared brush in my yard most of the morning and went for coffee around two. As I stepped into a small, eclectic bakery near the edge of the town Square, I spied the front page of THE SLATE COUNTY HERALD in a bin near the door.

"MINISTER SLAIN BY WIFE"

Under the definitive but somewhat premature headline were two pictures. One was a prim looking brunette standing with a taller man and two children dressed in loud Christmas sweaters. The other was a picture of a slightly younger Cherry Winter in front of a courthouse, perched behind a small podium, talking into a bouquet of microphones sporting the various station call signs and network logos.

Cherry was interviewed by Nancy Grace on Tuesday night and *In Session* the following day. She planted seeds about a sordid cult. And smiled. She offered more sizzle than steak and only enough steak to feed the 24/7 sensation machine that had turned the law into reality television and trials into sport. She wanted to keep it coming back and that meant giving it what it wanted. Quotes leading to more questions, not answers. The next week, the story was featured as a three-page photo and caption spread in PEOPLE magazine against a backdrop of southern religious intrigue and the hint of sex from a sexy defense attorney. Under pictures of Cherry, her client, the victim, his church and, of course, the children, it asked, "*Is Justice Blind, Blessed, or Blonde in the New South?*"

The case took on a life of its own. Her quotes became more memorable and outlandish. She swapped Tori Burch flats for Jimmy Choo stilettos and lip gloss for matte red tint. The case dominated the news and brought the national press to Forrest Springs in their droves. White news vans with bold letters parked at odd angles taking up every inch of the grassy lawn outside the courthouse and hoisted their antennas. Cherry's flamboyant façade procured extra face time with reporters. She rejected a number of reasonable plea deals from the D.A., sometimes not even taking them to her client, as her professional duty and the Canons of Ethics required. She flew to New York on Friday for an interview with Matt Lauer.

Hundreds of miles from The Big Apple, alone in a battered pleather recliner, I watched as the camera cut to Matt Lauer, who thanked Meredith and turned to "*the gripping drama that has captivated the nation, involving the murder of a controversial Baptist minister—leading to a string of unanswered questions involving mental, physical and sexual abuse by a man some in the small Mississippi town considered a messiah.*" He thanked Cherry for coming and she thanked him for having her. In response to his questions, she said almost nothing, but looked great saying it.

Two minutes and thirty-four seconds later, the camera panned to Al Roker, who was outside the studio trading quips with a bridge club of old women from Kansas before turning to the weather. It was going to be a beautiful day, hot and clear, in the mid-South, with only a single patch of scattered showers out of Arkansas.

2.

I WAS SURPRISED when Cherry called a few days later. I hadn't spoken with her since my first day in town. I was staining the rear deck of the old plantation house I'd inherited five weeks earlier. She must have gotten my number from the probate paperwork. She said she needed a break. Given the barrage of media coverage, it seemed like an understatement. I'd been following the case from my oversized shack. I suggested a quiet dinner at her place, given the still-shabby condition of my place, but she opted to go out. Tactically sound, she didn't really know me. We agreed to meet at a diner near her office.

I got to the Square early and watched as she walked down the sidewalk, phone glued to her ear, arguing, gesturing furiously with her hands. She folded her phone, slipped it into her oversized hobo purse and checked her lipstick in the side mirror of a car parked near the restaurant's door. An old man in overalls held the diner door for her. She thanked him sweetly. And smiled. His stare lingered on her as she walked through for a split second too long before letting the door slowly drift shut.

I stepped down out of my truck and walked to the diner. She was seated at a tall bar table. Clearly the center of attention, she didn't seem to mind. The men whispered about the case, the women about her outfit. The bar was covered in old license plates, toothpicks poked out from the ceiling and fans cut through the smoky air. Pure Americana. A TV over the bar was tuned to the Atlanta Braves game. I'd been a Braves fan for decades, even when they were perennial cellar-dwellers, but I'd lost interest in baseball. I watched football and boxing and was the rare soul in the South who favored the NFL over college football. In Atlanta, an architect friend who was an Ole Miss alum told me about The Grove, the *Walk of Champions* and the endless talent that lurked about in sun dresses and heels wholly unfit for soft grass or concrete and bleachers. It wasn't a top priority, but I planned to check that out at some point; Oxford wasn't that far away.

She waved to me, and I took a seat on the tall barstool next to her.

"Nice place," I said. We ignored the undercurrent of whispers. My presence fueled the stares.

"*Cody's* has been here for as long as I can remember; Old Man Cody died a few years back. His son was a couple of years ahead of me in school. He runs the place now." We each ordered a beer, and she ordered a plate of fried pickles for us to share. The menu was standard meat and three. The vegetable list included macaroni and cheese, cheese grits and most of the more traditional fried offerings: okra, zucchini, and mushrooms. My kind of place. Although there wasn't any seafood to speak of in North Mississippi, that didn't mean there wasn't fresh fish. Farm-raised catfish from just down the two-lane in Abbeville.

We made small talk. I had planned to avoid discussing the case. At least until the pickles arrived. Avoiding the case was more awkward than asking. People continued to stare. The beers arrived, followed by the pickles. She wrapped a napkin around her beer, took a long swig then took a pickle and dipped it in an unidentified sauce in a small bowl perched on the side of the plate.

She smiled when I asked casually, "So, how's work?" and kicked me playfully under the table. She parried with some info about the case, all of which I'd already heard on the news. I took a pickle and dipped it in the sauce. We talked about the house and the town. All she said about the case was that she hadn't slept more than two hours at a clip since the night the minister's wife called her. The sun cast gold and red shadows across the storefronts on The Square. We both ordered the catfish, followed by several more rounds of cold beer.

We stepped out of the diner onto the sidewalk and walked towards her car. She chirped the lock. The night shrouded her in darkness, but her eyes seemed to brighten. Alert. Prowling.

"I guess you'd better go home and try to get a good night's sleep," I said.

"Yeah," she said, stepping back up on the curb and looking at me. "I guess what I really need is something to tire me out."

Several hours later, I couldn't speak for her, but I was tired. Way, way too easy, I thought more than once. Her motives crossed my mind but, predictably, I decided to worry about them later. I never got the chance.

The next morning, I woke to the smell of coffee and the sound of her voice in the next room. I sat up in bed, spied the remote, arranged the pillows to support me and turned the TV on. A headache had arrived with the sun. I heard her give a curt goodbye. A minute later she entered the room with a mug of coffee wearing a T-shirt that reached her knees.

She handed me the mug and perched on the side of the bed. She glanced at the TV. She was probably hoping they were talking about the case. No mention. A pretty, blonde, fourteen-year-old, white girl from the Dallas suburbs was missing. She played the cello and loved her parents, her younger sister, and horses. A stern-looking sheriff in a green uniform and a cowboy hat was being interviewed. I thought absently of how many Black kids were missing in Atlanta at any given time without any media interest.

There were no pictures in the room. Not of her parents or siblings or a group of friends on some girls' weekend drinking margaritas. Not of a wedding party where she was the maid of honor. Not of her at her law school graduation. Nothing.

"You sure get quiet in the mornings," she said. I smiled at her and sipped.

"So, what's your day look like?" she asked.

"Dry wall," I said. "Just working on the house."

She looked at me and then looked down. Her eyes were wide, and she wasn't wearing makeup. It was like she was without her armor. She was completely vulnerable in just that T-shirt. No high heels, no designer suits.

"You know I like the fact that you don't know much about me… and I know nothing about you except that you are the kind of man who can just pick up and move from Atlanta to North Mississippi and live in a broke down mansion."

She was still looking down. She bit her thumbnail.

"You've seen me on TV, right?" she asked.

"Of course," I replied.

"Do you, you know, hear things about me around town?"

"Like?" I asked.

"Like, I don't know, about the cases I handle or about me and a certain former client." Her voice trailed off.

"You told me you do criminal defense, and I know about this one case because I've seen you on the TV news and read about it in the newspapers. But that's it."

She searched my face. I could tell she thought it was more complicated. Or maybe that it should be. She was tough.

"You tell me what you want me to know," I said. She looked relieved.

"You know there's stuff I can't tell you, client communications and all. There are other things I can tell you, but I need to know that you won't tell anyone else."

I took a sip of coffee. "I don't think I know anyone else."

She gave me a genuine smile, took the mug from me, and took a sip. She set it on the bedside table next to a clock under an ornate lamp. She lay down on the bed and rolled me on top of her. She had brushed her teeth, but I hadn't.

"I don't really know anyone else either," she said. "Or, at least, I haven't in a long time."

She wanted to know me just well enough to let the possibilities wash over her, but not so much that she'd discover something that would mean it couldn't work. She was a tough read. My take was that she justified shallow personal connections by telling herself that she had time for a husband and kids when her career went on autopilot. There's no such thing as plenty of time unless you are out of dreams. She wasn't. But she was hungry.

3.

WE DROVE AWAY from The Square for less than a mile, pulled into a gravel lot and parked between a Slate County Sheriff's Office cruiser and a Mississippi Highway Patrol interceptor near the door of a barnlike structure. "Duffy's" was painted on a large but faded wooden sign on the roof.

She left the windows down, the keys in the ignition.

"You're not going to take the keys?" I asked. "Or roll up the windows?"

"This isn't Atlanta. It'll be fine, come on, I'm hungry."

We walked in. There was the smell of bacon in the air. We sat in a booth.

A woman in a red T-shirt poured coffee.

"Thanks, Miss D.

"You're welcome, honey. You gonna remember the manners your mama taught you and introduce me to your beau, or do I have to embarrass you?"

"Too late," Cherry said, stifling a laugh. "I was fixin' to, and he's not my beau. He's Dan Stock, the new proprietor of Magnolia Ridge."

Miss D welcomed me to Forrest Springs, took our order and was gone. She took a pot of coffee from the orange tray she had set on the table behind us and poured cups for some loggers sitting near the front. At least they looked like loggers, what did I know?

"The house has a name?" I asked. "You never mentioned it."

"Of course, all good Southern homes do. Yours has been called Magnolia Ridge for as long as I can remember, probably as long as anyone around these parts can remember. The history of the name escapes me."

The cops were sitting in the booth directly across from ours. The Sheriff's Deputy was fat. The Trooper was in shape with a thick neck. They looked up once or twice before focusing on us. Cherry nodded to them. They left before us but didn't stop to speak.

"Fan club?" I asked, as they walked out the door without paying and pulled their cars out onto the road, fast and in opposite directions.

"I'm a criminal defense attorney. Most cops don't love me, you know that, but..." Her voice trailed off.

"But?" I asked.

"Well, the Deputy—the large guy in brown, was my high school boyfriend. First love, first whatever, prom date... all that stuff."

"Interesting," I said, raising my eyebrows. Large was being kind. "Weren't you a little out of his league?" I took a sip of coffee.

"He wasn't fat back then. Played linebacker in high school. He was a big deal around here." She looked down, buttered a biscuit, and ran a knife with strawberry jam across the top.

"You must have been a big deal around here, too," I said. She looked up and smiled, this time without teeth, taking the compliment gracefully. She had a lot of experience accepting compliments. Not as much lately, though, it seemed.

"It's been a long time since I talked to anyone who doesn't already know everything about me," she said.

It's been a long time since I sat in a restaurant without a gun, I thought. We ate and then Cherry drove me back to The Square to my truck. She dropped me off and told me to call her later; she was late for an appointment. As she pulled away, I could see the vanity plate on her Mercedes SUV: Mississippi tag—2XJPRD—Slate County. I backtracked through a maze of backroads to my tattered estate.

I unpacked for a couple of hours, intermittently refilling my Duffy's to-go cup with whiskey. There was a lean-to shed behind the house that was wired for electricity. I took a pair of bolt cutters and snapped off a rusty combination lock. It would do. Three hours later, after clearing the cobwebs, and hammering down stray nails, I carried my rifles and shotguns into the shed. I'd pick up a new lock later.

I heard a car and turned see a green and white sheriff's unit rolling slowly towards the house. I stepped back into the shed and grabbed a long rifle with a scope. I walked about ten feet, stood behind a tree and aimed the rifle at the car which had stopped just beyond one of the curves in the driveway. I closed one eye and trained the other through the scope. Two men sat in the Ford Crown Victoria. The deputy from the diner was in the driver's seat in his brown uniform. The other man was thin, with a hawkish nose and a receding hairline. He wore a white shirt instead of brown like the road and court deputies wore. That usually meant a boss. I watched them watch my house. After a few minutes, the car backed down the driveway to the road and drove away.

I drove to a local co-op for supplies and spent the rest of the day nailing loose shingles on the roof. The sheriff's cruiser drove by twice that afternoon. The car slowed each time but didn't stop.

4.

THE HOUSE WAS coming along. Slowly. The small armory in the shed was operational. I had installed a keypad lock on the interior door. The drywall took a week, the painting another, and the yard and grounds would be a work in progress. I replaced the appliances and retiled the kitchen.

I saw Cherry a handful of times during the weeks that followed. She was exhausted, only in small part because of me. Although they hadn't found the missing girl in Texas, media interest in Cherry's case had piqued once again as more details about the minister's congregation had come to light. She spent half of her time giving interviews, the other half in back-room, off-the-record negotiations with the local DA. Originally, she had planned to push for a speedy trial, but no longer. The more time the press had to uncover the seedy facts about the congregation and the victim, the better. Nancy Grace featured the case twice more and mentioned it almost daily. The minister was emerging as a David Koresh type figure. Allegations of relations with young girls, polygamy, and amphetamine fueled all-night sermons about Armageddon were followed closely by the small community, some of whom would ultimately be in the jury pool. And the county prosecutor knew it. Cherry would assert a classic defense in Mississippi: *He needed killin'*.

The sex was great. The nights were restless; both of us were used to having the center of the bed. A month to the day from our first night together, I deemed Magnolia Ridge worthy of company. We sat on the back porch on wicker chairs under a newly installed fan.

We pulled from cold bottles of beer and ate pizza. The night was unusually cool for July, the mosquitoes unusually merciful.

Cherry hadn't planned on staying over and had nothing to sleep in. She was already upstairs in my bedroom. I heard the television. I grabbed the last two bottles and the pizza box; there were two slices left and the crust bones. The bedroom was spacious, but not as large as the vaulted ceiling and eight-foot-high windows made it appear. There was a fireplace. Original. The tile was sand-colored and slick. The walk-in closet off the bathroom had been a butler's den. Inside was an extra bureau of drawers, a floor safe and the other items one would expect to find in a closet. Next to the safe was a cardboard box.

I didn't see her when I walked into the bedroom. Some of her clothes were piled on the floor next to her boots. I glanced into the bathroom and from the mirror that covered one wall, I could see her standing facing the bureau with the top drawer open. She wasn't snooping, just looking for a T-shirt to go with the pair of shorts she was already wearing. She pulled one of my old favorites over her head and shut the door to the bathroom. A few minutes later, I heard the toilet flush and the sink run. She turned off the water and stepped into the bedroom, past the fireplace. She hung her bra over the back of a chair and crawled into bed.

I slept better than usual. The paranoia I'd developed on the street was fading. Slowly.

I felt something tighten on my wrist. Metal. I opened my eyes. She was kneeling on the bed, staring at me. She was holding the other handcuff in her fist. She pulled at it. Gently.

She was wearing a sweatshirt with an embroidered Atlanta Police Department Emerald Society logo. She had laid out a small collection of items on the bed. There was a badge case next to a gold badge. Most cops have more than one badge. One is for the uniform and has the clasp. The other is flat-backed and is kept in a leather case for off-duty. When I left the department, they only asked for one, so I gave them the one from my uniform and kept the other, which I'd paid for out of pocket anyway. She had opened the case revealing my

ID with a much younger picture of me, taken while I was in the academy and the numbered silver patrolman's badge. The unnumbered gold badge was the one I received when I worked the Olympics in '96. We only wore it during the Olympics. It wasn't in a case. My *Red Dog* coin was in a small box she had opened. I saw the seal and the words: *Speed. Stealth. Strength.* I took it out and flipped it over. I read the acronym: *"Run Every Drug Dealer Out of Georgia."*

My mind raced the way a mind does when you know you haven't lied but must employ creative arithmetic to form a cluster of half-truths into a whole explanation. Cherry had finally asked me what I did for a living in Atlanta, and I'd told her that I had worked for a towing and repossession company. This was a half-truth, like telling a new widow that her husband was lying down in the other room. It was the job I had done for about nine months while I waited for the police department to process my application.

She smiled. Curious. "I went to get a sweatshirt, opened a box on top of the safe, which is another conversation, and found this. Do I need to put the other handcuff on you or are you going to tell the truth?"

"Like a magic lasso of truth," I asked.

Her eyes brightened and her smile widened.

"Something like that, but if you don't have any rope handy, I think handcuffs will do."

She tugged at the cuff on my wrist again. She wasn't mad; almost playful. I told her my story. She dropped the cuff, crossed her legs, and listened. An hour later she slipped out of the sweatshirt and dropped it on the floor. She dressed, told me she would call later and left. I walked to the dresser, found a handcuff key, unlocked the cuff from my wrist and took a shower. I called her around four and then again around seven. No answer. I left a message on the first call but not the second. She had always called when she said she would. I was surprised I hadn't heard from her and called her four times between nine and eleven-thirty.

I waited until midnight to drive over to her house. As I turned a corner, blue light spit against house windows and careened off the painted metal of the parked cars on the tree-lined street. The source of the lights was not a mystery to be solved. Police.

5.

AN AWKWARD MAN with liver spots and an old Springer Spaniel named Toby had found her. She was in her car. The car was parked in her driveway. She had been shot twice. The car doors were locked, and the rear window of the SUV was splintered but intact; the film of tint held it upright. Her bloody scalp was slumped against the driver's side window. Blood streaked down the inside of the window glass. A clean shot. A trained shooter.

A crowd of onlookers clamored up near a cluster of deputies who were doing a half-assed job of holding them back. I parked as close as I could on the curb beside a large tree. I had my window open, and I could hear snippets of conversation. Toby's owner was holding court with a small throng of locals. I watched as they took the body out of the car and placed it onto a rolling gurney. Seemed quick to move the body.

Cherry was covered with a starched sheet. A black Dodge van with white stenciled letters on the door indicating *Slate County Coroner's Office* followed a sheriff's cruiser presumably en route to the county morgue.

I watched from my truck as the vehicles drove away. The house and part of the yard was cordoned off with yellow crime scene tape, but there were still too many people milling around the scene inside the porous perimeter. I saw the white-shirted man I had learned was the Sheriff talking to a blonde man wearing a seersucker suit and a bowler hat. I knew he was blonde because he removed his hat as the gurney rolled past him on the crushed stone walkway leading from the house. He held it to his heart. At best a gentleman, at worst, and much more likely, a politician. Under the suit he wore a light, powder blue shirt and a broad pink tie with a perfect knot. He walked up to a thin man with an athletic build in a brown suit who wasn't wearing a tie. A gold badge hung from the man's neck. He was holding a notebook. Detective. I watched him for a few minutes as he took notes and listened to the man with the tie. The detective reached into the inside pocket of his coat to pull out a pair of rubber gloves. As he did, I could see the wooden grip of an old-school, snub-nosed .38 tucked into a paddle holster. The detective wore it cross-draw fashion. He put the gloves on and knelt next to the car, taking the crime scene in at different angles. I made a mental note to find out who the men were. Then I drove home.

A few hours later, I awoke to a single loud knock followed by another and then a more rapid pounding. I sat on the edge of the bed and tried to focus on the clock on the bedside table. My view was obscured by a bottle of Eagle Rare bourbon and two pill bottles. I stood. I could see over the bourbon. Just shy of four a.m. The hammering continued. I slipped on shorts and a T-shirt, went downstairs, and opened the door. The fat deputy and the detective I'd seen the night before were standing on my porch. The detective looked more harried than the first time I saw him. He looked like he'd been up all night. Which, of course, he had. He wasn't wearing the suit jacket and his sleeves were rolled up. The badge that had been hanging around his neck was now clipped to his belt.

"Mr Stock, sorry to wake you," the detective said in a smooth voice. "I'm Sam Browning, Chief of Detectives for the local PD. I'd like to ask you a few questions."

I glanced past him and saw four more deputies and a gaggle of town cops standing idly in my yard. I glanced back to the fat, boorish deputy. "Chief" of Detectives... how many could there be, I thought. I sensed that Browning would rather not have the deputy with him, but since I was probably a murder suspect I figured they weren't taking any chances.

"Mind if we come inside?" Browning asked.

I didn't answer, just stepped back inside through the door I'd left open. As I took another step, I heard Browning ask, "Mind if we frisk you for weapons?" If Browning meant it as a question, it was a rhetorical one to the deputy. He stopped me by putting a meaty hand on my shoulder and gave me a rough pat down.

"Really?" I asked after he pushed me a couple of inches away from him with a light shove when he had finished. "I just got out of bed."

The deputy looked like he wanted to give me another shove. He sneered through flushed, fleshy cheeks.

"Can we sit down?" Browning asked, shooting a glance at the fat deputy.

I walked towards the kitchen to a wooden butcher's block table. I sat and Browning chose a seat across from me. The deputy leaned on the counter.

"You going to read me my rights?" I asked.

"We're not there yet, Mr Stock. We're still in the *preliminary* stages of our investigation." The word *preliminary* seemed to stretch Browning's southern accent to its outer edges. "As you can imagine, it isn't often we have a murder in Forrest Springs." Browning looked at me. What he meant, of course, was that there weren't usually murders in Forrest Springs unless there were newcomers.

My mind raced. Usually, I'd talk to cops. I hadn't done anything wrong, but sometimes that doesn't matter. In their minds, they had PC. Probable Cause. Not the type we learned about in the police academy or the kind the lawyers talked about in court. Their PC was that I wasn't from Slate County, or even Mississippi. I was new. Unknown in a town where everyone had been accounted for long ago. And they'd seen me with her.

After a few minutes, they realized that I wasn't going to tell them anything and the circus retreated. Two agencies and probably half the on-duty cops in the whole county at 4 a.m.? A show of force; the emphasis on "show." I needed a lawyer. The only person I'd gotten to know in Forrest Springs in the past five weeks was a lawyer. Unfortunately, she was dead.

Browning thanked me for my time on the way out, apologized for stopping by so early, or late, and shook my hand. He seemed like a good cop, maybe he'd been on the job somewhere else before coming to Forrest Springs. The deputy told me not to leave the county in a strained, threatening voice. Like he just had to say something on the way out. Fat-ass had been watching too many TV shows; I'd go wherever the hell I wanted.

"Screw you," I said. I slammed the door and it ricocheted in the jamb. Through the peephole, I could see him turn back. His jaw was tight; his face flushed as he stared at the door. Browning reached out and grabbed the fat man's elbow. I could hear him say something but couldn't make out the words. The deputy turned and headed towards the patrol cars.

I took a couple of pills and stood at the window, sipping slow on a glass of bourbon. I thought about Cherry for a while. I poured another glass of bourbon and thought about myself.

6.

I SLEPT FOR a few hours, woke up and pushed a button on the TV remote. I picked up an odd collection of local stations through my satellite service. I flipped to the NBC affiliate out of Tupelo to watch the early news. A woman with smoldering eyes and hair so black it was almost blue sat next to an older man with silver hair, a cracked chin and a large Adam's apple. A small box with a silhouette body with a chalk-line around it and the words "MURDER" appeared over her shoulder.

"A well-known and sometimes controversial criminal defense attorney was found murdered last night in the driveway of her Forrest Springs home." She went on to give a bare-bones recital of what the police had released in a written statement and a short interview clip with the lead detective—Sam Browning—the same one who had been at my house a few hours earlier. I watched another quarter-hour of news as I waited for coffee to brew. I spiked it with bourbon.

I pulled a pair of boots on and walked out to the shed. I entered the code on the keypad and stepped into the side room. I flipped a light switch. The fluorescent light I had installed began to hum as the long cylinder bulbs came to life. I scanned the wooden wall lined with rifles and shotguns. The pistols were stored in blue plastic boxes stacked on a workbench. Ammunition was in deep bin drawers on each side of the bench. I walked out to the driveway, drank coffee, and waited for my new car.

A few days earlier, I had bought a 1971 Plymouth Duster from an old woman whose husband died three years earlier in a hunting accident. I saw an ad in one of the newspapers covering Cherry's case. She wanted about a quarter of what it was worth. I paid her twice what she was asking. Cash. The same kid who had brought me back from the truck rental place my first day in town had agreed to tow it over. He arrived ten minutes early. He was a pale white kid with a sleeveless *Elvis Festival* T-shirt, work gloves and a fading "Dixie Forever" tattoo. He still reeked of the same dank odor. He was still spitting Skoal-juice into a plastic Dr. Pepper bottle. He unloaded the Duster. The key was in it. I reached through the open window and turned it. The car cranked, missed once and then roared to life. It backfired twice. The hood rattled under the cotter-pins holding it down. It spit dark exhaust fumes. It had a hood-scoop that was trimmed with rust. Stuffing seeped out of the seats. Its previous owner had kept it under a green tarp for three years. All things considered, it was in pretty good shape. I reached back in and turned the key. I'd driven one a few years earlier. The car would idle up hills. The kid left. The air cleared.

I pulled the cotter-pins out and raised the hood. I set my coffee on the roof and planned the Duster's resurrection. The rest of the pot of coffee and what was left from the half-empty bourbon bottle later, I showered. I and drove into town after tucking a .38 Smith & Wesson K-frame into my boot.

I stopped at Duffy's and got a seat at the counter. A couple of State Troopers were seated in a booth. No sign of the fat deputy. I was sick of the local news. A rusty-looking guy in a tall John Deere hat had left a USA TODAY. I scanned the front page of the colorful paper. The story of Cherry's murder was on the Associated Press wire.

I ate pancakes topped with butter, drenched in syrup, and framed with sausage links and grits and drank black coffee for an hour. Out of habit, I reached down a couple of times to my ankle and felt the grip of the gun. One of the Troopers walked out. The other one was talking on his phone when his colleague left. Ten minutes later, Miss

D. was refilling my coffee when the fat deputy strode in, his uniform wrinkled and his belly hanging over his belt. He sat in the booth across from the remaining Trooper. I could feel the men glaring at me. I glanced over my shoulder at him once. His eyes were deep-set, and I still couldn't tell if they were foolish or sly. Either way, the eyes of a dangerous man. Or a desperate one. I ordered another stack of pancakes and picked up the SPORTS section.

Later, I drove from Duffy's to the NAPA auto parts store and bought parts for the Duster. When I came out, I saw the deputy parked across the street in a dirt lot next to a bank. His deep-set eyes were covered by mirrored aviator sunglasses. As far as I could tell, he didn't follow me home.

I brewed a pot of coffee and pulled another bottle of Eagle Rare bourbon from the cabinet next to the stove. I worked on the Duster most of the afternoon, took a one-hour nap and awoke at five o'clock.

On the TV in the bedroom, a different anchor—a light-skinned Black girl—led the broadcast with "Breaking News." A young man in an NBC NEWS windbreaker stood in the rain in front of a long, windowless cement building. He reported that Amanda Smith had been found dead in her solitary cell at the Savannah Creek Correctional Facility, a privately-owned lockup on the opposite side of the county. The man said that according to police, Smith had been found two hours earlier in her cell. Although the cause of death had not been officially determined, early reports indicated that Smith had intentionally overdosed on prescription medication. A press conference was scheduled for ten the following morning. Give them a chance to get a story together for the national media, I thought.

I stretched out on the bed and waited for it to get dark. I thought about calling an old friend, decided against it, and fell asleep watching a *Hogan's Heroes* rerun. Like Sergeant Schultz, I was beginning to believe I knew nothing.

I woke up three hours later, took a shower, dressed in dark clothes, strapped the gun on my ankle and drove to a Taco Bell in front of a Walmart wedged in between a Captain D's and El

Charro—a generic yet "Authentic" Mexican Restaurant. It was several hours past dusk. I got a couple of burritos and chicken tacos at the drive-thru and washed them down with a Diet Coke. Dusk had turned into a dark, moonless night.

I drove by Cherry's house. There was a sheriff's car parked on the curb. The crime scene tape was gone. I didn't stop. The house was still off limits. I drove downtown and parked in the alley on the north side of Cherry's office behind a dumpster. There was a side door. As expected, no alarm. The lock was easy to pick and in less than two minutes, I was inside.

I walked past the conference room where I'd signed the inheritance paperwork for the house. Her office was in a back corner. I doubted anyone would be able to see the overhead light from the street, but I left it as dark as possible. I took a small flashlight from my pocket. Her desk was neat and free of clutter. Nothing personal. On top of an expensive desk-pad was a single file folder with "SMITH, Amanda" typed onto a small label on the side tab.

I opened the folder. Inside were three stapled pages, a copy of the police report. Four bankers' boxes with the same name in Sharpie were stacked next to the desk to the side of an empty trashcan. I opened the first. Empty. The remaining three were empty as well. Who folds and marks four boxes before the first one is even needed? Implausible. The file on the desk was at a careful right angle. There was a clean, sterile smell. Lemon scent. This could be a trap, I thought. Three large grey file cabinets lined one of the walls. They were divided alphabetically and, surprisingly, at least to me, unlocked. I opened the one on the right: Q-Z. As expected, it was meticulously organized. My file was in its place between files marked with the names "Simmons" and "Stramm." There were two folders inside the larger file. I pulled the first out and held it open. Tucked and folded into a brown envelope was the Magnolia Ridge inheritance paperwork I had signed at Cherry's office. She didn't usually do estate work but had been friends with a great-uncle I'd never known, or even heard of. She did it for free. As much I as liked getting free legal work and jumping into bed after an early dinner on a first date, she had been killed before I'd had a chance to really delve into her motives.

The second folder had the initials "V.S." These initials meant nothing to me. Yet. I opened it. There were two holes punched at the top and scrapes in the brown paper that indicated that a metal clasp had previously held paper inside. But it was empty. I pushed the file back in between the others. There was no reason to take it. Shutting the drawer, I heard it click. I backtracked to my truck and pulled out onto a deserted Main Street.

7.

IT WASN'T COMPLETELY deserted. As I turned and crossed over the railroad tracks, a dark vehicle pulled out from behind a parked car. The driver waited a couple of car-lengths before turning the headlights on. It looked like a van. I figured he wanted me to get over the tracks so I wouldn't see where he'd been parked. I drove over the tracks and took a small side street that ran alongside a local Christian radio station and a feed store. I could see as the vehicle crossed over the tracks. I was right; it was a van. Dark blue or black. There was some type of lettering on it. It stayed with me, but didn't gain, even though I wasn't going that fast. It was following, not chasing. I reached down and pulled the .38 from the holster. Easy to carry, but it only had five shots. The barrel wasn't even three inches. Even with the hollow-point ammo, I'd have to wait until someone was close to shoot at them. It didn't come to that. I pulled into a SONIC Drive-In and the van passed. I ordered an oversized Route 44 Diet Coke. A blonde, waif girl with big hair brought it to me. I sipped at it and watched two high school girls flirt with a long-haired man in a yellow pickup truck. I went home.

8.

MY ONLY FRIEND in town was gone; her most famous client was in the morgue. Death loomed in the humid air. I didn't feel like waxing poetic about it, but I'd been in a slow-motion of sorts since I'd learned about Cherry. I didn't feel like sleeping. When someone you care about dies, you don't sleep. You pass out, maybe, but you don't sleep. I had cared about Cherry as much as any woman I'd ever known. Except one. I had loved the idea of the possibility of a life together with Cherry. A future. A promise beyond a tattered house in a bland town. I didn't love either of their mothers, but I loved my children. And, just like the kids, I knew I wouldn't miss Cherry for long. It wasn't in my nature. I could be alone without being lonely. I missed my job. My identity. And, sometimes, a 'her' from my past.

I'd been run out of Atlanta. There was a reason to leave; the question now, being in the crosshairs of the power base of this nasty little town, people who appeared willing to kill me: was there a reason to stay?

The logical thing to do would be to leave. Now.

Then I remembered back to my earliest days as a cop. It quickly became clear there were two types of cases where the arrest was easy but the prosecution usually pointless: bodega shoplifters and domestics. Why people ever shoplift at chain stores is beyond me. Their security guards come to court. Hit mom-and-pop bodegas. The owner usually works the place open to close and there's no way he's going to close the place to go to court and wait a few hours to testify about a stolen Malt Liquor and a few bags of potato chips.

Then there's domestics. Usually, she wants him out for the night more than she wants him arrested and in jail. Or, even if she wants him arrested late at night by morning's early light the love—or at least co-dependency—has been rekindled. Or the first of the month is coming and she needs his check or stamps to care for her kids or get her a fix. She won't come to testify. Maybe she'll accept a protective order but then she invites him back in. Never run the victim in a domestic through the system. Half the time she'll come back with a bench warrant or two for failure to appear in court from the last time you locked him up. But you don't want to have to arrest her because then you must deal with Child Protective Services which means hours of waiting. You can't leave all the kids with him. They're all hers but they're not all his.

But that doesn't mean it's the woman's fault. Almost never. Nothing grates at a beat cop's soul more than hopeless domestic situations. Women. Trapped. 'Just leave,' sounds easy but in the real world, it's near impossible. But the law is the law. A badge gives you a lot of authority but few options.

When they stripped my badge, they took away my authority but expanded my options. Now, I was going to do what I always wanted to do on those calls.

Where the law ends, justice begins.

Too much thinking. Whatever I was going to do, I wasn't going to start tonight. I needed a friend. If I couldn't get that, then I needed a place where I could have a chance at desperate trim and cold beer. Maybe just cold beer. I hadn't been to a bar since I'd moved to Forrest Springs, but I had heard of a place from a guy I'd talked to at Duffy's. Seemed like a good guy. A guy like that didn't know much about anything, but he knew everything about one thing. His town.

The blues lived and breathed deep in the Mississippi Delta, some ninety miles due west of Forrest Springs. North Mississippi Hill Country Blues had a shallower breath than its Delta cousin, but an equally deep soul. The place was called The Rust Club, and it sat on a one-lane cracked asphalt strip off a two-lane road. It was squat and wooden. Stairs crept up the right side of the building to a clapboard door. Blinking Christmas lights hung across the façade and dipped down where the roof sloped. Oddly angled white painted signs adorned the building.

I walked in. A heavyset Black guy with dark sunglasses and a black mesh ball-cap with "FROG" written across the brim in green letters sat on a stool. He held up his palm, fingers outstretched.

"Five," he growled in a deep voice. Dollars I assumed.

I handed him a well-worn bill and walked past. The place wasn't crowded, but it wasn't empty. Two Black women, one fat and one skinny, both in bright dresses, danced between the tables in front of the jukebox. A small window was cut into a wooden door between the main room and the kitchen. The beer list wasn't complicated. Painted by hand in red:

Light – $3.00

Heavy–$3.00

Budweiser Only

Get Over It—No Bitching

I peeled a five from the money in my pocket and handed it to the man standing on the other side of the door.

"Heavy," I said. He nodded.

"Thanks, have fun," he said in a voice almost as deep as the man at the door. He handed me a 32-ounce plastic bottle of Budweiser and two singles. I threw one of them in a plastic pitcher with "Bail Money" written across the front. I walked in the direction of the jukebox and sat at the last table under a poster for an R.L. Burnside show back in the mid-eighties. There was nobody else at the plastic picnic table. I twisted the cap off my beer, took a swig and sat down.

I watched as people danced and listened to the music for the next four hours. I got up three times. Twice for beer, once to piss in a splashy metal trough in a cramped bathroom. I had a slight buzz. It came on more slowly with beer than bourbon. The difference between low tide and crashing waves. I was ready for another piss and another beer. The place was filling up. Still, nobody had sat down at my table. Or talked to me.

She walked in just as I stood up to leave. I sat back down. Petite with lean curves and smooth skin, she started to dance slowly, her hands wandered up her sides and down her hips. Moves like liquid metal. She danced for a song and went for a beer. I watched her and as expected, the man in the kitchen didn't charge her. Bud Light. She placed her hand on top of his as she took the bottle and smiled for him before moving away, back towards the dance floor. Seeing me watching her, she drained her beer likely for courage, waited two songs and then shimmied over. She sat down, put her elbows on the table and leaned towards me.

"I don't know you," she said in a purring voice. "And I know almost everyone who comes here."

"Almost?" I asked. She smiled at me, and I smiled back. She drained her beer.

"Buy me a drink," she said.

"You don't pay for your drinks," I said.

"Buy me one anyway," she said.

"And you'll wait here?" I asked, standing up.

"I'll wait," she said. I walked towards the kitchen.

The place was filling up; there were three people ahead of me

"One heavy, one light," I said when I got to the window. I paid. The man gave me my change. I tossed another single in the tip jar and turned back to the table. She had kept her promise. I saw her wave to someone across the room. We drank the beers, walked outside for her to smoke a cigarette, and ended up in my truck.

She lit another cigarette and held it in her right hand. It shook slightly. She took a couple of forced puffs and turned towards me, resting her hand above the knee of my jeans. I brushed it away. She began to cry. The drags on her cigarette and her advances had been forced. Deliberate. The tears were not. In the bar, she had looked college-aged, though certainly not enrolled anywhere. The tears made her look younger as her makeup began to dam below her eyes. Dark streaks escaped and ran down her cheeks. Snippets of a story about a man beating her if she came back empty-handed emerged. The fear seemed genuine, the story rehearsed.

"How much?" I asked.

She looked confused but stopped crying. "For what?"

"For nothing," I said. "What were you expecting?"

"That depends on what *you* were expecting, but I usually get fifty, more in the rooms than in the trucks, less at this place than at Cowboyz. I only come here Thursday nights."

I looked at her arms. No tracks. She didn't seem to be hooking because she was hooked. She didn't appear to be jones'ing. Even the cigarettes seemed like a prop. An excuse to get outside the bar.

"What do you make in a night?" I asked.

"That depends," she said again. "On the place. On the night. Less than a hundred and I get hit." She said it matter-of-factly. Resigned. As the awkward minutes passed, the story seemed more real. And she looked even younger.

'Not my problem,' I told myself, as I handed her three twenties. She didn't look me in the eye when she reached for them. I gave her two more.

"What's this for?" she asked.

"A night off," I said. She looked up and tried to smile. Her teeth were white. And straight. She hadn't grown up on the street. Most likely a runaway. She opened the door and stepped down out of the truck.

She answered a question I hadn't asked and told me her name was "Tasha." She said it as if she'd only been using the name for a few months. Or weeks. Or days. Or hours. She walked back inside. I drove home.

As I drove, I thought about how often I'd used money on the street to solve the problems I'd found, or at least put them on hold for another day. Almost every cop I knew had paid for a cheap hotel room for someone for a night or two after a nasty domestic, bought a Greyhound ticket to get a woman with fresh black eyes down to stay with her sister in Savannah or a cousin in New Orleans, bought diapers or shoes. More often, money bought information.

Confidential Informants, or CIs, weren't usually the nosey altruistic upstairs neighbor you see on TV looking out the window at all hours, they wanted either money or a break on some charge. Cops traded a lesser charge on one perp for a more serious one on another. It was basically an on-the-street plea bargain between perps and cops instead of perps and prosecutors. It's smoother without the lawyers.

A protective order was a piece of paper; money could buy distance and time and sometimes that's what it took. On the street, I'd done what I could with what I had. Which hadn't been much at the time. If I ever had more money, I'd do more.

A Meatloaf song on the radio pulled me out of my thoughts. I focused on the road in front of me, one of the seemingly endless flat roads cut into the cotton fields. I thought about what I would—or wouldn't—do for love. If I ever found it again.

9.

LIKE THE HOUSE, the Duster was coming along. Slowly. The carburetor was sticking. I was under the hood, almost to my shoulders. I didn't hear the car pull up the driveway until it had almost stopped. I saw the headlights extinguish. I killed the engine. A woman I hadn't seen since my first day in town stepped out. Cherry's receptionist. Victoria Speer.

A dark-haired woman in her early twenties, Cherry had told me that she worked the hostess desk at an upscale restaurant in Memphis on the weekends. She stepped away from her car and walked towards me. As her silhouette emerged from the darkness, I could see her features take shape from the shadows. Long legs. Tight jeans. Leather boots. She gave me a forced smile, unlike the one in Cherry's office weeks earlier.

She stopped. "Mr Stock," she said and began to introduce herself.

"I remember you, Ms. Speer."

She seemed relieved.

"Your visit is a nice surprise. Would you like a drink?" I asked.

"It isn't a social visit, but I'll still take a drink," she said.

I noticed for the first time that she was holding a small leather attaché case, gripped in nails as groomed and polished as Cherry's had been. We walked up onto the porch; she sat down in a rocking chair and placed the case on a wicker ottoman.

"Beer, bourbon, both? All I've got. I'm assuming a drink means alcohol?"

"Good assumption," she said. "Beer." Her drawl was intact, but her voice was drained and hollow.

I went inside and grabbed two beers. I brought along a bottle of bourbon and two shot glasses just in case. Her voice sounded like it needed more than light beer. I twisted the caps off and handed her one of bottles. I set my bottle and shot glasses on the worn wood next to my rocker and sat down.

"What brings you to Magnolia Ridge, Ms. Speer?"

She glanced around. "Well, it's such a fine example of an old southern plantation home Mr Stock, I couldn't resist." She smiled, genuine this time. "But from Cherry's description, I have to admit it looks a lot better than I thought it would. Better than that old car." She was flirting. Sort of.

"What really brings you out this way, wrong turn?" I asked.

"Unlikely, Mr Stock. I've lived in Forrest Springs my whole life, except for two years at the University of Georgia."

"Just two, what happened?"

"Nothing *happened*," she feigned offense, "I graduated, just spent the first two years at junior college, lived at home.

"Doesn't mean it won't end up being a wrong turn, though, so to speak," I said. She smiled. Coy.

"Really, what brings you out?" I asked again. She motioned for the bourbon silently as she took a last, long swig of her beer. She picked up the case and put it in her lap. I poured two shots and offered her one. She unzipped the case and handed me a thick file before taking the shot glass.

"Cherry told me to give this to you if anything happened to her," Victoria said.

"When?" I asked.

"The day before her body was found," she said, taking a long sip of the whiskey.

We drank two more shots and two more beers while I scanned. There was no name on the side tab. It was the Amanda Smith defense file. The real one. The moon slid behind charcoal clouds. The porch fans crept around. Okay on whiskey but low on beer, I stepped back inside and turned on some music. Too loud in the house, it was just right on the porch. I stepped back out, handed her another beer, and sat back down. Victoria watched me. She was getting drunk on purpose and knew she couldn't drive home. She was beautiful, and it was late. And she was scared.

I had three spare bedrooms without beds. I woke up on my couch downstairs. I had overcooked Victoria and allowed two beers and two shots too many. I had carried her up the winding steps to the bedroom and placed her in the bed. For some reason neither of us understood the next morning, I'd taken off her watch and set it on a table near the bed.

She walked downstairs just before six, her hair and eyes sleepy. I opened my eyes as she softly wished me good morning. She placed an earring into her right ear. We drank coffee and exchanged cell phone numbers. She said she had to look for a new job, but she'd call or stop by later. Either was fine. I walked her to the door. I heard her say that it looked like rain right before I closed it.

I listened as her car engine faded as I poured a second cup of coffee, this one spiked with bourbon. I didn't notice she'd left the files on top of the made bed until I came out of the shower. I sat in a towel on the edge of the bed, listened to the rain outside and studied the files. Three hours later, I dressed and headed to Duffy's for breakfast.

10.

DUFFY'S WAS ALWAYS either packed or empty. The only constants were grease and cops. The pancakes were as fluffy as the coffee was bland. At least it was hot. As I drank a cup and waited for my pancakes, I saw two familiar faces. The fat deputy and one of the men I had seen the night they'd found Cherry's body. The man with the seersucker. Same powder blue shirt and bowler. This time the tie with the perfect knot was light purple. I glanced up at them. The dapper gentleman said something to the fat man, who craned the rolls on his neck to turn and glare. I stared back for a second and then looked over them, out the large front window, and rested my eyes on the van I had seen the night I'd broken into a dead lawyer's office. The one that had followed me.

I realized I had seen it twice before. The first time was the same night I'd first seen the dapper man. The night they found Cherry's body. I saw the white letters across the body of the van and the Slate County seal stenciled on the driver's side door. "Slate County Coroner's Office." The window of the diner was slightly tinted and with the sun's glare, I almost didn't realize that someone was sitting in the driver's seat talking on the phone. He stepped out right as I was about to turn back to my pancakes that were just arriving. He had the tensile strength of a farmer. Faded tattoos littered tight, vein-ridden arms. The tattoos were likely either from prison or time in the military. Or both. He walked in and sat with the fat man and the dapper man. He handed the dapper man a newspaper.

The older of the two waitresses filled my mug and I sliced into the pancakes and fatty bacon. I ate slowly, adding butter and syrup as I went. There was a small mirror underneath a green wooden frame that held the first dollar Duffy's had ever taken. It was so faded I half-expected George Washington to look younger in his portrait. As my mug was refilled, the three men in the booth got up and walked out. They didn't pay. How does this place make any money, I thought? I turned and watched them go. The man perched his bowler on his head at the exact moment he crossed over the door's threshold. A bell rang.

The man with the veins got in the van and drove away. The other two men spoke for a few moments. The fat deputy nodded back towards the diner a couple of times before getting into a patrol car and driving out of the lot, spitting gravel. The dapper man pulled a cellphone from his belt. He spoke with an expressionless face, walked over to a gleaming white Lexus sedan, took off his hat, and got in. As he drove past the window, I could see a magnet on the Lexus that matched the one on the van's door. I ordered another half-stack and another small plate of bacon. I walked over to the booth and grabbed the paper that the prim coroner had left. A USA TODAY.

I finished the pancakes, drained a plastic cup of water I hadn't asked for, dropped a ten on the counter, and stood up. I left the paper on the table I'd taken it from, in case the coroner returned for it, and walked out. The sun was a quarter way across the sky. It was Tuesday morning. Humid.

I started working on the Duster a few minutes before ten. Brakes. The Duster was jacked up. Front right. I was on a roller underneath the car. I had Springsteen playing in the background. *Jersey Girl*. Right as they were dropping her brat off at her mom's and heading out into the moonlight of the Garden State, a fat man with black boots hit me with a wrench. My face slammed against the muscle car's underbelly. I could only see the man's scuffed boots as I felt blood pouring into my right eye. He hit me twice more in my knee and jammed the silver wrench into my ribs. I could barely breathe. He swung again. I gripped the axle and rolled out into a short stack of tires resting against a tool bench, hauling myself upright. My right eye was closing. I could see the fat deputy through the blur of my left. He dropped the wrench; he didn't want to kill me. This felt like a warning.

I threw a looping punch that grazed off his chin and dug into his shoulder. He pushed me hard against the tires. I bounced back into him. He hit me in my already tender ribs. I buckled. He grabbed me by my collar and slung me across the garage, off my feet and onto the hood of the Duster. The back of my head banged against the hood scoop. He kept his right hand on my collar and punched me with his left. He let me slide off the hood and kicked me again in the ribs as I landed.

He pulled a Beretta 9mm from his duty belt and pushed it into the deepening gash near my closed right eye.

The man with the hawkish nose walked into the garage. He'd been waiting in the car.

"Mr Stock, Mr Stock," he said, in a southern drawl more exaggerated than most. "Magnolia Ridge. Just lovely." He held his hands out like he was greeting a friend. He wasn't.

"I have an uncle that lived on the other side of your property; your kin used to let us hunt over here when I was a boy. Deer. Even coon. Nice piece of property to *inherit*." He enunciated the word. "Funny how that's been working out for folks. You, that carpetbagger, coon-ass police detective. Out of the blue. Just like that. Out of nowhere. Like wind just blowing into our little county out here in the sticks."

"Well, some people are just lucky," I said. I pushed the pistol away from my head. If they were going to kill me, they'd have done it already. The deputy started to move it back towards my temple. The sheriff nodded. He slammed the pistol into its holster and snapped it in.

"Funny thing for a bleeding man with only one good eye to say."

"I'm nutty like that." I cupped my eye. I could feel the blood. I needed to get to the hospital before I lost the eye.

The sheriff read my mind. "You could lose that eye. I used to box; did you know that Mr Stock? Light middleweight. In the Army. Doesn't take as much as folks think to lose an eye."

"Thanks for the advice and the history lesson, but you can still kiss my ass."

"You seem like a smart guy, Mr Stock. You ever watch cable television? A&E?"

I didn't answer.

"They have this show where folks flip a house. I think that's what they call it. Make some money. You should do that. This is a pretty place; a little dated, maybe. Nice name and all."

"Sounds like a plan," I said, trying to focus on anything. The blur in my left eye was getting worse. A concussion from banging my head on the hood scoop was likely.

"Do what I can, Mr Stock. Do what I can." He reached down and helped me to my feet. I leaned against the Duster. I had no balance. He nodded again to the Deputy who walked away towards the car.

"Thanks," I said once more, not meaning it. Again.

"The question isn't whether you're leaving Slate County, Mr Stock. It's where you're going and what you will leave with. You can flip this house and walk away with some money. A lot more than you paid for it."

"Or?" I asked, the answer obvious.

"Or you can die. Right here in Slate County. In a place where you've got no friends, no kin. Best case, buried in a pauper's grave at county expense. Or maybe not even that... maybe not even that Mr Stock."

"Subtle. So, you recommend flipping it?" I asked.

"That'd be my suggestion." He smiled. For a second, I thought he was missing some teeth. I realized that looking through one blurry eye, they were just brown. Or green. "You bein' one of my constituents and all, I had my deputy call you an ambulance. Shame about you hitting your head underneath that car. You're leaving town, Mr Stock. You mention my name at the county hospital and you'd better leave today. Nobody will believe you anyway. And you know it."

I nodded. He was right. At least about that.

"Good day, Mr Stock."

I nodded a second time. I could hear the ambulance. The sheriff walked back to his car, walked around to the passenger side, and got in. It drove off. The car reached the edge of the driveway as the ambulance was pulling in. The two vehicles met for a few seconds, and I saw the deputy wave to the driver as he pulled onto the road and out of sight. The ambulance driver waved back.

My right eye was closed. I worked my way around the car and leaned against the trunk. Two paramedics got out of the rig and walked towards me. A man and a woman. The man carried a small orange and white case. The woman's long brown ponytail was pulled through a generic EMT baseball cap.

11.

I WOKE UP in a hospital. I saw the ponytailed paramedic standing in a hallway behind a large pane of frosted glass, talking to Detective Browning. A nurse in blue scrubs tapped her finger against the bag connected to the I.V. in my left arm and smiled when she saw my eyes open. A metal clipboard, my chart, was hanging from the bedpost at the foot of the bed. She picked it up and scanned it. I could see her left hand. No ring.

"Welcome back, Mr Stock. And how are we feeling today?" Her voice was like syrup. Only elementary school teachers and nurses talked like that.

"What day is it?" I asked.

"Friday. Morning. You came in on Tuesday. Head injuries. Concussion."

"Sounds right," I said. "It hurts to breathe."

"You'll be up and about in a couple of days," she said.

"When can I go home?"

"That's up to the doctor. I'd guess tomorrow, or Sunday. But, again, it's up to the doc. He'll be in shortly. The detective," she nodded towards Browning, who was now standing in the open doorway, "...he wants to talk to you too. You're extremely popular, Mr Stock." She smiled and walked out. As she walked past him, I heard her say, "He's all yours, Detective."

Browning pulled a chair up to the bed and sat down. He took a notebook from the pocket of his short-sleeved dress shirt. White.

Paisley tie. Like a lot of cops, Browning wore clothes so long they eventually came back into style. He flipped the notebook open.

"Hit your head while working on the brakes of your car, is that right, Mr Stock? That's what the sheriff and his deputy told the paramedics when they arrived at your residence."

"Sounds right." I looked him in the eye.

"Here's the thing, Dan, it seems like you hit your head in the front resulting in the gash above your eye and then hit your head again resulting in the blunt trauma to the back of the head resulting in the concussion. Inexplicably you also have three broken ribs. Was the car pissed at you?"

"Not that I know of, *Sam*." He had switched to my first name, a good technique to establish familiarity during an interview. I had read his name in the newspaper and seen it on TV after Cherry's murder, so I used it too. Us being on a first-name basis and all. He was a good detective, I could tell.

"Where's your sidekick?" I asked.

"Sidekick? Who am I, The Lone Ranger? What sidekick?"

"Your partner, the fat-ass you brought to my house that night."

His smile said he despised the fat deputy too. And I could tell that he thought it was probably the deputy, and not my car, that had kicked my ass.

"He's not my partner. I work for the city police department; he works for the county sheriff. Amanda Smith's husband's murder was in a part of the park that's just inside the town limits. Mississippi Bureau of Investigation could have taken it because it was a state park, but we caught it. Sort of. The sheriff is a constitutional officer of the state and the police chief is appointed by the city council and mayor. Sheriff is the top dog in any Mississippi county. So, that night, the sheriff called my chief and told him that someone from his office had to birddog the investigation. So…"

"So, you had to bring him?" I asked.

"So, I had to bring him," he confirmed. He nodded a 'you know how it is' nod. I did.

"Anything else you want to tell me, Dan?"

"Like?"

"Like, I pulled the radio transmission. Coincidentally, that same Deputy called the ambulance. And from what the paramedics told me, both the deputy and the sheriff were leaving your house when they arrived."

"So?"

"So," he repeated with frustration in his voice. It was staged. He knew I wasn't going to tell him anything. "Really? Is this the story you're sticking to, Dan?"

"What's wrong with it?" I asked.

He looked at me, almost smiling. Verbal judo.

"The Deputy and the Sheriff didn't respond to the call before the ambulance. The Deputy called it in." I gave him a blank look. "So, what's wrong with it, is what were they doing at your house? Not just the Deputy. The Sheriff himself."

"I'm just a likeable guy. People gravitate towards me, Sam. What can I tell you?"

He stood up. "More than you are, that's for sure. You have your reasons, Dan. Just watch your six. That's all I can say."

"All you can say?"

"All I'm going to say at this hospital. Like I said, watch your ass."

"If I stand up, you can watch it for me. These damn gowns."

He smiled. "Well, free morphine. Enjoy it while you can. Stay safe, brother." He handed me a business card and walked out. I couldn't tell if he knew I used to be a cop. He knew more than he was telling me. And I knew more than I was telling him.

He was right about the morphine. It kept me from missing the pills and bourbon that I plowed through on a normal day. The doctor cleared me to go home on Monday. Said I was lucky I didn't lose the eye. I didn't feel lucky. I didn't have a way home. The nurse with the blue scrubs and sweet smile gave me a ride. A ring had appeared. She saw me looking across the car to her hand propped on the steering wheel.

"I don't wear it when I work."

I nodded like I thought it was a good idea. It probably was.

"Well, you wouldn't want to leave it in anyone."

She didn't get it at first, and then she laughed. Well, I'm not a surgical nurse, but I suppose you're right."

We rode in silence until she pulled up my driveway and stopped near the short stairwell to my door.

"Here we are, Mr Stock."

"Call me Dan," I said.

"Next time I will, Mr Stock."

I thanked her for the ride and made my way upstairs to my bedroom. My head and ribs throbbed. I squinted to examine the stitches around my right eye. It was still partially closed. I looked like shit. I felt like shit. I dropped into bed and slept with the windows open and the overhead fan on high. I slept, but not well.

12.

THE METAL BUILDING had been erected almost dead center at the highest point of a rugged 50-acre plot. Two buses, with "Primitive Baptist Church of the Redeemer" painted in block letters on them, sat dark and idle on one side; a small cluster of cars were parked in spaces directly in front of the main entrance. It was just past eleven on a Wednesday night. Mid-week service had ended an hour earlier. The masses had gone home, leaving only the council of elders to meet in a large conference room outside the office of a dead preacher.

His office inside hadn't been touched since his body was found weeks earlier. Pictures still sat on a small credenza near the desk, including the same image the newspapers had run the morning Kevin Smith had been killed. The Smith's: Amanda, Kevin and two kids. One girl. One boy. Garish Christmas sweaters. Broad smiles. The preacher's *King James* Bible sat open on an expensive desk pad in the center of an antique desk. Revelations.

Nine men. All white. Most bald or balding. The meeting was short. Like every recorded vote in the church's history, the vote would be unanimous. Contentious meetings had lasted deep into the night and the recorded vote was always unanimous. Always. This meeting would not go deep into the night. It started at eighteen minutes after eleven, and by half past, Clifford Greer had been chosen as the new lead pastor. He fit. It was time for the church to move on. There were souls to be saved. And money to be made. And secrets to be kept. Not in that order.

Next morning, Clifford Greer moved his belongings into the office. He dropped the pictures from the credenza into a cardboard box and replaced them with photos of his own wife and kids. His kids, one girl, one boy, were dressed for Easter service. The boy had dimples. The girl had light blue ribbons in her blonde hair. Both kids looked like their mother. Neither favored their father in any way.

Clifford Greer sat down at his desk and called out to Nancy, a widowed woman who volunteered as a receptionist two days a week, to bring in the most recent ledgers of the church's finances. She entered the office seconds later. She was young for a widow, mid-thirties. Attractive. She locked the door behind her. He had time. He'd get to the finances later. And back to Revelations.

Or not. Two nights later, a National Park Service Police Officer found a man dead in a car leased to him by the Primitive Baptist Church of the Redeemer, eleven miles outside Tupelo, Mississippi on the Natchez Trace, a highway running between Jackson, Mississippi and Nashville, Tennessee. The "Trace" as it was known, had a somewhat sordid history as a well-known destination for deep-in-the-closet homosexuals.

He'd been shot twice in the head. The Trace was federal land. The Park Service cop called the FBI, who called the Tupelo Police Department for assistance until they could get an agent over from Oxford. A Tupelo homicide detective with fifteen years' experience looked at the preacher's body slumped against the driver's side window streaked in blood. His suit pants were down. The Park Service cop, a young guy with a reddish-blonde high and tight haircut watched him.

"What do you think, Detective?" he asked.

"Same as you. A homo-cide. Some queer getting head out here on The Trace. Nothing new. Shot in the head. Close range"

"Motive?" the young cop asked.

"Who knows? Maybe the shooter was being blackmailed for money for being gay, maybe for head. Maybe both. Who knows? Gets tired of giving non-reciprocal hummers to the Vic, acts like he's going down and shoots him when he's distracted whipping it out.

Could be anything. We'll know more once we figure out who's going to run with this thing. I'm sure the U.S. Attorney in Oxford is dying for this one. We got ID on this guy?"

"Yeah," the young cop said. "I thought I would let you run it through PD dispatch. Park Service system can be a tad slow."

He handed a driver's license to the detective. The detective pulled a radio from his belt underneath his suit jacket, keyed it, gave his unit number, "D-David 18," and conveyed the information.

"Stand by," he was told by a woman with a curt voice. The detective was surprised when a man's voice responded instead of the dispatchers.

"Unit 3 to D-18,"

The detective gave a quizzical look to the young cop. "Weird. Assistant Chief, boss named Logan," he told him before speaking back into the radio.

"Go ahead Unit 3."

"Make a 20 to the precinct. Landline."

"10-4," the detective said. "Something's up. Doesn't even want me to use a cell. Got to find a payphone and call my boss. Stay here."

The detective drove off to find a payphone which were becoming increasingly scarce. The young cop watched the car with the body of the dead preacher.

13.

IT WAS DARK when I woke. The phone was ringing. I kept my eyes closed and reached across the sheets to find the phone by sound. It vibrated in my hand as I picked it up. I glanced at the small, glowing screen, recognized the number, and answered.

"Dan? Dan is that you?" Victoria Speer's voice was high and panicked. "I need help." It didn't take her too many more words to convince me she was right. She did need help and it wasn't the kind of "help" I could phone in.

"Where are you?" I asked.

She told me.

"I'll be there as soon as I can. Wait for me. Don't do anything. Don't call or talk to anyone." I thought absently how many times Cherry had given this same advice.

A few days had passed, but my head still throbbed. I was dizzy. But this couldn't wait. I reached into the bedside table to get a small .38 Smith & Wesson I kept in an ankle holster. It was missing. My thoughts were cloudy, but I was sure that I'd put the gun in there. I'd seen it. I didn't have time to think about it.

I splashed water onto my face and got dressed, before walking to the kitchen and shoving my feet into a pair of boots. Outside, I opened the door to the shed, punched numbers onto the keypad and entered my makeshift armory. I pulled a Glock .40 from its pancake holster, made sure it was fully loaded, chambered a round, returned it to the holster and shoved it in the waistband of my jeans. I got in my truck, pulled down my driveway and turned left.

NEW ALBANY WAS in Union County, 55 miles due east of Forrest Springs. Surprisingly, for a small town, four highway exits were assigned to it. I exited right, drove down a short slope, and pulled into a Petro. Eighteen-wheelers were lined up like dominoes beside the truck stop on the far side of a set of industrial scales and diesel pumps, running lights aglow like algae on coral reefs.

I drove the wrong way through the covered diesel pumps and saw her car parked far in the back, next to several large green dumpsters. I pulled up, got out of my truck, and into her car. The overhead light was on. I turned it off.

She was still as panicked as she had been on the phone. Shaking. Frantic. She tried to speak, but the sobs filled her throat before the words could escape.

"I… I… I killed him. He's dead. In… car," was all I could make out. She was even less composed than she had been on the phone. She looked ahead, her stare thousands of yards past the steering wheel.

"Who's dead?" I asked. Asking that question was like picking up a violent hitchhiker. Intentions pure. Consequences always undesirable. I tried to convince myself not to get involved. Let it go. I'd slept on my own couch for this woman. She finally turned her head. She had the same look I had seen a thousand times on the faces of battered women. Afraid. Trapped

"I shot him," she said.

I thought back to something my grandfather had always said when we sat down to a breakfast of my grandmother's eggs and bacon. "The chicken is involved; the pig is committed." I was committed. Or I soon would be.

When she stopped crying, she told a story. A hell of a story. Cherry had told me once that Victoria made extra money up in Memphis at an upscale Italian restaurant. It wasn't her only part-time gig. She had another part-time job. Actually, her sister had a part-time job in Atlanta. Victoria had a *part*-part-time job. In Atlanta. Her twin sister was a prostitute. Not a streetwalker; a very expensive call-girl. A grand a throw; five thousand for the night. At places like The Mark, the Buckhead Ritz Carlton, the W Hotel off I-285, and the Westin Peachtree Plaza—the place with the revolving roof-top restaurant. The conventioneers were usually at the Sheraton and Hilton Hotels, down off Courtland Avenue. At first, her sister was the evil twin, but after twenty minutes it became clear that it had been Victoria who'd opened the door for her sister.

Cliché, yes, but when Victoria was at the University of Georgia in Athens, 70 miles from downtown Atlanta, she put herself through school on her back. Or knees. When she graduated, her twin took over her clients. Her johns. Some of them knew it was a different woman, some didn't. Either way, none cared. Two months ago, Victoria's sister had got sick. Morning sickness. She took care of it at a clinic in Midtown Atlanta. A night later, she wasn't ready to work. She called Victoria, who asked her if it was someone she'd remember. Her twin said "No," that the client wasn't a regular, only came in once a year. He had visited the past three years; came to Atlanta for a Convention for non-affiliated Baptist Churches. He paid double. Double, even triple the price usually meant kinky, multiple girls, or pain. Her sister assured her that it was none of the above. Just a guy that imagined someone else when he screwed his wife and needed to refresh his memory every twelve months. Nothing unusual. Other than the chicken-pluckers and the furniture wholesalers, Baptists spent the most annually on sex: direct and passive. Prostitutes, strip clubs and hotel room porn. Victoria took her place. At the Hilton off Courtland. She was right. Nothing kinky. Quick. He even paid for the good stuff out of the courtesy bar.

Months later, Victoria accompanied Cherry Winter to a preliminary hearing for Amanda Smith. She saw the man from the Hilton. He was seated in the third row. He saw her. He found out who she was. She found out who he was. He called her at the office three days later. They met on the Natchez Trace two days after that. They assured one another that they would keep each other's secrets.

She didn't hear from him again. Until a few hours before she had come to my house that evening.

He was nervous. He told her that he was taking Kevin Smith's place as head pastor at the church. It was a sick, wretched, evil place. A cult. Pure and simple. Victoria knew that being promoted meant he was a very sick, wretched, and evil person. It was in the job description. She went to meet him. Unlike the first time they had met on the Trace, he asked for sex. He said he would pay. She knew he never planned on paying. She smiled and agreed. She reached over and cupped the bulge in his pants to convince him. He unbuckled his belt and pulled his pants down, revealing white briefs. He put his head back and closed eyes he'd never open again. She pulled a small .38 out of her purse and shot him twice in the head.

14.

I FOLLOWED HER back to my place. Why the hell hadn't I just told her to drive to my house, I thought, as I pulled up my driveway. Crying women sapped me of logic. She went inside. The Duster was still propped up on the jack in the barn. I checked the mail and walked into the house. I could hear the shower running. In the kitchen, I grabbed four bottles of beer from the refrigerator and a bottle of bourbon off the counter. I walked upstairs to my bedroom. She was in the shower. The door to the bathroom was open. I walked in. I could see her silhouette behind the cloudy glass.

"Beer?" I asked her.

"Huh?" She couldn't hear me over the shower. It didn't seem to bother her that I was in the room though.

"Beer?" I said again. Louder.

"Thanks." I saw a still slightly shaking hand come up over the crest of the shower screen. I put the cold bottle in her palm. She lowered it out of sight.

"Thanks," she said again. Her voice had also calmed. Some. It was sweet again. Even a southern accent isn't sexy when there is a fear behind it. And her voice was sexy—sort of a throaty southern.

I walked out of the room, drained the water from a short glass by the bed, and replaced it with three fingers of bourbon. I opened a beer, took a sip of the bourbon, and chased it.

The water stopped. She walked out of the bathroom wearing two towels. One wrapped around her head, one covering her torso. No makeup. She looked clean. Scrubbed. It was easy to forget that standing in front of my faux fireplace was a part-time prostitute who had recently killed a clergyman. Even if she was an innocent hooker and he was a guilty preacher.

"So, I'm not sleeping on my couch this time?"

She walked up to me and held her lips up to mine. She smelled like the cheap shampoo I use. She emitted a misty heat. I could feel it when my cheek touched hers. Her skin was smooth. I hadn't shaved in a week.

"T-shirt, boxers, shorts. What have you got? Can I raid your closet?"

"Be my guest," I said, thinking of her former boss. "Right back through the bathroom."

"I am your guest," she said with a playful smile, before spinning around and retreating into the bathroom.

"Through the door?" I heard her ask.

"Yeah." Where else could it be, I thought, above the garage?

I took another sip from my bottle and walked back over to the nightstand, poured another glass of bourbon, and drank some of it. Then more beer. I looked down at the nightstand, hesitating. Sure enough, when I opened the drawer, I looked down at my missing .38 in the ankle holster. Picking it up, I cupped it in my hand and worked the cylinder loose. I pushed the catch forward. Two spent shells. Three intact hollow-point rounds. The rounds were law enforcement only. I pushed the gun back into the holster and placed it back in the drawer. I rubbed my index and middle fingers against my thumb and felt the dust. I shut the drawer, poured another glass, and turned around.

Victoria was standing at the bathroom door looking at me. She was holding a pair of boxer shorts and a T-shirt in her right hand. The towel was gone from her head. She pulled the towel away from her body with her free hand. It dropped to the floor. Her eyes never left mine. Until my eyes left hers. Which, of course, was the point. I allowed my glance to linger and then looked away.

I sat on the edge of the bed and sipped at the bourbon. She stepped into the boxers, pulled the T-shirt over her head, and slipped under the covers. We finished the beers and most of the bourbon before falling asleep. I woke up an hour later and turned my head towards her. She had rolled into me. Her face was inches from mine, her arm draped across my chest. I could feel her breath. If fear turned her on it would have been a hell of a night.

All I could think of was The Trace. She'd killed him on federal property. Could mean the FBI. They sucked at kicking in doors but were great at forensics. It would take some Quantico egghead about four seconds to realize that the round was hollow point. All they would need was the gun. And it was in a drawer less than two feet from my head. She was trouble. Like that hitchhiker you should leave on the side of the road. But I didn't leave her by the side of the road; trouble was now in bed next to me asleep.

Sleep ended when the shotgun blasts erupted. We both jumped. I knew what it was, she just knew it was loud. I rolled her off the bed onto the floor.

"Stay here," I hissed, and moved towards the closet. The K-frame .38 in the drawer was a short-range weapon. At best. I moved through the bathroom into the closet. The leather motorcycle jacket was hanging from a stiff metal hanger. I put it on. I reached into the inside pocket and retrieved a .44 Desert Eagle. Three spare magazines in the opposite pocket. I moved back out through the bathroom. Victoria had listened. She was right there on the floor where I had left her and appeared to have little interest in moving.

"Believe it or not there's a revolver in that drawer right behind your head. Take it out, and if anyone but me walks back through this door, shoot them. You've got three shots left."

I slipped around the door and pulled it closed behind me. The shotgun blasts continued. I could hear glass breaking on the front side of the house. Moving through the kitchen to a small porch that housed cleaning chemicals and a washer-dryer stack, I crouched and reached up. I unlocked the dead bolt and slid out into the darkness. Tall shrubs lined the house to the right. I stayed low. The grass was wet under my feet from a recent shower. I reached the edge and peeked around the widest patch of shrubs. Four men. Three blasting away with shotguns at the front of the house. Glass continued to break. I could hear the buckshot ricochet off the old wooden planks of the front porch. The fourth man was standing in front of the barn pumping rounds into the exposed shell of my Duster.

I could barely make out the outline of the grille of a dark van parked in the grass just off the driveway. Running lights on; headlights off. I closed my left eye and focused the .44 on the man standing near the barn. I watched him through the night-sights. He pumped and fired the shotgun three more times. I didn't have a good shot. Yet. He didn't make me wait long. He moved away from the barn in the direction of Victoria's car. He walked behind it. The shadow of his torso perched over the car's hood. I pulled on the slack in the trigger, moved the gun down and to the left, and trained the night-sights on the small square outline of the car's gas cap cover. I breathed. And fired. Four shots. Five. The man dove down behind the car's left quarter panel. Six. Seven. The large rounds ripped through the car's shallow metal. A fire sparked. Nine. Ten. The other men had run to the van. Out of the corner of my eye, I saw doors open. And close. The van's engine cranked. It cut wide around a large oak tree and barreled down the driveway and onto the road. Nice friends. Eleven. Twelve. The car exploded. Orange and blue flames roared through the bleak Mississippi darkness. Bugs were scorched. The flames spit up inside the passenger compartment. I walked back in through the tattered front door and walked up the steps.

"Vicki," I said in a loud voice. It was the first time I had ever called her Vicki, but it seemed like our relationship had probably progressed to a more casual place. I opened the door. "It's me."

She was sitting up on the bed, sipping from the now lukewarm beer she hadn't finished earlier. The revolver was resting on the pillow next to her.

"I like the look," she said. I stared at her, confused.

"No shoes, no shirt, boxers, leather jacket. Hot." She smiled a brave smile.

"I think I pull it off." I grabbed my money clip off the nightstand and fished Browning's business card out of it. I picked up my phone and punched in his number. It rang. I was about to fold it shut when I heard a sleepy voice.

"Browning. What?"

"Browning, Dan Stock. Got a little situation out at my house. Don't want to go into too much detail over the phone. Some asshole burned himself up trying to steal my friend's car."

"Hate when that happens," Browning said. "By the way, it's really been great having you in town, Stock. Be there in fifteen."

I set the phone on the nightstand next to his card.

"He'll be here in fifteen," I said. "Quickie?"

"I would have, until you called me Vicki," she said. "Don't call me that," she said seriously then lightened back up and half-smiled, "Rhymes though…" she said.

"I'll settle for bourbon on the porch" I said.

We walked out to the side porch and sat in the rocking chairs. We sipped at the bourbon until we saw the headlights of Browning's car. It turned up the driveway and pulled towards the injured house.

I told Browning the story. He believed most of it. He spoke into a radio he took from his belt. He gave a vague description of the situation to the dispatcher. Within ten minutes, city and county cruisers littered the yard. Dead body. No choice but to call the coroner's office. Twenty minutes later, the same dark van returned to the scene of the crime. We only paid attention to the charred car and the crisped dead body. It was pitch black. Crisp flashlight beams danced in my yard. It was easy to ignore the house and the Duster. So, we did.

All the men except Browning glared at me. All the men except Browning lied about not knowing who the dead man was. Or who he had been. I waited until they all left. I flipped a switch near the door and lit an exposed bulb hanging down on a long chord from a rafter above. The Duster was beaten but not broken. I'd finish the brakes and put the tire back on in the morning.

I walked back towards the house. I could see Victoria's silhouette sitting on a chair on the porch, where we had sat waiting for

Browning. She was sipping bourbon. I joined her. We napped in the rocking chairs and watched the sunrise.

"Sorry about your car," I said, but she had fallen asleep.

15.

IT WAS EARLY. I opened my eyes and looked at the empty rocking chair beside me. I walked downstairs and smelled coffee. She was in the kitchen drinking from a white *"Don't Mess With Texas"* mug I'd picked up somewhere. Probably Texas.

"Good morning," she said, smiling bravely. The gravity of the night before had obviously begun to descend upon her. She pulled another mug from the cabinet, filled it with coffee and handed it to me. I took a sip and watched her sit down in one of the chairs. She rested the mug on the table and pulled her hands away from it slowly. She was thinking.

"What am I going to do?" she asked.

"Get out of town." It sounded cliché, even to me. Like a movie. But it had become cliché because it was very often good advice.

"For how long?" I saw a tear run down her face. Another cliché. Teardrops in her coffee. She hadn't ever considered leaving Forrest Springs again. Not really.

I didn't answer her. I couldn't. I didn't know the answer. I should have asked her why she'd taken my gun. But I didn't want to know.

I added more coffee to the mug and pulled a bottle of Bailey's Irish Cream from a cabinet. I poured the Bailey's to the mug's brim and held the bottle out to her. She nodded and I topped her mug up. She buried her face in her hands. I walked upstairs and rolled the combination lock open on the safe in the closet. I pulled a metal box out off the shelf inside, rested it on the safe, opened it, and pulled out a stack of twenties crushed by a taut rubber band. I removed a

Ziploc bag with two prepaid cell phones inside and pushed the metal box back in, closed the safe and rolled the lock.

I walked downstairs. She was brewing another pot of coffee. It had just begun to drip. I handed her the money. Her sad eyes grew wide for a moment. "How much…?"

"A grand," I answered.

"What do I have to do for that?"

I smiled, didn't answer, and closed her hands around the stack of bills.

"You need to leave today. Don't go home. I'll check on your place later. Use the money to buy what you need."

She nodded as I spoke. I opened the plastic bag, took one of the phones out and handed it to her. There was a label with a number affixed to the back of it.

"Use this cell phone to call me. The number to this cell phone," I held up the one I was still holding, "is on the back." I flipped it over. "Don't use any other phone. Understand?"

She turned the phone over and glanced at the label. I waited for her to nod. She did.

"I'm really sorry; I know this isn't fair to you at all." She was emotional, but she said this without emotion. Simply. She kissed me on the cheek and ran her free hand down my shoulder. She walked upstairs. I sat down at the table and waited for her. When she returned to the kitchen, I led her out to my truck. She slid behind the wheel.

"Wait a minute," I said, and walked over to the barn. I entered the code on the keypad, walked inside and took a 9mm Glock from the cabinet. I returned to the truck and handed it to her. She had the same look on her face as when I had handed her the money a half-hour before, but she didn't ask any questions about the gun or the fact that she was taking my truck. She drove away. I went back inside and put the prepaid cell on the nightstand next to my cell phone.

16.

A PHONE WAS ringing when I stepped out of the shower. For a second, I thought it might be Victoria calling. I hadn't heard from her in a couple of days. It wasn't the prepaid one. I picked up the phone and looked at the screen. 404. Atlanta. It was a number I'd used before, but I couldn't place it right away.

"Yeah," I said.

"Stock." Unlike the number, I recognized the voice immediately. Brett King. Atlanta. Homicide.

"Brett, what's going on?"

"You first. Nobody seems to know where the hell you went. One day, you're on the street, Red Dog, dope interdiction, high-risk warrant squad. Next day, in the wind. Gone. There was that one thing, but everyone figured it would blow over. Guess not. You got out of the Blues, I assume?"

"Sometime, when I'm back in Atlanta. I'll buy you a couple of pints at Manuel's," I said after a short pause. I knew the pause told Brett we weren't discussing it over the phone. He took the hint.

"Probably a better story in person anyway," he said.

"Where'd you get my number, Brett?" I would have given Brett my number, but I hadn't.

"Where the hell you think?" I knew. He got it from her. I doubted Brett would go to the trouble of getting the number if this wasn't important. It wasn't social. I knew that as soon as I heard his voice.

"I've got to ask you a couple of questions. About a .38." I sat down on the bed. I could feel the wet towel under my ass.

He asked the name of the town I was living in. I told him.

"Forrest Springs… anywhere near Tupelo?"

"Relative to rural Mississippi, pretty close."

"There was a shooting. Somebody threw out a perfectly good white guy on a federal highway cutting through a couple of states. I found it on a map. The Natchez Trace."

"Yeah," I said. He knew I already knew what he was talking about. Brett was a good friend. An even better detective. He paused, I left it at 'yeah'.

"Anyway, shooting on federal land got the FBI involved. They ran the gun through ATF Came up with an owner. You remember Beckett?"

"Vaguely," I said. Beckett was former Tampa PD, now with ATF in Atlanta. For a fed, he was a good guy. "Beckett called you?"

"About two hours ago. Ballistics kicked back a possible match. And then your name. Tied it to an off duty shooting you were involved in about three years back. I'm sure you remember."

I did.

Like most cops, I had carried a second gun. Some beat cops carried three. A backup. Known by the more police-cynical types as a "South Florida throwdown." As in throwing it down in some unarmed perp's dead hand when a cop puts someone down. I carried the .38 under my armpit, the holster hooked to the straps on my bulletproof vest. Most folks don't know that the buttons on a cop's uniform are just for show. There's a zipper there. You can unzip it quick and reach into the shirt. That was on duty. A 9mm gets bulky to carry 24/7. Sometimes off duty, especially in the heat of an Atlanta summer, I wore the .38 on my ankle. It was primarily a defensive weapon. Two-and-a-half-inch barrel, and you had to almost be on top of the perp to take a shot; good for shooting someone off you, worthless at almost any range.

I'd been in East Atlanta. Where Memorial and Moreland meet just off I-20. A shitbox bodega. The kind of place that sells nothing but beer, mostly forty-ounce Schlitz and Old English, and cheap liquor. Ripple. Mad Dog 20/20. A place where all the potato chips were two years expired and it didn't matter. A place that sold crack kits. Small paper bag, brillo, open-ended glass tube. I was on the way to meet up with her. Didn't feel like going anywhere better. I got out of the car and headed to the door. I wasn't drunk. Yet. I heard the cop before I saw him. He was yelling at someone.

"Drop it!"

I instinctively crouched down behind my car. I pulled the .38 off my ankle. Seconds later, a strangely spotted-looking man backed around the corner of the bleached-out white building. He had a big semi-auto pistol; black glazed, against the temple of an anorexic-looking Black woman in a paper-thin dress, with scraped knees and burnt fingernails. Of course, I didn't know all of that. Yet. The gun was in his right hand, his left arm held her in a headlock. Tight. He was backing towards me. I stayed crouched. The cop was too far to take a headshot. Or at least I hoped he thought so too. The cop kept yelling. The man yelled back. In a coarse voice.

"Fuck you, you cracker cop mutha'fucker. I'll blow this bitch's head off. You know I will cap this bitch." Yes, people really do talk like this.

I believed he would do it. My radio was in the car. I was surprised I didn't hear sirens yet. We weren't more than two miles from the Zone Six precinct. Maybe they didn't want to spook the guy. He was geeked up on crack. He kept backing towards me. When he was less than two feet away, I rose from behind the car, put the small-frame revolver to the back of his head and fired. He slumped. She screamed. The cop looked surprised. He kept his gun trained on the perp lying in the concrete. It wasn't clear why. Blood ran from the gaping hole in his head down a slight slope towards a blue dumpster with cracked paint and gang graffiti. Death was a foregone conclusion.

I crouched back down, opened the cylinder on the .38 and set it on the ground. The cop finally holstered his gun and walked up. He was on the job in East Point, a town outside Atlanta, to the southwest. I hadn't been sure what he was doing in uniform working an off-duty job in the city and never found out. Patrol cars bounced into the lot and parked at odd angles; blue lights careened off the windows of the bodega and the vertical metal bars that covered them. The woman was still screaming.

"Shut up," I remember saying. Wasn't the most diplomatic community-policing I'd ever done, but she was geeked up too. I glanced down at the dead man. He was skinny. He looked spotted because he was a Black man with impetigo. I found out later his street name was 'Pinto'.

A supervisor in a white shirt walked towards me. A Lieutenant I knew. He knew me. I liked him, even though he was bat-shit crazy. Zone Six evening watch shift boss. He was holding his gun at his side. Finger straight, out of the trigger guard. He knew I was a cop, but I still put my palms out so he could see them.

I'd replayed that story in my head so many times that it took about half a second to run it through again. I heard Brett ask another question.

"You still got that gun?"

"I'll have to look," I lied. "Do the Mississippi feds have this yet?"

"Not yet. Beckett can stall for a day or so, say they're running it deep; that he hadn't gotten a hit yet. But, hell, he's ATF and he's got to give it to the FBI at some point."

"Anything else?" I asked.

"Not from me, brother. Isn't my case. I just got a call from an old friend of ours and wanted to catch up."

"She ask why you needed the number?"

"No. Knows neither of us are exactly the greeting card type. Knew I wasn't just calling to catch up, so she didn't ask. Too smart. Might not want to know. Don't read anything into it. I'm sure she still cares."

"Yeah, I'm sure you are. I'm not. Wait, you mean you lied to me? You didn't just call to catch up? I was so touched."

"Screw you, stay safe," he said. He hung up.

I took some pills, drank some bourbon, and took a nap. Or tried to. I stared at the ceiling. Watched the fan make its orbit. I hadn't thought about her in a while. She hadn't been a relationship but an addiction, a chemical reaction. A physical craving for someone I instinctually knew was an emotional toxin. After her, I was like a heroin addict. Other women were the methadone that did nothing but get me even. The high was long gone

17.

VICTORIA'S CALL WOKE me the next day. I answered the prepaid cell on the fourth ring.

"It's me. I just wanted you to know where I was."

"Well?"

"Atlanta, had to talk to my sister."

That made sense. She paused for a second. Like she was deciding whether to tell me something important. She didn't, just told me to be careful and hung up before I could tell her the same.

As the line on the prepaid went dead the other phone rang.

"Yeah?" I answered, unfolding the phone.

"Dan? Browning. I think we should meet. Talk. Off the record. Away from Forrest Springs."

"I agree," I said, even though I hadn't really been thinking about it.

"Name it," he said. He was convincing me that the meeting wasn't official. Not part of a formal police investigation. When I first heard his voice, I thought maybe they had the information out of Atlanta linking me to the shooting on The Trace. Or they had something they thought linked me to Cherry's murder. But he'd have come to the house. Not an out-of-jurisdiction meeting fifty-some miles away.

I didn't know too many places out of town. The only place I could think of was the Petro station where I'd met Victoria a few nights before. We agreed to meet that night. He told me to name a time. So, I named one.

"See you at eleven," he said, and hung up. I folded the phone. I went to the kitchen, opened a fresh bottle of Jim Beam, and mixed it with Diet Coke and ice in a plastic cup. I went to the porch and thought about the two dead preachers, and the cult, and about women I'd met since I'd moved out to nowhere, even the married nurse. Then I thought about myself, took a handful of pills, and gulped down what was left in the tall cup. Whether I would end up in jail or dead had a lot to do with how much I could trust Sam Browning.

I had a call to make. One I wasn't particularly looking forward to.

Jamie Manning was a narcotics investigator with the Sheriff's Department in Harrison, Mississippi's southernmost county. I dialed her number from memory. She answered. I could tell she was driving, maybe in a convertible. That was a nice thought. I wondered absently if she could see the Gulf of Mexico.

"Manning,"

"Chy," I said. I doubted she had my number in her phone. But, as far as I knew, I was the only one who called her Chy.

"Dan Stock, and I *was* having a good day. I wish I knew someone else with a 404 prefix."

She'd cried and screamed out of anger the last time I'd spoken with her five years earlier. The time before that she hadn't screamed, only cried. Out of hurt. Betrayal. When she realized I'd lied to her—and I had. We met when I attended a narcotics interdiction course at the RCTA, the Regional Counternarcotics Training Academy, in Meridian, Mississippi. It was the only time I'd been to Mississippi before I moved to Forrest Springs. Meridian was straight across I-20 from Atlanta, so I had seen nothing of Mississippi except for the Interstate and the NAVY installation the RCTA was housed on. It was a month-long course. Advanced training. Cutting-edge stuff. I started calling her Chy after the first week.

It started out as Chyna, comparing her to the female professional wrestler who steamrolled the men with her freakish strength and high-peaked biceps. With repetition, Chyna was cut to Chy. Jamie was strong and athletic but bore no resemblance to the square-jawed, leather clad bruiser. But she loved pro wrestling and told me with a smile that I'd always be second to the late Bam Bam Bigelow in her heart of hearts. I figured she was teasing me as Bigelow—a surprisingly agile hardcore champion known as the "Beast from the East"—was also an almost 400-pound, gap toothed behemoth with a flame tattoo spanning his bald dome. Her nickname was cast when she volunteered to take the battering ram on a warrant exercise and splintered a door on the first swing. It's more angle than strength. She predictably said it was for "Doll," as in "China Doll" but we knew the truth. She was nobody's doll.

We slept together every night after the second.

"I've got a situation. I need some information."

"Well, of course. I want to do anything I can to help *you.*"

She hadn't hung up, so I was way, way ahead of the curve. Deep cuts turn into scars. Scars fade over the years. There was as much sarcasm as spite in her voice. And maybe a little curiosity.

"You driving?" I asked.

"Yeah. What do you want, Dan?"

"Can you see the Gulf?"

There was a pause. "*What* do you want?"

"I need some information about a detective in Forrest Springs. Guy named Browning."

"Forrest Springs…? Wait, Mississippi? What's that got to do with you?"

"I live there," I answered.

"Live where? Forrest Springs, up in North Mississippi? You're kidding me? What are you doing there?"

"Long story. Well, actually a short one, but it can wait. I've got to meet this guy in a few hours. Thought you could reach out, maybe give me the broad strokes. I just need to know if I can trust him. Big picture-wise." I gave her Browning's full name.

She paused for a second. "You don't trust anyone but yourself."

"But you'll get the information?"

"Do what I can. I'm not going to break a nail doing it. Not for you. Not anymore. He's a Mississippi cop?" she asked.

"He is now. I get the feeling he's worked somewhere else. Somewhere bigger."

"That's quite a lead. You said Browning, right? Sam? You figure Samuel, common spelling on both?"

"Yeah," I said.

"Got anything else?"

I couldn't think of anything for a split second; then I did.

"The Sheriff called him a coon-ass or something like that. What's that?"

"Louisiana," she said. "Might help. I'll start there. Anything else?"

All I could think to say was thanks, so I said it.

She confirmed that my number was in her phone and said she'd call back as soon as she could. Her hostility was somewhat tempered by the raw efficient curiosity of a detective. She knew I'd only call her if it was important. Or at least if I thought it was. Now she'd at least want to see if I was right. Even if just to shove it back in my face if I wasn't. That and she had to be damn curious about why I was living in Forrest Springs. She hung up.

I sat on the porch and watched the heat. It felt like it was watching back.

The day traded the night a red sunset for a full moon. I showered, dressed in jeans and boots. The mercury had dipped a dozen or so degrees, so I put on my leather jacket, the one APD had issued me when I worked a motors detail on a motorcycle during the '96 Olympics. Not 100% sure why I needed it during an Atlanta summer, but it was a hell of a nice jacket. You could barely make out the indentations from the stiches where the APD patches and American flag had been sewn on before I ripped them off. I retrieved the files Victoria had delivered from Cherry's office from underneath the mattress. I left at nine thirty; I wanted to be there first. Battered shell aside, the Duster roared to life. I rolled out of the garage, barely tapping the pedal. I stretched her out a little when I hit the blacktop. The Duster drove cocky. Solid. Detroit in the 70's. Immediate; not even that millisecond hesitation waiting for turbo to kick in. I took a couple of back roads to a two-lane which spilled out onto I-78. I headed east. The highway was almost deserted, apart from a couple of tractor-trailers and a car hauler with "Spanky's, Baldwyn, Mississippi" painted on the door.

Every fifteen miles or so a cluster of hotels, gas stations and the occasional chain restaurant cropped up over the tree line. I passed a battered trailer that advertised the services of a palm reader named Madam Sol.

I took the same exit I'd taken before, cut onto Highway 15 and hung a sharp left into the truck stop. I was early. Browning was even earlier. I saw his brown sedan backed in near the rear of the lot flanked by two green dumpsters to the left and a row of semis on my right. He lowered his window as I pulled to a stop and killed the engine.

"Get in," he said.

I picked up the files, got out of the Duster, walked around the back of his car, and climbed in. I closed the door. There was a thick manila envelope resting on the dash above the steering wheel. He handed it to me. I returned the favor and gave him the files in my hand.

"The missing Amanda Smith defense file" Browning didn't look surprised when I nodded.

"I figured that the one in the office was a skeleton file. Knew there had to be more. Where did you get it?"

"Victoria, her assistant, brought it to me," I said.

"That was nice of her. I'm sure that delivery was a hell of a lot more fun than meeting me in the parking lot of a truck stop. I assume you know where she is?" He looked over. I nodded. He looked back down at the file resting in his lap. He pulled the stack of papers and pictures out of the expandable file.

The pictures were on top. Browning looked at each one at a steady pace. Not lingering on any photo. He didn't seem surprised. He had either seen it all before, or already knew what went on in that church. Or both. I figured it was my turn.

I unclasped the outer envelope and pulled a folder and a smaller envelope out. I rested the folder on the envelope and flipped it open.

"You want me to read, or you want to tell me what I'm looking at?" I asked.

"What you're looking at is something I probably shouldn't be showing you," he said. Inside the envelope were several pictures. The one on top showed four men standing in front of a tank in desert camouflage. I'd seen two of them before. The tallest of the men wore the kind of goggles I guessed tank drivers wore. He was my favorite sheriff. The shortest man was holding an M-16. He would have been a widower when Amanda Smith was killed. If she hadn't already killed him. I didn't recognize the other two men.

"So, the Sheriff and Preacher Smith are old Army buddies, huh?" I asked.

"They were, and that's just scratching the surface," Browning said. I scanned through some of the files. Browning didn't say anything until I looked up. He was right.

We skimmed our respective files in silence for a while.

"Okay, I'll ask again. What am I looking at?" The paperwork was mostly investigations with long narratives. One of the files was a collection of official police reports that had been filed, complete with stamps and numbers. A lot of the narrative didn't appear to be attached to a particular report or official investigation. Nothing stamped. No numbers. It seemed to be a compilation of Browning's personal notes.

"I'm not reading all of this from a dome light… give me the short version," I said, "For now, at least."

He pointed down at the folder in his hand. The Amanda Smith defense file Cherry had compiled. He was skimming Cherry's notes of what Amanda had told her about the cult.

"This is in line with what I've found out since coming to Forrest Springs," he said.

"Which is?"

"The church is a front. It's a cult, without a doubt, but it's also a front. For dope, guns, but mostly for a human trafficking ring that spans all the way from Arizona to Georgia. The girls are mostly from Mexico."

"That's a long reach," I said.

"It all goes back to the photo," he said.

"The one with the soldiers in front of the tank? I asked. "This one? I held it up. Of the Sheriff and Kevin Smith and a couple of other guys?" I held it up.

"Right, the other two guys are a cat named Gus Lambert and a guy called Sangre. I don't have a full name on him."

"How's it work?" I asked.

"Sort of like a Walmart approach to smuggling, guns, dope, trafficked girls, whatever. They supply small towns all over the South and leave the big cities to the competition. Word is that Sangre is the Mexican connection. He picks up the girls in small villages all over Mexico and smuggles them north across the border. The girls are shipped into Arizona. That's where Lambert takes over. He's part of a big-time OMG—outlaw motorcycle gang—called the White Werewolves. They then smuggle the girls from Arizona towards the South. First stop is usually here in Forrest Springs where the sheriff takes over. The church-slash-cult is the front. They house the girls there, under the auspices of an orphanage, runaway shelter, whatever. The details aren't as important, really.

"So, the church isn't just a front, the people there actually believe in it?" I asked. He nodded.

"Oh yeah, the sheriff, Sangre and Lambert are in it for the money, they're smugglers, pure and simple."

"And Kevin Smith?"

"Smith was, and his followers are, deranged as hell. Word is that Smith set the church up to be a front for the fencing operations of the smuggling ring and then started to believe his own diatribes. The church started out pretty standard for an evangelical, non-affiliated primitive Baptist church. Then, somewhere along the way, it veered off into polygamy. Sex with young girls, all-night sermons about Armageddon, the ultimate judgment. You get the picture. At some point, Kevin Smith became a true believer."

"In what?"

"In himself. He believed he was the Messiah. Or a prophet at the very least."

"The young girls?" I asked.

"Depends on which ones you mean. The young girls they were pimping out, it doesn't look like he ever went after them. They were product. But…"

"But?"

"But Kevin Smith was a pedophile plain and simple. I got a friend at the Veteran's Administration who did me a solid. I couldn't get any physical records, but he alluded to the fact that there was something in Smith's file about some incidents with underage girls in countries he had been deployed to. Not much on paper. No charges ever filed. With that kind of access to young girls in his church, I figure he came up with the idea that they had to be "blessed" by him. You can guess the rest. I am not even sure how many wives he had."

"I know one wife who killed his ass."

"Probably for that very reason. We don't know much about Amanda Smith. Not sure how much she knew when she originally hooked up with him, but at some point, she'd had enough of him and decided that it was time for him to go sit at the right hand of the Father or wherever she believed he was headed."

"What now?" I asked.

"Now, we look at these files, and figure out what we're going to do."

"What makes you think I want to do anything?"

"Call it a hunch," he said. "I checked you out when Cherry was killed. Before I came to your house that night. From everything I've gathered, you were a hell of a cop. Stand up. Guys just treading water for steady pay and solid city benefits don't work Red Dog." I had no idea where he was getting his information.

"And you?" I wanted to change the subject. "This isn't your first stop out of the academy I'm assuming." His stubbled cheeks dimpled. But it was a sad smile.

"Louisiana State Police, eighteen years, early out. Six on patrol, six in investigations, last six as a supervisor."

"And this? Forrest Springs PD?"

"I left the State PD a little earlier than expected. Some internal stuff. My wife was an Episcopal priest. She'd wanted to get out of Louisiana for years, and a growing parish over in DeSoto County needed another priest. They offered it to her. We moved three days after I took the plaques down off my office wall. That was five years ago. Two years later, she died. A year after that, out of the blue, the Police Chief in Forrest Springs offered me a job. So, I sold the house in Olive Branch and moved to town."

I wondered absently what his 'internal stuff' was.

"So, what now?" I asked again, after a memorial pause for the death of his wife and the consequences of his choices.

"It isn't a matter of what, it's a matter of how."

"How to do what?" I asked, but we both knew the answer. He ignored the question and countered with his own.

"Any ideas on where to start?" he asked.

"One," I said. "See the second picture?"

He held the stack of photos up and flipped the first one over to focus on the second. He held it up. I nodded. It was a Polaroid of a girl taken at a hospital. He lowered it and studied it.

"Yeah, I remember. The Sheriff brought her into the ER for treatment. Said she got into an argument with one of the other girls at the church. The ER nurse didn't believe it, but she didn't have much to go on, and it was the Sheriff's story. So, I went over there once, asking some questions about the church, and she gave me the picture. How can that help? I've never even seen her."

"I think I know where we can find her."

"It's a start," he said.

"Call me tomorrow." I opened the door. As I walked around the back of his car he pulled away. I drove home. I wanted to trust Browning. I was at eighty percent when I closed my eyes that night.

I took the picture of the four men in front of the tank, folded it and slipped it into the leather jacket's deep inside pocket where I often kept my backup gun and sometimes, when I worked an off-duty job in uniform, a flask of bourbon.

She called before dawn and kept it short.

"What?" I said, as I answered the phone and rolled my head on the pillow to focus on angular bright red numbers of the clock. Four-fifteen.

"Dan, it's Jamie,"

"I like it more when you nudge me than call Chy, but Good Lord, what are you, Amish?" I asked.

"You can trust him. If he calls me, I'll tell him he can't trust you."

"You wake up hating me, huh?" I asked.

"Fall asleep that way, too," she said and hung up. It dawned on me that I really needed that information before the meeting, but I wasn't about to say anything. Not that she had given me the chance.

18.

MY BEST LEAD was the girl. Tasha, the girl from the Polaroid, the one I met at the Rust Club. I left at dusk. It wasn't dark enough yet. I pulled off the highway into a parking lot with washed-out blacktop fifty yards past a green sign with white letters: "Bone, Mississippi – 4 miles". Bone was a small town a few miles off the road leading to the juke joint.

I'd heard about Norma Jean's, a small bodega run by an octogenarian convinced she was Marilyn Monroe's twin separated at birth. She'd legally changed her name years before. Her belief was genuine, the resemblance nonexistent; I was sure no Kennedy brother had ever called for her company. I'd heard about Miss Monroe's store. Two old Christian women made biscuits and red-eye gravy each morning, except the Sabbath. If the pious women had been there on Sundays, they would have seen Norma Jean bootleggin' beer and whiskey in violation of Mississippi's blue laws.

The floor was splintery sheets of plywood that had been laid at odd angles, leaving gaps of exposed dirt. The building was wood; two abandoned gas pumps perched out front like headstones to an economy that had died a slow death. I parked the Duster in front of a propane tank and got out.

I walked towards the building. Groups of Blacks, young and old, were clustered throughout the parking lot. Half were smoking, half drinking and half doing both. Their stares followed me to the door, and I picked up new ones as I stepped inside. I took a bottle of low-shelf whiskey off a high shelf, paid for it, and walked out. The same stares picked me up as I walked back to my car. The moon slid behind a cloud. It was dark enough now.

I drank from the bottle as I drove. I pulled off the highway and crossed over railroad tracks. The blacktop turned to packed gravel, then to loose gravel, then to dirt. I spotted the building and parked a couple of car lengths behind a purple Oldsmobile Eighty-Eight with spinning rims and dual exhaust pipes that shined even in the blackness of the Delta night.

I slouched a little in the seat, resting the bottle between my knees. It wasn't as crowded as the time before. Twenty-five minutes later, a cat crept out from beneath the Oldsmobile's dual exhaust. Thirty-five minutes later, the girl who had introduced herself as Tasha walked out of the joint, trailed by a light-skinned Black man with a paunch and a fedora. They made the surveillance easy. They got into the Oldsmobile. The man must have cranked the engine. The shiny exhaust pipes shimmied, and the cat bolted into the woods.

I took another swig from the bottle and waited for her to get out of the car. Less than ten minutes later, she stepped out and lit a cigarette. The Oldsmobile drove away. I honked the horn in a short clip and flashed the headlights. I could only make out the outline of her dark skin as she wandered further from the green and red Christmas lights strewn across the building. The red glow from her cigarette grew larger through the front window of the Duster. She opened the door and got in. She wasted no time placing her hand on my right knee.

"I'm not here for that," I said. She reached for the door handle. To her, talk wasn't cheap. It cost her time, and time was money. Money kept her from getting hit.

"Wait," I said. "Close the door."

She looked over her shoulder at me. The sadness in her eyes escaped from behind the layers of heavy makeup. I held up a hundred-dollar bill folded lengthwise. She pulled the door shut. The first time I had been in my truck, not the Duster. I couldn't tell if she recognized me until she spoke.

"You gonna give me more money for doing nothing, Mister?" The echo of a voice that was decades older than the young hand she had put back on my knee was even sadder than her eyes.

"I just need you to introduce me to some of your friends, Tasha" I said, instantly realizing it was a cruel choice of words.

"I don't have any friends in Mississippi," she said, looking down, her voice trailing off. When she looked up and said, "Except maybe you," it was almost a whisper.

I asked her a question. The tears accumulated with her words, so she kept her answer short. And brutal.

I told her what to tell the men that came to pick her up at the end of the night. She nodded and got out of the car. I backed down the road until the dirt turned into gravel, then turned the car around. I crossed back over the railroad, moving onto the highway, and picked up speed. I passed the store. The crowd in the parking lot had grown denser. I passed the sign. Ten minutes later, I pulled into a motel that was two eight room buildings that faced one another. An empty pool with a sagging fence sat between the structures. Past the deep end of the pool there was a small office advertising vacancy in partially lit neon.

I'd checked in earlier. Fake name. Cash. The old man hadn't asked for ID. I took a pair of black gloves from a tactical bag on the passenger seat. I had two keys in my pocket each attached to a plastic disk with a white stenciled number.

There was a small white Baptist Church next to the motel. I parked in the rear of the church, walked past a large liberty-style bell surrounded by roses, and went into room 11. I sat at the table in the dark, propped my boots up and sipped what was left of the whiskey. Then I waited, watching room 2 through a slice between the crusty drapes.

I expected the van. I was right. The wide tires gripped the gravel as it lurched to a stop. On cue, two front doors opened. The side panel slid back. A guy I'd once heard being called Nails at Duffy's stepped out. Another man climbed out the passenger side. He held a baseball bat. The driver pulled a large revolver from his waistband. The men walked towards the door.

They stopped and turned when they heard a car approach. Its headlights cast fallow light across the men and threw their shadows onto the parking lot. It was a dark blue Ford sedan. I'd seen it before. The Sheriff sat in the passenger seat; the fat deputy drove. It rolled up and the man with the bat and the man with the gun traded words. The sedan drove off, red lights disappearing into the darkness.

The batman kicked in the unlocked door and the men walked into the room. In less than a minute they walked back out through the door, which now swung only from the top hinge.

The driver got back into the van. He pulled the door closed. Hard. The man with the bat yanked the girl from the back of the van. She slumped as he dragged her. She was handcuffed behind her back and naked below the waist. Her dress was ripped. I could see a red bra.

The man dragged her through the threshold. I opened my own door, picked up the gun resting next to the empty bottle, chambered a round and stepped out into the parking lot. I stepped underneath the concrete steps leading to the upstairs rooms. A shot clapped from the inside the room. Before I could step through a bush and around a metal barrel trashcan, the man with the bat appeared in the door and hustled into the van. He pulled the door shut on its tracks and got in the van, slamming the door.

The van backed up and thundered out of the lot. Again, I watched red lights disappear into the darkness. This time only one. One of the van's taillights was burnt out.

I ran to the room. The water was running. Tasha was in the tub. Her shirt was ripped off. It was soaked in the bloody water near her feet. Her head was slumped back against the faucet. The running water diluted layers of thick red blood. I turned it off.

The wound was gaping. There was a hole in her head near her left eye socket. Half her head was blown onto the tile behind her. I looked at her. She was young. She was beautiful. But she was dead.

19.

I RETRACED MY steps to the car tucked behind the church, pulled the gloves off, and drove away. There is a small creek to the east of my house. Black Creek. I stopped the Duster on the bridge and stood a while, thinking. I'd wanted to find out who was pimping her out. I thought she'd give them the message and they would come. I should have guessed what they might do to her. I threw the gloves in the creek. I didn't have blood on my hands. But it was on my heart. And would stay there.

I drove towards Magnolia Ridge. I was a mile from the creek and a mile from the house when a car pulled in behind me. Red wig-wag lights popped in the dark. A blue light attached to the passenger side visor pulsed. I stepped on the gas; the Duster pulled away from the Ford. I made a hard right into my driveway; I could feel the Duster's rear-end slide out behind me. I accelerated to straighten the car. I stopped near the shed and opened the door. I didn't think I could make it into my armory. I crouched as I exited the car and moved to the front of the Duster. I pulled the Sig from its holster and pointed it at the approaching car. I focused on the far-red dot of the night sights; the two rear red dots blurred in my open eye. The car stopped. Two words echoed from the PA system. A name.

I lowered the gun as Browning killed the lights and stepped out of the car. "You've got trouble," he said, and Professor Harold Hill's first day in Iowa flashed into my mind—*With a capital T and that rhymes with P and that stands for pool!*

"We can't talk here," he said. "Follow me."

"Give me two minutes," I said. Browning nodded, walked back to the Crown Vic and dropped into the seat. I covered the short distance to the shed and opened the door, grabbing a tactical bag off the seat. I heard crisp beeps as I entered the code on the keypad to unlock the interior door. Inside, I took two AR-15's, a Remington short-stock 12-gauge shotgun with a combat strap, and two Sig P226 9mm pistols. I unzipped the bag, placed the ammo inside and slipped the two pistols into a separate pocket on the outside. It took two trips to load the weapons I wanted into the Duster's trunk.

It took almost five times longer than I'd promised; I was almost ready in just under ten minutes. I walked to the house, went upstairs and into my closet. I gathered some clothes and toiletries and shoved them into a large duffel bag. I took the lockbox from the top of the dresser and a metal attaché case from the top shelf in the closet.

The duffel bag on my shoulder was heavy. I carried everything back downstairs and returned to my car, emptying my arms into the trunk. I held up a single finger for Browning to hold on and give me one more trip into the house. I walked into the kitchen and loaded a cardboard box with whiskey bottles and two short glasses. I grabbed a couple of cigars from a humidor near an empty wine rack.

As I followed Browning away from the house and down the driveway, I glanced in the rearview. I wasn't sure if I'd ever see the house again. And I wasn't sure I even cared.

Browning led me on a Minotaur's maze of crisscrossing dirt roads joined by four-way stops, most of which we rolled through. If either my instincts or Chy's information was wrong, this could be a death march. Fifteen miles and ten minutes later, Browning pulled up to a gate that led to a narrow driveway, which disappeared into a cluster of trees a quarter mile from the road. Browning got out, worked the dial of a combination lock, pulled the chain away, and opened the gate. I followed him through the gate. As the driveway squeezed into the trees, I saw a cabin. He pulled up beside it. I parked next to him. We both got out.

"What's this place?" I asked.

"Place you can use for a while. You sure as hell can't go home," he said.

"Whose cabin is this?"

"Friend of mine from New Orleans. He's from up this way, went to Southern Miss to play ball and ended up with NOPD. Family cabin. He says nobody's been up here in a while."

"You think?" I said, when we walked in the door. The cobwebs were thick, the dust thicker. It had a dank smell. I wondered if the place had electricity. A silent question Browning answered by opening the refrigerator. I saw the light. Empty. Fortunately, he had a six-pack of beer in his hand. He pulled a couple from the plastic webbing and tossed me one. We walked out onto the porch. He sat in the lone chair, and I leaned against a post. We both took long gulps of cold beer.

"There's a warrant out for you, for murder," Browning said.

"Who'd I kill?" I knew the answer, but I wanted to find out what Browning knew.

"Young Hispanic girl. Called herself Tasha. They don't know her real name. Sheriff thinks she's probably a runaway from Memphis."

"Why do they think I killed her?" I asked.

"You mean what was your motive, or are you asking what evidence they say they have?"

"The evidence."

"They say you were seen with her at The Rust Club a couple of times, including just a few hours before she was killed. The handcuffs are police issue, and you used to be a cop. That, and the manager of the motel gave them a positive ID that you paid for two rooms, including the room she was found in, the afternoon before she was murdered. By the way, that wasn't the smartest thing you've ever done."

I shook my head. "I wanted to see who would come looking for me. I didn't have any idea they'd kill her."

"You didn't think they were that dangerous?"

"No, it wasn't that. I knew they were dangerous, but she made them money. They were pimping her out. Girls aren't like dope or guns; you sell it and you've got to go get more to keep selling it. Same girl can make you money over and over, night after night. For months, even years. I didn't think they'd kill her because she was product."

We talked strategy for a half hour or so and killed two more beers apiece. When it was time to leave, he stated the obvious:

"You'll need a different car," he said.

"Agreed," I said. I figured he had something in mind. I was right.

"There's a turnaround leading down to Pritchett's Lake. Follow me over. I left a car near the boat ramp. An SS Monte Carlo."

I nodded. We got back in our cars. I followed him through a different maze of roads. This time, I paid more attention, so I'd find my way back to the cabin. He rolled to a stop near a sign—Pritchett's Lake—with an arrow to the left. He stopped, got out and walked back to my window.

"You'll see the car; one's the cabin, ones the car," he said, and handed me some keys.

I nodded.

"One more thing," he handed me one of his business cards. "On the back."

I flipped it over.

"Stan Fite, he runs the towing service."

There was a number. Local prefix. I help up the card without a word. I didn't recognize the name. Why should I?

"He's a friend; only one I told you'd be out here."

I nodded.

"Stay safe, brother," he said.

"You too."

He got back in his car and drove away. I headed down towards the lake. There was nobody around. I parked the Duster next to Browning's loaned Chevy, opened both trunks and transferred the cargo, including the tactical bag. I took a long look at the calm, flat lake. I left the Duster parked near the lake and drove away.

20.

I RETURNED TO the cabin, stretched out on the cot, and napped for an hour. I drank whiskey and dozed in the chair on the porch. I thought about what I had to do. And how I would do it. First, I had to figure out the players in this redneck rogue's gallery. I heard an owl. Something rustled behind the tree line, and I aimed the pistol into the darkness. It was nothing. Still thinking, I drank whiskey, smoked a cigar, and fell asleep in the chair.

The chirp of my cell phone stirred me.

"You ok?" Jamie's voice was frantic. Even concerned. More ice had thawed.

I blinked awake. "I'm safe, what's up?" I asked.

"You're not safe. You're wanted."

"I know, for killing a young girl, right?"

"What young girl? There's a high priority BOLO out for you for killing Detective Browning."

"Browning is dead?"

Killed on a traffic stop. They think. Back road out in the county. Shot in the head. Close range."

"Why do they think I did it?"

"Because he was found next to your Duster. His car was gone when a couple of Sheriff's deputies found him. They figure he pulled you over, approached the car, you shot him and then you took his car."

"Bet they don't have a key," I said.

"Maybe you took it," she said playing the hypothetical game.

We talked for a few minutes. Then we hung up.

The Monte Carlo was quieter than the Duster, but not as fast. I drove down the passageway between the trees, through the gate, and out onto the road. The road dipped and climbed for several miles. A gray Ford approached. Mississippi Highway Patrol.

I wasn't in my car; wasn't sure I'd be made. I passed the Trooper on a bridge. No such luck. As soon as the Trooper rolled off the bridge, he turned, and the light bar came to life. Like plugging in a Christmas tree. I heard the siren and hit the gas. The Chevy thrust forward. The Ford gained. This was bad. The BOLO must have included vehicle information. I wasn't sure how. Last I'd heard, they thought I was in his detective's car. So, somebody gave them this car's details. No other way Highway Patrol would have information on this Chevy so quickly unless they had included all of Browning's vehicles. I didn't even know if it was registered to him or not.

As I topped the crest of the hill, I could see a second Crown Vic. This cruiser was a slick top—no light bar on top. Red and blue light pulsated from the front grille.

There was a small post office on the right beyond a small cluster of abandoned construction vehicles. I accelerated, approached the intersection, crunched the brakes, and took a hard right onto the side road. The post office went by in a blur. The Trooper behind me had gained and stayed with me into the turn. I checked my rearview mirror. The man was large. I could make out a hulking shadow with mirrored aviator sunglasses. In my side mirror, I saw the slick top turn hard to its left. Behind it was a third Highway Patrol car I hadn't seen until now. This was messed up.

The side road was a two-lane, lined with telephone poles. I passed an electric power plant behind a large square fence and a blue water tower, then under a concrete overpass with the spray-painted names joined with crude hearts. I imagined that most of the memorialized lovers still lived in the area. Married. Divorced. Either way, I doubted that many of them still shared a love worthy of graffiti. I passed a silo. A convenience store appeared on the left on the near side of a railroad crossing. A decrepit motor home was parked in a dirt lot across from the convenience store. It was for sale. I turned into the lot. Dust kicked up. I slammed my boot into the brake pedal and sunk it to the floorboard. I pivoted the car, the rear end sliding to the left until I faced the three police cars.

The lights were bright; the sirens grew louder as the cars loomed in the Chevy's wide front window. They split as I gunned the engine and headed back to the highway. The wide tires caught the pavement as I crossed from the dirt lot back onto the asphalt of the two-lane. The gas pumps were deserted. A lean woman with vein-ridden arms and hair like a gray bird's nest stood outside the front door, smoking a cigarette, and drinking from a jar.

I steered the Monte Carlo underneath the canopy over the pumps. The police cars had fallen back in line behind me. I shot around the building and out onto a single lane road that ran alongside the railroad tracks. I saw the light bar from the lead police cruiser in the rearview mirror. I followed the road until another crossing appeared. I took it and crossed the tracks. The houses on this side of the tracks were closer together and run down. Another cliché. Two of the first five had full-sized refrigerators languishing on the front porch; four had clotheslines in the rear, the fifth sported a sagging above-ground pool that had turned into a makeshift bird bath.

Sirens in this neighborhood weren't rare. People sitting on their porches looked up, not in concern, but grateful for at least a quick distraction from the heat; didn't see the law chasing a white man in these parts much. A green pickup truck shot out from an intersection I had almost cleared. Squeezing behind my speeding Chevy, it was a good job the driver had at least slowed for the intersection, because I hadn't. He honked as I passed, and obviously didn't see or hear the police cars when he took a sharp left. The first police car slammed into the pickup truck. The other cars stopped. I slowed, hoping to see either the Trooper or the truck's driver step out. I saw the Trooper's door open and said a quick prayer.

Going to war with a crooked sheriff and his cronies was one thing. Running from legit cops was another. Cops and civilians alike were getting hurt, even killed. This was already out of hand. And it was going to get worse.

21.

THE LEAST I could do was find a car I knew nobody was using. The Forrest Springs Police Department sat off the town square. It was a long, single-story building. I watched from a bank parking lot two buildings away for twenty minutes. No activity. After thirty, a black and white Crown Victoria pulled up in front of the building near the flagpole. A young officer in a dark uniform stepped out. He left the car running and the headlights lit. He walked into the building carrying a metal clipboard. Four minutes passed. He walked out and got into the car. He drove out of the lot and took a left. I waited another ten minutes. No activity.

I didn't creep. I didn't run. I simply got out of the Chevy and walked to the rear of the building. A half-moon cast a murky glow on the pavement. An eight-foot fence bordered the parking lot to the rear of the precinct. Three industrial air conditioners sat at the base of the fence. The largest was almost three feet high. Smart. I stepped up onto the unit, grabbed the top of the fence, and hoisted myself over. I dropped onto a small patch of grass and crouched down. None of the windows on this side of the building were lit. Most likely detectives' and supervisors' offices.

Cherry's Mercedes SUV was parked in a spot on the far side of the lot. The driver's side window had been removed. I moved towards it and crouched by the door. An alley of light from a streetlamp shone on the SUV. It gave the white paint a dull shine. I could see that the driver's seat was covered in a large plastic bag. The headrest had been removed, mostly likely coated with brain matter.

I opened the door and slipped behind the wheel. The car smelled antiseptic. Sterile.

The keys were part of a murder investigation. They should have been carefully logged into a locked evidence locker. So, I knew they would be tucked up over the visor. I pulled it down and caught the keys. Sad, but typical. I looked out across the parking lot to the precinct. No activity, so I pulled the Mercedes out of the lot, and waited until I had turned out onto Second Street to switch the headlights on. Before the console lit, I saw a red light in the shape of a gas can. The SUV was low on gas. I drove over to the bank parking lot, opened the trunk of the Chevy and the rear hatch of the SUV and swapped the equipment, tactical bag and guns.

I drove to the cabin.

I smoked a cigar.

I drank bourbon.

I slept, but not well. I was up before five. I drove away from town. I stopped at a small gas station with a red roof. The pumps didn't take credit cards. I had to guess which side the gas cap was on as I pulled up to the pump. I guessed right, passenger side. I inserted the nozzle, flipped the metal guard up and squeezed the trigger. Nothing. I looked across the small lot through the glass walls of the store. A short man in a stained white T-shirt with an ample gut stood behind a counter. He looked out, saw I was white, and the pump magically worked. I filled the tank.

I stepped into the convenience store. I heard a bell behind me. Two short racks of groceries sat to my right. A couple of tables and random folding chairs sat in the back. The tables were covered in a stiff, plastic, red and white tablecloth. A black ashtray and metal napkin holder sat on each table. There was a long glass case to the right of the counter, glazed with a haze of grease clouding bins of scrambled eggs, a variety of biscuits, gravy, sausage, and bacon.

"Biscuits fresh?" I asked.

"From scratch, just this morning," the man said as if he had baked them

I noticed for the first time that the man had a toothpick in his mouth, clenched between uneven teeth. I ordered a chicken biscuit, a fried steak biscuit, and a large black coffee. The man punched at the cash register. I paid cash, and the man handed me my change. I traded two of the quarters back and grabbed a local newspaper on my way out. I walked back to the car.

The biscuits were wrapped tight in thin plastic. I got back in the SUV, took enough sips from the coffee to top it off with bourbon, and unwrapped the chicken biscuit. It was good. The steak biscuit was better. The roads were empty as I drove back to the cabin. The story about the accident was on the front page. The Trooper was fine. Airbag. The woman was in critical condition at a local hospital. Other details were scant. A sergeant at the local Trooper barracks confirmed a chase but nothing about who they were chasing. There was a picture of the police cruiser buried in the bed of what turned out to be a silver Dodge pickup truck.

I topped off the half-empty coffee cup with what was left in a bottle of Eagle Rare, said a short prayer, and took a long swig. I drank until it was time to sleep or slept until it was time to drink again.

I woke up, took a long shower, and left the cabin at midnight.

22.

I EXITED THE highway and pulled into the parking lot. At the jook joint Tasha had mentioned Cowboyz. At the time I didn't know either what it was or how it was spelled. I found out later it was like the badlands of truck stops—a rolling border town. It sat at the top of a hill on the west side of the exit. There was nothing else in sight, except for a couple of self-storage units and a discount tire place.

The rigs were parked in long rows. Some lit, some dark. Men in overalls and mesh baseball caps walked between the trucks and the main building. I took another pass around the scales. I saw the shadow of the van in the collective glow of lights emanating from the parked trucks. I had missed it when I first pulled in. Or it hadn't been there yet.

I rolled to a stop near the side of the building, next to a cluster of propane tanks. The van was parked at the furthest end of the lot, beside a dumpster and a short row of pay phones, facing the opposite direction. The panel door was open. I watched three girls make trips between the van and the rigs. They were all Hispanic. Young. Thin. They wore tight white T-shirts and denim skirts, spindly legs climbing up into the rigs as the doors were pulled shut. After a short time, the doors would open, and the girls would retreat from the rigs and drop to the concrete of the parking lot. Each time, they would return to the van before they went to their next john.

As the minutes crept into the third hour of the surveillance, one of the girls walked from a truck, stepped into the van, and didn't come back out. Fifteen minutes after that, a second girl climbed into the van and didn't get back out. End of the night shift, apparently.

The third girl climbed down out of a silver and red rig and started towards the van. She was halfway across the lot when a four-door Ford sedan pulled up alongside her. The driver spoke to her through the passenger window. I recognized him, even from a distance. He was fat. She got into the car. It did a wide U-turn under some truck scales and pulled in behind the van. The fat man flashed the headlights and gave a chirp of the horn. On cue, the side panel door of the van slid closed, and it rolled away. The sedan followed it to the edge of the lot. The van pulled back onto the road and headed towards the highway; the Ford took a right.

I drove around the opposite side of the store, fell in behind the Ford and followed it for a couple of miles. The road was deserted. I could only get so close. The car took a left turn into a parking lot. I passed it by and saw the sign for a funeral home. I rounded a corner, so I was out of sight and took the next left into a Mexican restaurant. It was done up in yellow stucco. A ceramic burro, with "Welcome" painted across it, sat near the road. There were no cars on the side of the building and only one in the back. An old Cutlass sitting on three tires and a cinderblock. I killed the lights and pulled alongside the tree line that separated the funeral home from the restaurant. I got out, walked into the woods, and followed a path. I could see the sedan framed by large trees and obscured by small ones.

The car was running. The interior dome light was on. The fat deputy inside was distracted. I didn't creep. I didn't run. I walked to the car at an angle. I could see the back of his head. He had the seat pushed back as far as it would go. His window was open. His eyes were closed. I couldn't see the top of her head until I was less than a foot from the car. Predictably, it was in his lap. His brown uniform pants were bunched down against his boots. His legs were pasty and hairless and as fat as the rest of him.

With a pistol in my hand, I stood in the window. A shadow fell over the car. She opened her eyes and looked up. Her shirt was unbuttoned. Her eyes grew wide with fear, but she stayed completely silent. She scrambled out of the car. The fat deputy only opened his eyes when she pulled her mouth off him.

"What the…?" he said, his voice throaty and surprised. He glared and rolled his head over his right shoulder, trying to see her in the darkness. "You little…"

He still hadn't seen me. I pulled the hammer back. It clicked. He turned towards me. His eyes grew wider than hers. I fired. First, he died. Then he slumped against the door. I opened it. I pulled him halfway from the car. Gravity did most of the work. The girl had walked around the back of the car. She stopped and stood completely still. I stepped over the body and reached into the car. A twelve-gauge shotgun was attached to the roof over the front seat. It unhooked much like a fire extinguisher. I pulled it free and chambered a round. The fat Deputy's shoulders were on the ground. An organ he would never play again was exposed. I took the shotgun and held it against his center. I looked at the young girl with dark skin and even darker eyes. Her pupils drew tight like a cat's. She stepped forward, put her finger inside the trigger guard and pulled. At least he was already at the funeral home. An open casket was unlikely. I dropped the shotgun on top of him. The girl followed me back to my car without a word. I could hear the leaves and brush under our feet in the silence. We got in. I started the engine and eased out around the restaurant. I saw another burro with "Gracias" painted on it at the exit. I pulled back out onto the road.

"Think they'll buy it as suicide?" I asked. She smiled, but as though she was ashamed to.

I looked over at her. She had buttoned her shirt and smoothed her skirt out under her.

"You hungry?" I asked.

She nodded. We ate. We didn't talk much, but she told me what I needed to know. As always, it starts with the names. And I had names.

The Catholic church was on the side of the road. A lone Buick sat in the driveway near a sidewalk that led to the rectory. I told her to wait ten minutes and then come inside. The front doors of the church were unlocked. I walked past the Holy Water. Stained glass has moods of its own, and the overcast afternoon gave the church a somber feel. I stared at the glass, following it up to the apex of the windows. Stations of the Cross lined the walls, a large crucifix hung over the altar. The tabernacle was gold. The rug down the center aisle was purple. I glanced at the rug, looked up at the crucifix. Catholic churches have a reverence; the weight of tradition, the guilt that comes with faith tempered with the hope of redemption.

Father Joe Santos heard me walk through the oversized door. He was a Cuban. The kind of man with rough hands and a soft demeanor. He came through a door to the side of the choir pit. He was short and squat. I'd heard about him, but never met him. He gave a silent wave and approached me. He had a slight limp and a graying goatee.

He got close enough for me to hear his voice, spoken just above a whisper at a respectful volume. He saw, and I noticed, that I had blood on my shirt.

"Confession?"

I turned to the confessional, walked to it, opened the door on the right and sat down. He did the same but sat in the room on the left. We slid the wooden doors aside to expose the screen between us that we shared.

I started an untraditional confession with tradition.

"Bless me, Father, for I have sinned. It's been a lifetime since my last confession."

"Whose lifetime?" he asked.

"Mine and some people that aren't with us anymore," I said.

"I understand," he said. And I got the feeling that he did. I'd understand just how much later. But not yet.

I told him about the girls. The one in the car and the others. And the Sheriff. And what I'd heard about the cult. He wasn't as shocked as he should have been. He said he could help. I told him about the Deputy. We talked about sin and lust. Forgiveness. And redemption. He believed in it. I didn't. Not for the men involved in this. Maybe not even for me.

We walked out of the booths at the same time. She was sitting in one of the furthest pews. She looked small and even younger, swallowed in the dark wood. The stained-glass cast shadows like colored jellybeans on the canvas of her dark face. I gave the priest my cell phone number and shook his hand. He blessed her. Then me. I left.

She was safe. Relatively. I drove to the cabin. I drank, and smoked, and watched as darkness became shrouded by blackness. I fell asleep with a short glass of bourbon in my hand and a cigar burning. I slept, but not well.

23.

IT WAS THE next night. I drove to the truck stop and watched the same routine as before. Three girls came and went. Back and forth between the van and the rigs. I waited until one girl got into the van and didn't come back out. Then another.

I slipped out of the SUV and walked between the maze of trucks until I was hiding myself behind one, near the van. I crouched behind the tires and watched as the third girl stepped out of the truck I was using for cover. She walked to the van. Seconds later the headlights came on and the van pulled out of the lot and hit the road.

I ran back to the SUV and followed at a distance. It drove for ten minutes and took a left onto a desolate county road that only led one place. The Church. I kept following. I parked and got out, walked along the tree line. The van stopped in front of the barn. The driver got out, his silhouette bold in the van's headlights. He cast a shadow on the barn's large doors. He unlocked a chain running between the door's handles.

As the nose of the van disappeared into the cavernous barn, I ran over and pushed myself flush against the wall outside the open door. A few minutes passed. I heard metal doors clank shut from inside.

The wall moved as the man pulled the door closest to me closed. His hand reached out across the threshold to close the other door. I stepped forward, grabbed it, and pulled him out of the barn. I thrust my other hand into his elbow, and he fell to the ground. I stepped forward with my right foot. I still had his left hand gripped hard, so I now stood over him. I drew my pistol.

"Don't make a sound," I said, moving the pistol closer to his head.

He nodded. I hit him several times with the butt of the gun. Blood began to seep from his head. He passed out. I dragged him by his collar into the barn.

There was normal barn stuff in there. Three stalls. No horses. One of the stalls had narrower bars, like a jail.

The girls were in the stall with the narrow bars. It was bare, except for eight woven mats lying on the swept floor. As expected, there was one more mat than girl. The girls looked to be between fourteen and seventeen. I used a key hanging on a hook to unlock the stall and told the girls to wait for me. As I walked out of the barn, I saw the girls wander out of the stall and look at the man lying unconscious but still alive on the floor.

I could see the church in the distance. I walked towards it, staying close to the tree line.

The church was housed on a large compound of bleached-out cattle land in the far northwest corner of the county. As I got closer, I could see the main building, a nondescript octagon shaped granite structure with high windows and deep grooves. The architecture could best be described as brutalist. It didn't look like a church. No steeple. No stained glass. It looked like a prison.

I glanced at my watch. 3:13 a.m. The lot was half-full. Strange. I was on a narrow path, skirting the tree line. Behind the main building was an old barn and a new house. I crouched down. Floodlights cast dull shadows on the dark building, like wet spots on cardboard. A metal fire ladder was bolted to a rear exterior wall. A red metal door was secure but unlocked. I turned the knob and opened the door a crack.

The kitchen was empty. It glistened. There was a large cutting block table that ran the length of the room between industrial appliances. The kitchen led to a small hallway which in turn led to a stairwell. I crept up the stairs. The stairwell opened out into area that appeared to serve as a choir loft. It was behind the pews facing the altar. The room was large. A man stood behind the altar in a purple stole holding up a large red book. I watched from the shadows of the room. The congregation was facing away from me. The minister was facing me. He spoke in a loud voice. Of a time of blessing. Of virgins and the apocalypse. Of sacrifice and community. And of redemption and death. He spoke with his free hand and gestured often to a cluster of girls in the first row, clad all in white, their heads and faces covered. They looked small and young. Behind them were couples, two by two. One man. One woman.

Must be the girls' parents, I thought. The preacher held the book flat in his palm and scanned the page. He looked up with his eyes squinted and his face flushed. He spoke a name. Elizabeth something. One girl nudged the girl on her left, and the nudged girl stood slowly. I saw her turn to look two rows behind her. She gave a crippled smile to a man and a woman. They motioned her towards the stage. She approached the preacher and knelt in front of him. He waved his left hand around her and held the red book high, chanting.

After a few moments he blessed her again, and she stood. He held her hand and walked her around a large, silent organ and disappeared through a door. Nobody moved. Seconds later, he reappeared, standing with her behind clouded glass on a raised platform behind the altar. Her head and face were covered again. Other than that, she was naked. I could make out her form. She couldn't have been more than twelve or thirteen. She stepped down until only her head peeked out from the crest of the water behind the glass in what resembled a human aquarium. I watched as he chanted. I'd heard of people speaking in tongues but never seen it. Until now. At least, that's what I thought it was.

After he stopped speaking, he held the girl's hand as she walked up and out of the water. He towered over the child as they disappeared. Almost ten minutes passed as the congregation sat in silence. A woman walked in from behind a curtain, sat at the organ and began to play a grim recessional.

The crowd filed out a row at a time. Front to back. I saw the woman the little girl had nodded to hesitate for a moment and look back at the door her daughter had disappeared through. The man did not look back. He gripped his wife's arm. She faced away from the altar and walked out with him. The organ stopped when the room was empty. The woman at the organ stood and walked out through the curtain.

I moved across the balcony to the stairway opposite the one I had used to get up here and descended. I opened a door that led into the sanctuary and made my way along the wall to the front. To the side of the door the minister had used were three small steps I hadn't seen from the balcony. The steps led to the curtain that the organist had used. I moved out behind the altar. There was a gold box behind me that I figured was a tabernacle. It was covered in a large swatch of purple cloth trimmed in gold. I pulled the cloth from the top like it was a parrot cage. There was no parrot. Only snakes.

I dropped the cloth and left the church. I wanted to meet the minister, but the other girls needed to be secured. I had to leave the newly baptized girl in the church. I returned to the barn not knowing what I was going to do with the unconscious man.

It wasn't a problem. When I opened the doors to the barn, I saw that the man was dead. He looked like he had been bludgeoned with something. The three shovels lying by his feet were a clue. The girls scrambled back into the van. I drove through the open doors. I called the priest and told him we were on our way.

When I arrived at the Catholic church, the priest was waiting with two older women. Nuns. We left the girls with the nuns. The priest walked me back to the van.

"If something happens to me, find this man," he said. He gave me a name, Paul Silva, and a number. 313 prefix: Detroit.

His word was "if"; his tone was prophetic and echoed of "when". Everything had been said. We drove silently as the priest dropped me back where I had left Cherry's SUV. He took the van. I drove back to the cabin. I drank bourbon and smoked a cigar. A dog barked in the distance. I slept, but not well.

A noise outside the cabin woke me just before dawn. I grabbed a pistol and walked out onto the porch. A red tow truck was making its way up the rocky driveway, the tow hook swinging behind it. It stopped, and a man got out. I tucked the pistol into the back of my jeans and started down the short steps to meet him. As far as I knew, only one person knew where I was. Browning's friend. He was an older guy with a paunch and long arms. He wore thick glasses that hung from his neck by a chain. His mesh baseball cap had the same logo as the truck's door and the same words: Fite's Towing.

We traded names. His was Stan Fite, which I already knew. He held out his hand. We shook.

"You're Browning's friend?"

He nodded. "I met Browning when he joined the police department a couple of years back. We used to fish together. I run the tow service the cops use. Browning told me you were out here. Said I was the only one who knew."

I nodded. He told me a little about what was going on and then added, "I never believed you killed him. I was the one who towed your Duster when they found Browning's body. I heard a few things that night."

Just because he was Browning's friend didn't necessarily mean he was my friend. But I trusted Browning enough to give Stan the benefit of the doubt. And I wasn't swimming in good options for backup.

"What brings you out this way?" I asked.

Stan told me what he'd seen, wished me good luck, and left. I watched the tow hook swing as he drove away. The sun began to rise. Predictably. I took a restless nap until my cell phone rang. Before I could muster a groggy greeting, I heard the priest say, "They found me."

The line went dead.

I rolled to a stop in the church's rear lot near the van which was parked underneath a basketball hoop. Unzipping the tactical bag on the passenger seat, I pulled out a short-stock shotgun, got out and racked it as I ran to the rear door of the church. It was open. I made my way through the kitchen and then some type of community room. I found the priest in a small office off a long hall. He was lying on the floor, bleeding from his chest. I knelt over him. He was in shock. Dying. There was a lot of blood.

He stared up at me. His eyes were glassy but focused.

"Where are the girls?"

"They went with the nuns. They're safe." There was no breath behind the words. He handed me a small prayer card.

"Who did this?"

"Lompoc," was all that could surface above his clipped gasps.

"What?"

His pupils retreated and pulsed. His mouth opened, but Lompoc would be his last word. His head slumped. He was dead. I said the short prayer on the card and left him. There was an old green wall phone in the kitchen. I picked it up and dialed 911, having no faith in who would respond. I set the receiver on the counter and left the church.

24.

I DROVE A town over and went to a diner. I sat on a red stool and drank black coffee from a white ceramic mug. I ate an omelet. I read another abandoned newspaper. I was alone at the end of the counter. I called Jamie. She answered on the second ring.

"Dan, what's up? You ok?" The thawing had continued, and her voice was softer, but still guarded.

"So far," I said. "I need some information. Some of it might be a long shot."

"I'll try," she said.

I gave her the name and the Priest's last word.

"Lompoc? What's that?" she asked.

"I don't know. All he said."

"Spell it," she said.

"L-O-M-P-O-C. But I'm guessing."

"I'll reach out," she said. "Be careful, Dan."

"You too, stay safe. Thanks, Jamie." It didn't feel like a time for nicknames. I hung up. I drank three more cups of coffee. The place was empty, and the waitress sat at a far booth, chain-smoking and reading a magazine. She looked up from time to time. I held up my mug. She started to get up and then sat back down. She motioned to the coffee maker, and I stepped behind the counter and refilled the mug myself.

That night I drove back to the church compound. I rolled the Mercedes to a stop and parked it, partially shrouded in a cluster of evergreens. There was no briefing. No dry-erase board. No tactical plan. I got out, opened the rear hatch, and unzipped a large duffel bag. I pulled out a shoulder rig with the Sig and released the clip. Full. I pushed the magazine into the gun with my palm until it clicked. I draped the rig over my shoulder and pulled the straps tight against my belt.

The church lot was half-full. Again. Strange. It was 1:50 in the morning. I took the same door to the same stairway to the same balcony. I watched the minister. He spoke in a baritone. Fire. Brimstone. Ministers and politicians know the formula: fear breeds money. The audience sat transfixed. Hands held low. No palms stretched towards heaven. No 'Amens'. The potency didn't derive from originality. It ended with the same ceremony with a different girl with different parents. She was as young but with dark hair. I waited until the people filed out. When the music stopped the organist extinguished the candles and walked out, leaving an eerie silence.

I waited ten minutes and walked down the opposite stairwell and through the doors behind the now-silent organ. The hallway was empty. I moved past office doors on both sides. I racked the shotgun. I heard movement inside the next room on my right. The door was cracked. I eased it open. It was the side door to the main office. The minister's office. Behind a grand desk with one open drawer was a narrow door, wedged between oversized bookcases with thick bound volumes. The door was ajar, so I peeked through—once low, once high—and moved in to scan the shadows of the windowless room.

There was a large bed. Pillows. Candles. It looked like a sultan's den. One wall was lined with monitors focused on different parts of the church. He knew I was coming. The young girl, who had been baptized minutes earlier, knelt on the bed. She was wrapped in a white sheet. I held my index finger to my lips. She pointed with her eyes to an open door leading to a spiral stairway. Sickly light escaped from the floor below. I looked at the girl. She looked at the shotgun.

"Get dressed, go home," I said, as I moved towards the light. I peered down the stairwell. Nothing. I leaned tight against the metal rail. The stairs led into a large concrete room, some type of bunker. One wall was lined with shelves holding food, water, provisions of all kinds and boxes with medical and hazmat symbols. Two new portable generators sat in a corner. Several gas cans were arranged nearby. The room was lit by naked bulbs under thick mesh wire and had a smell—something dank and overwhelming. Paper. Ink. Almost like the smell of a van crammed with marijuana, but it was flatter, drier. It was the smell of money, a lot of money. The pallets were stacked higher than the shelves. Bundles of cash sat on the wooden bases wrapped in plastic. There was movement.

A man stepped out from behind the shadow cast by the tall pallets. He raised a gun, fired, and missed. I lifted the shotgun and pulled the trigger. The man ducked behind the money. The buckshot crashed into the corner of one of the bundles. Shards of paper and plastic kicked and scattered like dandelion puff in a strong wind. I moved forward and braced against one of the bundles of money, crouching down. I could see bare feet through the open area between the wooden base posts. I fired. The preacher's feet exploded. I rounded two corners, racked the shotgun, and pointed the bead at his head. He raised his gun but not at me. I wanted to shoot him. He beat me to it.

I reached into the hole in the plastic left by the shotgun blast as I passed and pulled out wads of hundreds. I stuffed what I could in the deep pockets of my cargo pants and made my way back through the bunker.

I unscrewed all the gas cans and picked one up before kicking the rest of them over. Gas poured out onto the glazed concrete. I carried the gas can up the stairs. I stood at the top of the stairs, propped the can on the top rail and emptied it. I pulled a wad of blood money out of my pocket, peeled off a bill and stuffed the rest back in my pocket. I pulled my lighter from another pocket and lit the bill, tossing it down onto one of the stairs below.

I stepped back through the narrow door. The sheet was on the floor near the bed. The girl was gone. I wanted to watch the place burn, but I didn't wait. I drove towards Fite's Towing but stopped and parked a mile away. I drank whiskey, smoked a cigar, and dozed while I waited for daylight. I didn't greet it in person and woke just before seven. I drove to the tow shop.

25.

UP WITH THE rooster, Stan was working on one of his own trucks when I drove through the gate. The cliché junkyard dog wasn't a tooth-baring, blood-thirsty mastiff. It was a dusty beagle that barely opened an eye as I drove within a foot of its tail. Fite pulled his head from under the hood and wiped his hands on a rough towel. He walked towards me.

"I need a car," I said.

"No problem. I've got something to show you."

He led me to a small office, walked to a desk in the corner, and picked a tape off the top of one of the stacks of invoices and empty pizza boxes. There was a small TV and a VCR on another table. He slid the tape into the player and pulled the knob on the TV. An image emerged after a couple of seconds of static—the rear of a sheriff's car. I remembered what I had been doing on the time and date in the bottom right-hand corner of the screen. I was waiting for a call.

The seconds continued to roll. I watched as a fat man in a brown uniform exited the car carrying a rifle. The car was parked in the driveway of a modest split-level house. Nice, more siding than brick, above-ground pool. Basketball hoop. American flag. This had to be from a security camera affixed to a nearby house. The quality was better than I'd expect from a system still recording to VHS. He walked towards the rear of the house. He braced the rifle against the brick corner of the house and stared into the scope. Several moments later, he pulled the trigger. His shoulder kicked slightly.

He walked back towards the camera. I saw a street sign as he backed out of the driveway and drove away. I recognized the name of the street and that it ran parallel to Cherry's. There were shallow woods between the two streets. Now, I knew what got Cherry and Amanda killed. Not completely sure who had killed them. Well, I was for Cherry, but not yet for Amanda. Stan never told me where he got the tape. And I didn't ask. It was telling the sheriff's deputy wasn't worried about parking in the private home's driveway or pulling off a hit in uniform.

I WANTED TO take my Duster but decided against it and left Fite's in an old Isuzu Rodeo he loaned me. "You know, Stan, this isn't my first rodeo…. actually, it is." He smiled but I wasn't sure he got the joke as he tossed me the keys.

I'd miss the Mercedes—it was a hell of a nice ride. But it stood out, especially with the vanity plate, and it was, after all, stolen from the PD, so it was time to let it go. I'd given Fite the keys and asked him to park it somewhere even the inept local cops would find it. I was three miles down the road when my phone rang. It was Jamie. She got right to the point. She spelled it. I had guessed correctly.

"L-O-M-P-O-C is a federal pen. It's a compound, varying levels of security, including maximum. It's on the central coast of California, Santa Barbara County. I talked to some people in federal Bureau of Prisons. I didn't have much to go on, with what you gave me, but, feds, multi-agency, I'd say this has to do with an attempted prison break a couple of years back. ATF had some people undercover posing as prison guards in the maximum-security pods. Deep cover, long-term. They had an attempted prison break; one of the leaders of the White Werewolves motorcycle gang, top cat inside, got sniped by a guard who turned out to be undercover ATF. Prosecutions followed, the ATF agent testified and then disappeared, most likely into the Marshals' Witness Protection Program. Werewolves took an almost fatal hit, inside and outside.

Guys in for short stretches in the minimum and medium security wings flipped. You can guess the rest."

"Anything specific about Paul Silva?"

"I couldn't get that much. Silva's a Deputy Marshal, been on the job awhile, moved around before landing in Detroit. A lot of the line Deputy U.S. Marshals I reached out to didn't know much about him. Even the ones in the offices he worked over the years. Even in Detroit. My guess?"

"Of course," I said. She had great instincts as a cop. And as a woman. Like everything, police work is about the human condition. You only need criminal laws for things that people want or want to do. Sex, greed, jealousy, ego, whatever. Jamie understood women and tolerated men, and sometimes that made for the best kind of cop. And woman.

She cut into my thoughts. "My take is that Paul Silva, and that sure as hell isn't his real name, was a handler for Witness Security. Basically, a shadow. My guess is that he was the Priest's handler, the ex-ATF agent who took the shot at LOMPOC that killed the Werewolves leader, Santos, Marquez, whatever his real name was."

"Marquez," I said.

"Whatever," she replied.

We talked for another couple of minutes. After we both said goodbye, I was about to flip the phone closed when I heard her voice again.

"Dan." I put the phone back to my ear.

"Be careful, it sounds like you're into some dangerous guys on this one," she said. "Promise to keep me posted."

She hung up before I could promise. It was nice to hear the concern in her voice. I kept driving. I saw a bridge in the distance.

I SAW THE van as I stopped at a red light on the far side of the short bridge on a windy road cut into the dense foliage. But I saw it too late. The headlights grew larger, and a sharp bolt of panic skated against my spine as I realized it wasn't going to come to a stop behind me. It swerved at the last moment, passed me on the left crossing over into the oncoming lane. There were no other vehicles in sight.

The van slid in front of me. The man I'd seen at Duffy's with the tight, vein-ridden arms, littered with faded tattoos. The man I knew as Nails. He stepped out and racked a shotgun. He moved around the van with an undertaker's gait. He fired. Shot plowed into the glass and metal of the old Rodeo.

I moved across the passenger seat, grabbed the door handle, and spilled out onto the pavement. He fired again. More glass shattered. The engine block provided the best cover, so I rolled onto my shoulder and held the Sig parallel with the ground. I closed one eye. I could see Nails' left boot underneath the van. His right boot was obscured by the tire. I could tell he was crouching because I could see the denim covering his calf leading away at an angle from his boot. I closed one eye and aimed. The boot was likely steel-toed, the leather terse and thick. I raised the Sig an inch and fired. The 9mm round plowed into the flesh and bone just above the boot. He collapsed to the pavement but had the wherewithal to move further behind the tire.

I figured he would predict I would come between the Rodeo and the rear of the van. Instead, I moved alongside to the front of the van passing the grille. I ducked under the rear-view mirror jutting out from the driver's side door. He was peeking around the rear of the van looking for me. I closed my left eye again. I could see Nails' balding head and the thin patch of hair receding back from the crown. I saw it one second. A second later, I pulled the trigger, and the back of Nails' head disintegrated to a flap of skin floating on top of a red pool of blood.

I looked around. I was standing between a discount tire shop and a generic, anti-Blockbuster video store. I walked back around the van and got into the Rodeo, crossed two lanes, and rolled it over the curb and the grass between the sidewalk and the road. The Rodeo dipped back down as I rolled into the parking lot and pulled into a parking spot in front of the tire shop. I grabbed the duffel bag from the backseat of the Rodeo, slung it over my shoulder, and jogged back to the van. I opened the rear doors. There was a small medical kit that looked like an orange-and-white tackle box. I wasn't not sure why a coroner would need a medical kit, but I didn't wonder too long or complain too much.

I opened it, pulled the floating shelves out and reached into the deep part of the box. I snagged a handful of rubber gloves, peeled two away and put them on. I pulled out a large roll of medical tape. There was a gurney with a sheet on it. I grabbed the sheet and left the gurney. For now.

The man's head was pouring blood. The wound gaping. I wrapped the stiff white sheet around his head. He looked like Casper the ghost. The sheet began to saturate almost instantly, the dark blood staining the sheet red from the inside.

I wrapped tape around his head in wide swaths until he looked like a mummy. I picked him up, dragged him to the back of the van, and pushed him into the space between the gurney and the van's interior left wall. I slammed the doors, ran around the van and jumped into the driver's seat. Just as I sat down and closed the door a vehicle approached. I put the van in gear and did a U-turn away from the oncoming vehicle. It took a left before it reached me; I rolled through the downtown area and took a left underneath a train overpass just beyond the discount furniture store that had been "Going Out of Business" for almost two years. I accelerated past the credit union, the water department and the county animal shelter and took a right into the small driveway leading to the morgue.

I backed the van to the rear door of the single-story brick building. The van made that annoying beeping sound until I slammed it up into "P." I turned it off and took the keys out of the ignition. The key to the back door was on the same chain as the van key. I unlocked the door and flipped the latch at the top so that I could open the other door. I opened the van's rear doors and slid the gurney out, letting it drop onto its wheels against the asphalt. I reached in and dragged Nails out by his boots and busted leg onto the bare gurney. I pushed the gurney into the morgue and threw a full row of switches up. Fluorescent lights pulsed on in sequence.

The inside of the morgue was boxlike. I saw an office marked "*James K. Pierce, Chief Medical Examiner – Slate County Mississippi*" in large letters, stenciled onto frosted glass. I rolled Nails past. The phrase, 'dead as a door*nail*,' came to my mind, and I smiled. The air was thick with the pungent smell of disinfectant.

I walked into the largest room. Two of the walls were paneled in stainless steel. Each had four drawers framed by the shiny metal. I opened the top left drawer on the wall nearest to me and pulled out the slab. Old white guy. I opened the top right drawer. Old Black guy. I opened the bottom right drawer. Empty. I rolled the gurney closer and moved Nails down onto it. I rolled him into the wall and shut the drawer. I was just about to walk out when I heard a sharp series of beeps from inside the drawer. I opened the drawer and rolled the gurney out. His cell phone was in the pocket of his jeans. I pulled it out. It was a text.

"WHERE RU? AT RANKIN'S – PULL UP – I'LL
COME OUT. U CAN FOLLOW ME OVER. JKP"

RANKIN'S GROCERY WAS a locals-only hole-in-the-wall barbecue place up East Main from the downtown Square past the Ford dealership, the State Highway Patrol barracks, and a row of churches. The pulled pork and hamburgers were great, the ribs were mediocre and the iced tea perfectly sweetened. They didn't sell alcohol, but that didn't mean that the town's men didn't drink it there at night playing cards and trading lies.

I turned off the light and grabbed an empty gurney from the hallway, rolled it out to the van and slid it inside, locking the door behind me. I started the van and rolled back into downtown Forrest Springs towards Rankin's. I pulled up to Rankin's large outside window.

I saw the Lexus with the Coroner's office magnet plastered to the front door parked directly in front. I flashed the lights. A minute later, the dapper man walked out in a seersucker suit, arranging his derby on his head. He gave a curt wave, unlocked the Lexus and got in. He backed out of the space then pulled past the van. I followed.

26.

HE CUT DOWN two alleys and came out between an estate jewelry store and a bakery. He took a left and drove through downtown towards the Ford dealership, passing under the highway and up the ramp to pick it up. I followed. He took the second exit, drove up the hill and took a left back over the highway. There was a tire wholesaler on the right and a large RV dealership on the left. A mile down, just past an old folks' home, the coroner took a right.

Another quarter mile down, the pavement turned to gravel, then dirt. We crossed over a small creek. There were cows behind the fence line to our right; nothing on our left but trees and open fields. He turned down another gravel lane. Some of the houses were abandoned, all were decrepit, a few barely standing. The Lexus stopped in front of a white clapboard house with a porch filled with plastic garbage bags and other assorted junk. Chickens walked around, pecking, and an assortment of dogs, some pregnant, all mangy, sniffed around the yard. He looked back at the van. I turned away before he saw my face and made my way into the back of the van. I squeezed around the side of the gurney to the right. I heard the coroner's footsteps coming around the van. I could hear him through the open driver's side window.

"Grab the boxes and carry them in. Let's get out of here, it reeks."

I waited. I heard a knock on the van's back door.

"Open up, Nails. What the hell are you doing in there?"

I reached for the inside handle of the door, opened it, and shoved. The door hit the coroner plumb in the forehead. I jumped down and pulled the Sig from the holster. He was groggy but still on his feet. I knocked the bowler off his head and replaced it with the well of the Sig.

"You into meth, too?" I asked. He was bleeding from his forehead, swaying, almost unconscious. I might have hit him too hard to get any information. I knew all I really needed to know. They were into everything, I was sure. I pushed him up into the van on the opposite side of the gurney. I closed the doors. I walked to the Lexus and took the keys from the ignition. A dirty, rail-thin, white man with long, stringy, blond hair and no shirt stepped out onto the porch. I tossed him the keys. He caught them.

"Got kids in there?" I hadn't seen any.

His response wasn't inspired. "Huh?"

"Keep the car," I said. I started to walk back towards the van. I yelled over my shoulder. "...and feed these dogs."

I got back in the van and pulled forward into the driveway beside a pockmarked old Mustang with no hood or trunk. It had more bond-o than metal. I backed out and pulled past the house. The now-not-so-dapper coroner stirred behind me. I drew the Sig, looked over my right shoulder into the back of the van. The coroner had opened his eyes. I was probably still within earshot of the man with the stringy blonde hair and his recently acquired Lexus when I pulled the trigger and buried a round into his Coroner's frontal lobe.

Back at the morgue, I followed the same routine and rolled the corpse past its own office. The drawer under Nails was empty, until I pushed the coroner into it.

I walked back out to the van, glanced in the back at the boxes he'd referred to. I hadn't paid much attention to them. As expected, the ingredients for meth. I hadn't seen the small black gym bag before, either. It was wedged halfway up under the seat.

I got back in the driver's seat and reached down behind the seat and opened it. Cash. Small bills. Probably a couple of thousand, wrapped loosely with rubber bands. I had plenty of cash left from the church. I had an idea.

I pulled in the driveway leading to the animal shelter. I stepped out of the van. Dogs were barking frantically from the cages to the sides and back. I judged people a lot by how they treated animals. Some of the best people I knew, in part, rescued themselves by rescuing animals. I didn't see any cars; the place was deserted this time of night. There was a mail slot in the front door. I opened the gym bag and stuffed the bills through. I could imagine the surprise in the morning when the shelter's most eager employee pushed the door open.

It was almost time to leave town. Almost.

27.

I CALLED FITE.

"Dan, what's going on?"

"Not much, I need a favor."

"Yeah, almost anything," Fite said.

"Almost?"

"Hell yeah, *almost*, I've got to live here after you're long gone."

"Good point," I said. I told him what I needed.

"That I can do," was all he said. "See you in a few." He hung up.

Twenty minutes later I pulled into Fite's Towing. Stan was sitting on the bed of a jacked-up Silverado pickup with oversized tires and *Yosemite Sam* mud flaps. A cigarette dangled from his mouth. The tip glowed. I stepped out of the van. He threw me a set of keys. He pointed towards a '98 Ford F450 tow truck with a winch and a rusty grille.

"Stay safe," he said, and took a long drag on his cigarette.

I got into the tow truck and fired the engine.

"Any idea where to look?"

"Some," he said. "Bennie Black runs an A/C and heating repair business out of a small warehouse. You know the place?"

I nodded. I'd seen it.

"A lot of the local men get together there at night and sit around and drink, lie, talk about wool they aren't pulling. Who knows? I'd start there."

"Good deal," I said. "Thanks." I backed the truck out, dropped it in "D" and pulled down the driveway leading away from the garage.

I DROVE TO Black's Heating and Air Conditioning. A few cars and more pickup trucks were parked in a haphazard pattern in the gravel lot surrounding the small warehouse. I parked on the far side of an Oldsmobile and a Ford. The Sheriff's slick-top Crown-Victoria was parked close to the small office door in the right-hand corner of the warehouse. It was time, but I had to wait.

There was a CB radio underneath the dash. I hadn't realized it was on. I saw the small green light. The volume knob was turned all the way to the left. I turned it halfway to the right. It was set to channel 4.

A couple of minutes later, I heard Fite's voice: "You on?"

"Affirmative," I said.

"Any big fish at that fishing hole I told you about?" Fite asked.

"The biggest. Thanks, brother."

"Stay safe," he said. "And if you need some company, check the glove compartment."

I opened the glove compartment. There was a bottle of Jack Daniels Green Label. I watched, waited, and enjoyed Jack's company. After the whiskey sunk four inches, the men began to trickle out. The Sheriff wasn't the first to leave. Or the last. He walked out, opened the Ford's door, and dropped himself behind the wheel. I saw the headlights come to life; they bounced against the dull metal finish of the warehouse door. He backed down the gravel driveway and plunged out onto the road, picking up speed. I eased the tow-truck onto the road behind him. I picked up speed. We started down a long hill. I narrowed the gap. A bridge came into view on the horizon of the flat road. I stomped the pedal down, the truck groaned and lurched forward. The Sheriff didn't speed up. Or slow down. I wasn't sure if he was paying attention to the headlights in his rear-view. I didn't know how much he had drunk; probably not as much as me. I took a last swig on the bottle of whiskey and tossed the almost-empty bottle out the window. I didn't hear it smack the pavement. The bridge was short. And rusty. And old. There was a small sign at the far end, "*Weight Limit 2 Tons*" which didn't do much good. By the time you could see it, you were on the bridge. I was only a couple of car lengths behind the Sheriff. He had almost cleared the bridge when my truck's grille plowed into the rear of his Ford.

The red and white plastic exploded, and the metal bumper folded into itself with a searing thud. The Ford seemed drawn to the truck for a split-second and then pushed away, sliding sideways. The Sheriff accelerated and righted the vehicle. The cruiser shot forward.

There was a short tree line to the left behind tall grass, an abandoned silo on the right and a water tower in the distance. The cruiser's lead had a short life. The metal on the inside of the wheel-well sliced into left rear tire and it began to unravel. The car's momentum hit a snag as the exposed wheel bit into the pavement. Sparks flew.

The cruiser left the road and rolled down a short embankment. It limped along a dirt path. I followed. The path led through a short clearing. A jagged fence, with posts like pointed spears, emerged from the tall, tired grass that enclosed a neglected family cemetery. One monument-style headstone peeked from the tall grass like a curious prairie dog. A collection of shorter headstones was barely visible in the thorny underbrush of grass and weeds. The cruiser crashed into the fence and came to a stop like a clenched fist slapped against a palm. I pushed hard at the wide brake pedal and stopped behind the cruiser.

It was time for a fight. Bare-knuckle. Carnage, not tactics. I was too tired for games. And too drunk. I stepped out and pulled the short-stock shotgun that had been held against the passenger seat with the seatbelt. I racked it.

The Sheriff's tolerance for any kind of dance was also minimal. He pulled his old-school wheel revolver from its deep holster slouched against his thigh and pointed it at me. I raised the shotgun and pointed it at him. At his angle, with the revolver, he needed to make a perfect shot.

He fired. He missed. I fired. I didn't miss.

The buckshot plowed into his throat and face. I fired again. More of the same. I fired again. More. Blood fought against his chewed flesh to escape, meet gravity, and spill out into the dirt. He dropped the revolver and slumped. He tried to stand and walk. He made it back to his feet, attempted a step and slumped again.

The Sheriff leaned against the fence. Words were useless and none escaped from the depths of his cavernous, exposed throat. He wheezed. He fell back. Part of the fence had been crushed when the cruiser hit it so that some of the spear tops had been bent and twisted. I hit him in the forehead with the butt of the shotgun. He fell onto the fence. The metal pierced through both shoulder blades, and one of the points plowed through the base of his skull.

I hated to disrespect whoever's family was buried in the dreary, unkempt cemetery, though it was clear none of the living members cared. I walked over to the cruiser. There was a paperback novel on the passenger seat, on top of a clipboard. I picked it up and went back towards the Sheriff. He had stopped pitching and violently convulsing; the pouring blood continued to seep from his now lifeless body. I glanced at the book's cover and flipped it over to scan. Odd time to do it but it didn't look too bad. Likely an overcooked plot about southern lawyers, deep pockets, and shallow ethics. But I'd never get the chance to read it. I opened it and shoved it down onto the sharp tip of the fencepost protruding from the Sheriff's throat. I returned to the tow-truck and pulled a gas can from the bed under the hook, went back to the body, unscrewed the cap and splashed gas all over him, soaking the pages of the paperback.

I pulled my lighter from my pocket and lit the book from the bottom. A very dry Viking funeral. I started to walk away. I looked back and noticed the dead man's boots. At first, they looked like regular leather. But they weren't. They were goat. Mad Dog Goat. Hand-stitched. Lucchese. A hell of a nice pair of boots. He wouldn't have much use for them where he was going. I would. I could feel the heat from the flames as I pulled them off his feet. I put them on and stuffed my old boots in the duffel bag.

I got back in the tow-truck and drove back to the tire store and swapped the tow- truck for my Duster. I stopped at a place called *Krebbs's Kwik Stop.* The place was half package store, half gas-station-convenience-store. I took advantage of both and grabbed whiskey, coffee, a large bottle of water and beef jerky. The ride would be long. I got started. It was just shy of midnight and a sliver of moon peeked out of a bruised southern sky.

A song floated into my consciousness as the flat roads unfolded in front of me. *I shot the sheriff, but I did not shoot the...*then I remembered. I'd shot that fat motherfucker too.

Part II

LOUISIANA, TEXAS & ARIZONA

28.

TROUBLE I DIDN'T need was seated in a diner next to a nondescript single-story motel in a small town in west Louisiana. You've seen one, you've seen them all. The motel and the town. Next to the motel was a dirt lot. Next to the dirt lot was the liquor store where I'd bought the rot gut whiskey that had led to the throbbing pain that gripped my temples. Trouble was leggy and blonde. Real trouble was the man seated across from her. Real trouble was not blonde. He was a Latino with pit bull genetics, a bald head, and a piranha tattoo swimming across his neck.

They walked out before me, and I watched them through the window. Arguing. I finished my omelet and ordered another cup of coffee. The couple had good arguing endurance. I finished the coffee. The check was under nine dollars. I left a hundred-dollar bill. Change was something from my past. At least for now. It was blood money. I really didn't want it. But even blood money is green. I walked out. A bell chimed.

"Get in the car," I heard him growl. He slapped her. Hard. This guy sucked. I could just about tolerate him yelling. Hitting her was unacceptable. He grabbed her arm. She writhed around, trying to get loose. She got away from him and started towards me.

"Can I have a ride?" she asked. "To get away from this *fucking psycho*." She turned her head back towards him and raised her voice to shriek *fucking psycho* directly at him. Predictably, this didn't exactly work to de-escalate the situation. The skin the piranha swam grew redder. The man started towards me. The woman got behind me. The man pulled a knife out of a pocket. I didn't have a gun. I'd just stopped in for breakfast and coffee. Stupid, but it turned out smart.

I'd fought guys with knives before. He held the knife dagger style, blade down. He brought his elbow back and up over his ear, raised the knife near his right eye and thrust it towards me. He was crazy and irate but not particularly proficient. I let the blade come towards my shoulder, pivoted and ducked down avoiding the blade, twisted my hips, and delivered a liver punch with my left fist. He buckled and fell to his knees. The knife was still in his hand, blade back.

He dropped the weapon as he tried to brace himself with his right hand. As I kicked the knife away, I saw the two patrol cars. They plowed to a hard stop in the loose gravel. Two corn-fed white cops stepped out and drew down.

"Don't move," the older of the two deputies said. He was relaxed. His gun, an old-school .38 revolver slung low in its holster. The other deputy was shorter. Young. Buzz cut. Oakley sunglasses, even though it was overcast. His gun, a slick Glock .40, was in his hand, gripped tight in a black glove. They handcuffed us. The older deputy walked me to his car.

"You gonna grab the knife?" I asked. He didn't care enough to be embarrassed. He didn't tell me to watch my head as he put me in the car. I gave him a fake name when he asked. He took me to the sheriff's office and put me in a holding cell. Alone. A half-hour later he returned. He opened the cell and stepped in. He left the door open.

"Here's the thing," he started, in a Cajun drawl. "I don't know you. I know him. The Mexican kid. His mama cleans up around the precinct. Has for years. She's probably illegal but she's good people, so we don't ask. He's a little touched in the head, as we say down here. Anyway, I'm sure it was his knife. No white man carries a knife like that. I'd be willing to forget it," he said.

Fine with me, I thought. They had searched me. Sort of. Nobody bothered to ask why a guy that looked like a drifter had a little over two thousand dollars in his pocket. The rest was in the car. There was more to this cleaning lady angle, most likely, but I didn't care. I needed to get out of there. If they printed me, who knows what would surface in the system. That, and the fact that Browning had a lot of friends in Louisiana who thought I'd killed him.

"Forgotten," I said. I stood up.

I walked past him out of the cell, and we left by a side door.

"Need a ride back to the diner?" he asked.

I nodded. I almost said the motel, but then he might go in, talk to the clerk, and figure out which was my car. Since it was full of guns and money, I really didn't want him to search it.

I sat in the front, next to him, but we didn't speak. He pulled up to the diner.

"Have a nice day," he said as I stepped out.

He handed me an envelope. I could feel my watch and a stack of bills through the envelope. He drove away. I opened the envelope and put my watch on. Like the waitress, the deputy ended up with a good tip. I was now a guy who looked like a drifter with five hundred dollars in my pocket. I went back to the diner and drank coffee. The waitress from the morning was gone. I took a cup to go, went back to my room and poured bourbon into the coffee. I took a nap. I slept, but not well.

A knock at the door woke me. I opened the door. It was the leggy blonde: Trouble.

"I need a ride," she said.

"You don't know where I'm going," I said.

"Doesn't matter," she said. "As long as you're leaving soon."

"I'll drop you off anywhere between here and Dallas," I said. She nodded. I checked out.

We got in the car and drove down the highway. We stopped to eat. I made a phone call. I talked to the man listed on the prayer card the Priest handed me before he died. He seemed to be expecting my call. I told him where I was and where I was headed. He said we could meet in Dallas in three days. We hung up.

She said she'd go with me to Dallas and then take a bus to Austin. She had friends there. We drank bourbon and beer, took our time, ate in diners, slept in motel dives and sport-screwed for three nights and two days. On the third day, I dropped her off at the bus station in a seedy part of Dallas. If the sex was any indication, I had faith she would help keep the Texas capital weird. I gave her some money. She walked to a large silver building.

I drove to meet the Priest's friend. I wished I had more information. Inverse relationship, the less information you have, the better it needed to be. I knew Chy was solid and I trusted her. But statistically, the cops and agents she was calling were men. Men who hoped they would see her again at some point. Men who didn't want to disappoint. Men who wanted her to owe them a favor. Men who wanted her to call back, which means they may not have given up everything they knew. I called Paul Silva.

We had agreed to meet at an hour before midnight on a Wednesday. He knew a place. A seedy strip club called The Kinky Kaktus in an industrial part of town. The buildings were shanty. Bodegas. Motels. Tattoo parlors. Strip clubs. Most of the signs were in Spanish. Most of the people looked like they slept on the street. Because they did. I gathered that the Priest's friend had lived or at least spent time in Dallas at some point.

He pulled up in a yellow minivan cab driven by a woman. Women cabbies are like baby pigeons and live armadillos. You know they exist, but never see them. The man I figured was the Priest's friend got out of the van. He paid the woman. I'd backed into a space in the L-shaped parking lot. I dialed his cell phone to be sure it was him. I saw him reach for it and answer, so I hung up and got out of the car. He saw me. We shook hands. We walked through large wooden doors. It wasn't the kind of place that had a cover. We walked past a beefy bouncer and paid a dark-haired girl for a pair of light beers in plastic bottles, pulled from a bin of ice.

He'd introduced himself giving me the name I already had: Paul Silva. Before either of us could say more, a stripper appeared in front of our table. I promised her that I'd buy a dance later. She walked away. The place wasn't busy. Our table was in a corner. He told me a story. When he finished, the stripper came back. I kept my promise and she walked me to the back by the hand. We walked through a large curtain and then through a smaller one.

"More private," she said looking over at her shoulder with a smile and squeezing my hand. A pro. The song began. She danced and peeled.

"You can touch me," she said, but I didn't. I had before, but I didn't feel like it. I kept thinking of Paul's story. She looked Puerto Rican. She was young, early twenties, with smooth skin, small cupcake breasts, perfect nipples, and a tight swatch of dark hair at her middle, and all I could think about was the macabre story I had just heard. She stopped dancing when the music stopped. I hadn't asked for a price; everything was negotiable at the Kinky Kaktus. I handed her a hundred-dollar bill and told her to keep it. She looked at the bill and then at me and smiled. But her eyes looked sad.

"Vaya con Dios," I said, as I handed her another hundred. She led me back out to the table, thanked me again and walked away.

Paul was drinking tequila. He took a final shot, stood up, and we walked out of the club. I turned out of the parking lot and took a silent left. We didn't need to discuss destination. Our trip through Texas began where Paul's story ended. The story plowed through my mind, as the expanse of Texas unfolded in front of me. I played it over in my mind. The eastern sky glowed red behind us and the desert flatness became the canvas of my consciousness.

The story had been gothic. Paul couldn't tell it any way but in a tense voice, his knuckles white against the bottle in his hand. The creases in his face had ticked to meet his reality. The story was complex, the message surprising. I thought the Priest wanted his friend to help me. The friend thought I was calling to help him. It was neither. And it was both. He knew we could help each other. And maybe save someone the Priest had loved. If she was still alive.

29.

PAUL'S GOTHIC STORY rumbled through my mind. Hacks don't run prisons. Gangs do. In LOMPOC, it was the White Werewolves. Outlaw Motorcycle Gang. OMG. Aryan-affiliated. Ruthless. The story began eleven years earlier. Back then, the Priest's name wasn't Santos. It was Marquez. He wasn't a priest. He was a sergeant with the U.S. Bureau of Prisons. A supervisor. He worked D Block. Hardcore. Maximum security.

The riot broke out on a Sunday after breakfast. The cells had been open so that inmates could go to their work details. The gun had been smuggled into the prison by a guard whose brother had a serious gambling problem and an even more serious methamphetamine addiction. The brother was into a small-time bookie in Phoenix for over fifteen large. The White Werewolves bought the debt. The guard smuggled the gun.

Their leader was a tall man with a long ponytail. Both of his arms were full-sleeved with hate tattoos. He stepped out of his cell and shot the first screw he saw. Then the second. Then the third. He took the fourth guard, a female, hostage.

The guard at the controls of pod eighteen was new. You never open the cells. Never. No matter how many hostages they take. All the guards had signed no-hostage agreements. They knew the score. The gang leader knew the score too, but he figured that the new screw would comply. He counted on it. He waited three weeks for the new guard to be cycled back to A shift in pod eighteen on D-Block on a day the female hack was working. The gang leader was right. The guard opened the pod and then all of D-Block. The riot was on.

The 'Blind Roost,' as it was called, didn't look like the rest of the towers. The cons couldn't see the guards. Not even all the guards knew it was there, only supervisors and members of the counterassault and high-intensity extraction teams. It allowed guards to perch and watch almost the entire yard. Marquez heard the alarm from his office. He headed up to the Roost. The gang leader came out of a side entrance on the southeast corner of the D-Block building.

Marquez took the gun from the guard working the Roost. Through the scope he could see the gang leader running with his female hostage. He was headed in the direction of a construction trailer just inside the prison's outer fence in an area off-limits to inmates. He was in the open, leading the hostage by the elbow. Marquez had a shot. He took it. The gang leader's head exploded. The female guard stopped running, brought her palms flat against her cheeks and screamed.

It didn't take the White Werewolves long to find out who took the shot. First, they found out his name. Then they found out that Marquez wasn't a sergeant with U.S. Bureau of Prisons, he was an ATF agent working deep undercover. In the following months Agent Marquez and U.S. Bureau of Prison Corporal Dana Lee Moon—the hostage—testified in open court about the inner workings of the White Werewolves. It was a crippling hit for the gang.

The top leaders of the Werewolves were peeled off like an onion. The ones inside were given longer stretches. The ones outside joined the ones inside. First, Corporal Moon disappeared. Then, Marquez did. The heir apparent to take the reins of the Werewolves was a man named Gus Lambert, who stood in the courtroom gallery watching as the sentences were handed down. He made a vow to find both Marquez and Moon and avenge their testimony. He knew it would take years. And it did.

The break came on April 23, 1999. The Werewolves had grown in members and power. They put money on the street, as much to get information back, as interest. She worked for a contracting company that specialized in data backup and transition. She was a winner. He was a loser. She had a master's degree and was senior management. Her son was a degenerate gambler, an alcoholic, and a high school dropout. He was into some bikers outside Phoenix for over forty thousand dollars. Her company was hired by the U.S. Department of Correction's Western Region to backup information and plan the transition for certain computer databases for Y2K. The data to be backed up contained classified personnel information.

At first, the Werewolves thought they could just get the mother to add money to commissary accounts of incarcerated Werewolves. Somehow, Lambert heard about it. He made a call. Dana Lee Moon had left the U.S. Witness Protection Program of her own volition. Her real identity was reinstated, and her retirement account information updated. It led them to a small town in Idaho.

She had never recovered from losing a baby. She was hooked on junk. They snatched her and brought her to Arizona. She was strung out, almost suicidal. She put up little resistance and told them where Marquez was. She had contacted him seven months earlier about her drug problem and lost faith. He was trying to help her. They kept her in Arizona and made plans to deal with Marquez.

30.

WE DROVE WEST. We stopped in the small town of Temple, Arizona. We found a diner and a motel. The town was small, the diner deserted, and the motel nasty. We ate and waited until the plates were cleared and the plastic cups replaced with chipped ceramic mugs. We sipped black coffee until the trucker in the next booth left and the waitress walked away.

Paul reached into a pocket and pulled out a short stack of folded pages. He unfolded them, smoothed them with his palm, and placed his cell phone on one edge. Several were photocopies of ATF files that had no place on the dingy table we shared. The pages were rap sheets, mug shots, field pictures, incident reports, and investigative notes about a full-patch member of the White Werewolves. Went by Tiki. He had been a confidential informant for Paul when he was a WITSEC handler. Paul had to find out if the Werewolves ever got a lead about the Priest's new life.

As I was reading, he pulled a folded brown envelope out of a different pocket and handed it to me. I pulled out a single sheet of paper and unfolded it. It was an internal report from The United States Bureau of Prisons, marked CONFIDENTIAL—NOT TO BE RELEASED WITH PUBLIC REPORT—LAW ENFORCEMENT SENSITIVE. The date of the riot was in the upper right-hand corner. It was two short paragraphs.

Dana Lee Moon, the female guard who had been taken hostage, the woman who was inches away from the gang leader when Marquez shot him, was three months pregnant. She lost the baby a day later. The details were scarce. No name listed for the father. I didn't need one.

"Priest was the father?" I asked. Not something you utter every day.

Paul nodded.

I kept reading. The second paragraph was circled in red. It ended:

"...Deputy U.S. Marshal Argiro reports that Jose Santos (formerly "Miguel Marquez"; herein "Santos") has indicated that he has re-established communication with Dana Lee Moon. (hereinafter "Moon"). DUSM Argiro has expressly discouraged Santos from continuing this, or any, communication, with Moon, who has left WITSEC. (Details in separate report). After consultation with USMS Witness Protection Program Senior Management Council determination, has been made that, while discouraged, this communication will not disqualify Santos for continued inclusion in the WITSEC Program."

The rest of the story wasn't long. Santos, who had been Marquez, had a short affair with a female prison guard, Dana Lee Moon. She got pregnant. He had planned to ask her to marry him on Friday, two days after the riot, one day after she lost the baby. He didn't. The riot changed everything. Marquez knew the White Werewolves would find out he was the shooter. He would testify against the Werewolves in open court. Then he would disappear. The baby had been the only reason he would marry her. Now the baby was gone.

Marquez entered WITSEC, moved to Mississippi, his name was changed and attended seminary as Jose Santos with the Paulists. It couldn't be a coincidence, somewhere in all of this, Santos must have found out about Smith and the Sheriff. I flipped absently through the pages, but I had all the information I needed, for now. As promised, the report about Dana Lee Moon was attached. I didn't bother with it. I felt better about it. The information I'd received from different sources was lining up and clicking in my head like the tumblers in a safe.

"Anything else?" I asked. I folded the sheets and handed them back to Paul. I knew what was coming. It always came back to a woman.

"Santos found out she was missing," he said. "He knew it had to be about him. Or at least he thought it was. He was right. Once they found out about her, they thought she could tell him where he was. They were right too."

"And now we've got to find her?" I asked.

"Yeah," he said. "She's missing. The Werewolves have her."

"So, to find her, we've got to find them?" I asked, knowing the answer. He nodded.

"They found Santos; we can assume she gave him up; any reason to believe she's still alive?" I asked.

He shrugged, but I knew we were going to look for her. In some way, the Priest loved her until he died. I'm almost sure of that.

"How are we going to find out where she is?" I asked.

"The CI, Tiki, from the papers. I reached out. We'll meet up tomorrow. I know a place."

We walked back to our rooms.

You go to war, you write a will. You eat your gun, you write a note. I debated with myself about which would be more appropriate. Instead, I lay down on the sullied comforter and drank from the bottle. I spilled bourbon on four days of stubble. I slept, but not well.

AS THE FIRST fingers of reddish haze began to reach from the horizon to the sky, I peeked between the stank motel curtains. I saw Paul talking on his cell phone and walking in circles. I joined him. Those fingers weren't even to the first knuckle when we drove out of the parking lot. The air was crisp but dusty. Paul navigated to a small-town east of Mesa. The place Tiki had arranged to meet us was called the Fourth Shift Tavern. It sat on a flat parcel of land between the road, a half-mile from an abandoned grain warehouse. There was a Harley Davidson Fat Boy near the door. We parked on the side of the building and walked in.

Tiki was a tall, thick, serious-looking man with a blond buzz cut. He wore sleek sunglasses in contrast to a pinched face. A sleeveless leather vest covered in patches was draped over a V-neck T-shirt. A chunky silver watch rested on the wrist of the arm not sleeved in biker tattoos. He had three earrings in his left ear: one less in his right. He was in a booth. He was drinking a dark beer from a large glass. Swinging doors to the left led into the kitchen. We walked to the booth and sat down.

We asked questions about the White Werewolves and about the girl, Dana Lee. He answered them. They had her. We asked where.

"A place out in the desert. Safe house. Hangout. Hideout. Whatever. Lambert calls it the Hornet's Nest. They cook and tweek out there. All meth. All the time. He's got her out there."

He told us where it was and about the closest town: Bone Junction, a day and a half away on the other side of the Superstition Mountains.

The man walked in the door and saw Tiki before any of us saw him. Paul saw the man before I did. Tiki saw him before Paul. The biker wore black jeans, had a shaved scalp and a goatee. He wore a black leather vest over a white T-shirt. Sunglasses. The tattoos on his arms and neck matched the patches and logos on his vest.

Tiki stopped mid-sentence. "Damn."

I glanced over my shoulder. All eyes locked. There was a charged undercurrent of still, silent panic. The biker turned and ran back out through the door. Tiki followed.

"Through the kitchen," I said. Paul darted through the swinging doors. I pulled a bill from my money clip, dropped it on the table and followed Paul. We came out a rear door into a parking lot near a row of plastic trashcans and a couple of dishwashers catching a smoke. We ran around the building and came up behind the Duster. I saw two hogs spit dirt and gravel in their wake before catching the grip of pavement and tearing out onto the highway with Tiki chasing. The Duster roared to life. I followed the motorcycles.

The bikers swerved like eels on the highway. Tiki was clearly the better rider of the two. The man looked over his shoulder as Tiki gained. The highway veered to the left. An unpaved road continued straight ahead. There was an open gate. The motorcycles shot through. I scanned a sign as we followed them through, "*Bragg Grain Processing.*"

The grain warehouse was one large building with several small buildings attached to it. An old cargo truck was parked on the side. Exposed ductwork and frayed electric wires crept alongside the exterior of the warehouse and ducked into holes drilled into the outside walls. The bikers shot around the building cluster to our left.

"Right!" Paul yelled.

I steered around a small offshoot building and a construction trailer. The two bikers had a longer path around the other side of the warehouse and now headed directly towards me. I pushed down on the accelerator. The Duster wedged into them; the man shot hard to his left; Tiki to his right. I jerked the wheel towards the man's Harley. It pitched. He laid the bike down or the bike laid him down. It jackknifed and skipped along the dirt like a pebble on flat water. The bald man crashed into the cracked dirt and rolled off the bike. I slammed on the brakes and came to a stop near the hog's front-tire. Paul's door was open before the Duster skidded to a stop. I heard the clap of a shot. And then another. And another. Paul was firing, the gun kicking as fast as he could pull the trigger. The man, still dizzy from the fall, limped towards a side door. A 9mm slug landed at the base of the biker's skull just as he started to close the red metal door behind him. He died with his hand still gripped to the knob.

Paul lowered the almost empty Glock to his side; I slung the shotgun over my shoulder. Tiki had unsaddled from his motorcycle and stood behind us holding a pistol. We stepped over the body. I grabbed the man by the collar and slid him against the pavement. There were tall stacks of grain in white bags with green lettering. I pulled him by his boots into the plant. The door wasn't wide enough to pull the man's hog through it. We unlocked a large electric bay garage door. Without power, it took all three of us to push it on its tracks.

Tiki walked outside and rolled the man's hog through the open door. It was almost as hard to close as it had been to open. We left the man next to his bike. Paul and I walked back out the red door. Tiki followed. But then stopped. As expected, there was grain on the floor of a grain processing plant. And dust. Tiki pulled a silver lighter out of a pocket, flipped the lid back with his thumb. Paul and I both began to motion towards him but before we could yell, he rolled the lighter to life and tossed it in through the large bay door.

We both gave Tiki an incredulous look as we watched him walk away from the blaze. He didn't notice. He gave us a half wave and kicked his Harley back to life. The rear wheel kicked sideways in the dirt until it caught on the asphalt. He roared away. We listened to the growl taper and then drove away. I looked at Paul. He looked at me.

"Just why?" I said shaking my head.

"Waste of a nice lighter in my opinion. That and there was really no reason to steal Mr Bragg's livelihood," I said.

"Good thing we hid the body and the bike, so we don't draw any attention to ourselves," I said as the fire swirled inside the plant like a cyclone catching on grain and dust, then wood and grain bags.

"You're worried about a lighter and some stranger's grain fortune," Paul asked. "I'm wondering who we just killed?"

"And why?" I asked. Good questions but I honestly hadn't thought about it; I was mesmerized by the inferno. I mean of all people, if Tiki thought you needed to die, he was most likely right.

"Let's go," I said. We went.

Small popping explosions were a prelude to a huge blast like cracked knuckles to a thunderous Tyson Fury roundhouse punch. We heard it when we were pulling out onto the road. After a few minutes the volunteer fire trucks with emergency equipment activated and sirens at full blast began rolling past us in the opposite direction. American flags snapped in the wind behind the rigs. They were pedal down. We were pedal down. We swapped the diner for a roadhouse next to a one-story motel advertising color television, A/C and "Free HBO,"—as if all three had recently been discovered—further down the road and got drunk.

I was enjoying a brand of whiskey I'd never heard of while scanning two blonde women across the bar trying to figure out if they were twins. I thought absently of Victoria. Paul was texting Tiki, still wanting to know who he had killed. And why. They went back and forth for a few rounds. He shook his head and picked up his glass for a first sip. Mine was empty. I waved for another.

"And?" I asked, not really caring.

"So, the guy that walked in, he was in Tiki's MC," Paul began.

"But we met far enough away from their turf to avoid that from happening," I said.

The guy is a White Werewolf but he's a Nomad, he's not with one charter, sort of a vagabond biker, so he can be anywhere according to Tiki," Paul said.

"And, with our luck, anywhere just happened to be the Fourth Shift Tavern," I said. My drink arrived. We clicked glasses in a silent toast. Paul and I didn't exactly look like cops. Seems like there may have been a less incendiary way to deal with the guy. No pun intended.

The next morning, we weren't quite sober when we checked out of another crusty motel. Bone Junction, the next town, was forty miles away. The Hornet's Nest was twenty-seven miles further on to northeast.

In the 1850's Bone Junction, Arizona was a bustling silver-mining town full of whores, whiskey, and silver. The silver was gone. The whores and whiskey remained. The road to Bone Junction was long and flat. The sun was high, the cactus sporadic. It was our kind of town. But we didn't stay. Our only stop was for coffee; then we kept rolling.

The highway stretched out like a long yawn north from Bone Junction to the base of the Rattler Mountains. The straight desert roads crisscrossed in jagged patterns. After eighteen miles, the only evidence of human existence in the dust and sand were motorcycle tracks. Sneaking up on a house built on a flat stamp of desert is a nightmare. There was a ton of shit that could go wrong. There was nothing else out there. The Werewolves came and went at all hours.

Meeting a single biker, or worse, a pack of wolves, so to speak, could be fatal.

We left the road and cut across the desert. We parked almost a half mile away and trekked towards the Hornet's Nest. An exterior stucco wall surrounded the house and formed a patio area between a wrought iron fence and the front door. There was a small break in the wall to the rear of the building that led to a door. A tall, chain link fence surrounded the entire house including the driveway. There was an open gate at the end of the driveway. The chipped land on all sides of the 'Nest was flat. As expected for an OMG hangout, motorcycles were parked all around the structure. They were all oversized and black. Chrome. Some had flames painted on their oblong gas-tanks. Some had long twisted forks. Some had saddlebags with metal studs and worn leathers. Some had World War I helmets hanging from their handlebars. All had chrome. They were all Harley's, not a rice-burner among them. My mind flashed to a T-shirt I had seen in a store on the Myrtle Beach strip, *"I'd rather have a sister in a whorehouse than a brother on a Honda."*

Tiki had described a shed to the rear of the building that they used to keep spare parts and tools. We both carried large cargo bags slung over our shoulders. We crouched and rested behind the shed. We could see the 'Nest at an angle. Tiki's description had been dead on. Except for the dogs. A pair of Dobermans roamed the yard. They wore studded leather collars attached to thick chains with plenty of slack. They stood as we approached and sniffed in our direction. They pulled at their chains but didn't bark. Yet.

"Are you freaking kidding me?" Paul hissed, almost with a laugh. "This mope remembers everything except for the two friggin' Dobermans?"

Paul was one of those people that swore but didn't really swear.

"We can put them down, suppressor, no problem," he said. "But damn things are big enough that their slump alone might alert everyone inside."

"Once we put them down, they might notice, and we'd have to go in strong," I said. I had figured we'd wait outside, let them leave, then go inside and put people down one at a time.

"Let them tip their hand," I said. "If the dogs start to bark and they come out and find us, we'll go strong from there. Chances are a group will come out, the dogs will bark, they'll figure they're barking at them and leave. Smaller the group inside, the better."

He nodded in agreement. Not that this was a great revelation on my part. We both doubted that they'd take her with them anywhere. We were right about that. Wrong about almost everything else.

31.

WE COUNTED FIFTEEN motorcycles parked in the yard. We waited. The dogs lost interest and slumped on their haunches and paws. Almost an hour had passed when we heard voices behind the stucco wall, and bodies flooded the patio area. Twelve men strolled out, followed by half as many women. Most were smoking. They mounted the hogs and fired them up. The noise was deafening. As predicted, the dogs barked. The bikers left. We could hear gears shift and engines wind and unwind. Until it was silent.

We'd hear them in the desert before they made their way back to the Nest, but we had no way of knowing when that would be. It was time.

We couldn't scale the fence with the dogs. At the least they'd bark and alert whoever was left inside. Unless they were worthless, they'd also attack. They didn't look worthless. The numbers had changed. We'd go in through the front gate and front door. If the man-hog ratio followed logic, there were less than a handful of people inside. We had no idea what part of the house she might be in. With larger numbers and spaces, short-stock shotguns would be in order. Coming all this way to rescue her and then killing her in a crossfire was like getting the *Apollo 13* crew into the atmosphere without burning up just to have the parachutes fail. We left the bags and opted for stealth.

We both wore tactical vests with extra magazines for our 9mm's pushed into the slots. There was a small snap for handcuffs and a loop to hold an ASP baton. There was a pouch for pepper spray. Mine was empty. I'd always hated that crap, even before an overzealous Georgia State Patrol Trooper had sprayed me during a scuffle with some doper down on Auburn Avenue during *Freaknik* in the mid-nineties. Hated it even more after. We wore black watch caps, black gloves, and boots. The dogs barked as we moved around the outside of the fence. We'd only shoot them if we had to. Fortunately, we didn't have to; surprisingly, they barked but never charged. We ran through the gate. We stood at the outside of the curved stucco wall, one of us on each side. The front door opened. I peeked low and could see a man coming out through the front door. I pointed two fingers of my free hand at my own eyes to indicate to Paul that I could see someone. He held up a clenched fist to show he understood.

A scab of a man with dark features stepped through the opening. He sensed Paul before me. His head turned to the right. He gasped as his eyes focused on the smooth black steel of the Glock pushed into the slight give of flesh in his forehead above the eyebrows. He started to scream, or speak, or make some kind of noise, but Paul just shook his head. No. He cocked the hammer. The biker was still.

"Don't speak, just use your fingers or nod," I said in an even voice barely above a whisper. "How many in the house?"

The man held up two fingers.

"Including the woman?" There was a spark of realization behind the man's pupils, which were the size of quarters. The biker nodded. Yes. We were right, she was here. Or, at least, some woman was. Paul lowered the gun a split second before I flipped the ASP baton open and hit the man at the base of his neck. He slumped. I handcuffed him to the fencepost.

The screen door hung on a single hinge. We stood on opposite sides. I nodded. He pulled the screen door towards him and stepped forward, so his back held the door open. He crouched down. If the front door was opened from the inside, he would shoot from a crouch. I'd kicked in enough unlocked doors on the job. Paul nodded. I reached around and gripped the knob. I twisted it with an inverted palm. It turned. I pushed against it noiselessly to check if the deadbolt was locked. I could tell by the give that it wasn't. I pushed the door open an inch. I pulled my hand away and nodded at Paul.

He placed his hand against the bottom of the door, extended three fingers and then dropped them one at a time. As the third finger dropped, he pushed the door open and stepped through the gap to the right of the door in one motion. I moved up and to the left. Guns at shoulder height. Raised. We moved through the short hallway leading from the door. Paul in front. I was a pace back on his right shoulder.

It wasn't the first time I'd entered a house uninvited to hear the unmistakable banging, thrashing, strained breaths, and clipped words that are the chorus of screwing. We stepped into the doorway and watched for a split second. We expected her to see us before he did. But she was on top, facing away. He saw us first and rolled out from under her onto the floor behind the bed. She stayed on the bed. Kneeling. Screaming. She was in the way, neither of us had a clean shot.

Lambert surfaced over the corner of the sheet and fired a shot from a pistol. I moved to the right. Paul moved to the left. There was no cover.

"Get out of the way," I yelled at her. The shot buried into a closet door between us. Paul was far enough to the left to take a shot. He fired. Lambert ducked back down behind the bed. The round shattered a low window. I stepped up onto the bed. Paul kept moving to his left. I took a step and saw Lambert facing Paul, ready to fire again. Time slowed and then almost froze. He never got the chance. I fired and buried a round into a gap somewhere below his left earlobe and his ponytail. I fired three more times. At the time, I thought it was probably three too many.

I saw her reach under a pillow behind my planted foot. I shifted to my left to try and see her face underneath me. Paul shouted.

"Dan, watch..."

I felt the knife pierce the fleshy part of the inside of my right thigh before I heard the word, "out."

She was on her back, but she held the knife overhead, dagger style. I'd seen it before. Her head was directly below me. I stepped off the bed. She lunged again. I was still only a few feet from her.

"Drop it," I said, as calmly as possible. Paul's gun was leveled on her, but I was behind her. I had a cleaner shot. I realized I'd probably have to kill her, but before the thought came to rest in my reality, she lunged. I shot. It hit her, literally, between the eyes. She was dead. Actually, deader than Lambert. We had both thought Lambert was already among the not-so-dearly-departed. We were wrong. He gurgled. Blood spilled from the side of his mouth like a Vatican fountain.

"What the hell?" Paul said.

"Stockholm syndrome," I said. Paul nodded.

"Big time," he agreed. "We came a long damn way to rescue a tweeker snitch. A traitor tweeker snitch at that.

WE DID A short walk around the cabin. It didn't take long to confirm that Dana Lee had been trading sex and information for meth. I stopped at a wall. I called to Paul; he was looking through the kitchen. He walked around the corner. I summed it up.

"RIP Wall,"

Paul nodded.

There were newspaper clippings about the shooting at LOMPOC. Zoom-shot pictures of the Priest in Mississippi. Courtroom sketches of the trials, of Dana Lee and Marquez's testifying. Old mug shots of the fallen gang leader. Satellite maps of north Mississippi focused on a rectory in Forrest Springs. The wall was full—all tacked to the white paint over a White Werewolves' logos in black.

Then there were the postcards and letters. A familiar return address. I didn't have the heart to read them all. The Priest had reached out. And she reached back. We took a final glance at the wall, nodded our heads, and walked back through the front door. We hit the man on the way out and left him slumped against the fencepost. But we took the handcuffs with us and made our way back to the Duster. His boots didn't interest me.

"Good thing we saved her," I said to Paul as we closed the doors. We allowed ourselves a laugh.

When the laughs turned to rueful smiles, Paul said, "I got more info on the fourth guy, Sangre." He told me about a woman who had worked Sangre undercover. On the border. A while back. She's DEA in Detroit. I've met her before, but I didn't know she'd been Border Patrol or that she'd worked this guy Sangre. Hell of a coincidence, I thought. It turned out to be just that.

We had to meet her in person. We needed information that she would never give over the phone. Neither of us expected her to. She said she'd meet us in Phoenix; she was already working on something in San Diego and said she would need a few days to head east. We got into town ahead of her. We arranged to meet at a Mexican restaurant next to a coffee shop two days later.

So, we had two days to kill.

Surprisingly, the only thing we killed was time and the only shots we took were filled with whiskey.

32.

BROOKE MONTGOMERY WAS waiting for us when we arrived at the Mexican restaurant between a laundromat and a coffee shop. We pulled into the lot and backed into a spot. I hoped I'd be able to see the car from inside.

She wore worn brown boots and a black *ZZ Top Eliminator* T-shirt. Her hair was pulled back; ringlets fell across her blue eyes. I saw her brush it away three times as we made our way across the pitted hardwood floor to the table.

She saw us, stood, hugged Paul, and shook my hand. She'd ordered a bucket of pale beer. A waitress brought it and some chips and salsa. We ordered food and made small talk until it arrived. Then she talked for almost an hour about Sangre. We listened, ate, and drank.

When she finished, we ordered another bucket of beers, talked about the DEA and Detroit. Paul got up several times to answer his cell. He walked away each time. He paced around the parking lot, barking into his cell phone. Through the window I saw him open the Duster's trunk where our gear was stored and reach in. I figured he was checking equipment. Each time he returned his stress level had risen. His face had flushed, a trim of sweat formed at the crest of his forehead. She asked me about Mississippi. We finished the beers, paid, and walked out.

I knew something was wrong, but Paul waited until we were in the parking lot to drop a bombshell.

"I've got to go home. My daughter is missing."

What could I say except we'll drive you to the airport? Brooke nodded but gave me a look with a raised eyebrow once she saw Paul glance back down at his cell phone. We walked next door for coffee. Paul and I took it black. She got some kind of latte. We walked back across the parking lot to her vehicle—a black GMC Yukon parked flush against the side of the restaurant. Brooke lifted the rear gate for Paul to get his gear. As he pulled it out of the SUV's cavernous storage area, I realized I had been correct back at the diner when I saw Paul transfer his gear to the Yukon. Last time I'd gone into my tactical bag for a phone charger and to check ammo all our gear had been neatly arranged. The bags were still arranged neatly. But differently. It seemed trivial when compared to a missing daughter. We drove Paul to the airport. He got his gear, the gate SUV's rear descended. Brooke hugged him. I'm not a hugger. I shook his hand. He walked into the terminal. After, we picked up a bottle of Eagle Rare bourbon on the way to a motel on the outskirts of Phoenix. We checked in. Two rooms. We sat at a small table in her room, talked about our plan, and drank bourbon while she told me her life story.

SHE'D GROWN UP in Pepper Pike, an affluent suburb of Cleveland, Ohio. During her first semester at the University of Pittsburgh, her father's paper dot-com fortune evaporated. A week later, he pulled his black BMW to the arc of their circular driveway, took a drag on a Cuban cigar, a few sips of Evian water and shot himself. Noteless suicide. No insurance payout. A mountain of debt. Thanks dad.

She stayed in school and took a job tending bar at *Smokin' Joe's*, a Southside joint frequented by cops. She drank with them often and went home with one occasionally. She met Dave, and then she went home with one all the time. He seemed kind. He wasn't. She drank a lot; he drank twice as much. They met around Thanksgiving. By Christmas, he slapped her for the first time. He apologized and promised not to do it again. She accepted. He'd lied. After a torturous New Year's Eve shift at the bar, they went home and got in a fight. He hit her again four hours into the New Year. This time his fist was closed. He apologized and promised not to do it again.

She didn't accept the apology or allow him the time to turn it into another lie. She left. She still liked cops, and the badges and guns on the nightstand, and the Kevlar vest on the floor. And even the handcuffs. Especially the cuffs, perhaps. She wanted it to be her world. She graduated in three and a half years, took on more shifts at the bar, and decided she wanted to go Fed.

A deep hiring freeze had yet to thaw, and only the United States Border Patrol was accepting applications. She filled one out and jumped through the hiring hoops. Eight months later she got the call, and two weeks after that she drove to Artesia, New Mexico for training. She was assigned to a post in Yuma, Arizona, out of the academy. Twenty-two months on the line, she was called to her Chief's office. He was there with a DEA Supervisor. From DC. They wanted her to do undercover work. Get close to a guy called Sangre. Badass. Former military. Ran guns, dope, and brothels. Human trafficking. They called it *Operation Mud Flap*. Something they explained later.

Undercover experience. Rare for USBP agents. She couldn't turn it down. And didn't want to. She traded her green uniform for clingy sundresses and knee-high leather boots. She frequented places Sangre did, waiting for him to notice her. He did. She worked him for almost a year until complications shut the operation down. She didn't elaborate. She couldn't go back to the southern border. And didn't want to. She liked dope cases. The freeze was over. She took a position with DEA in Detroit. And here we were.

There was no way we could fly with the equipment. We had to drive. We'd leave the next morning. Early. The bottle was empty. I walked back to my room. I slept, but not well.

IT WAS EARLY. She insisted we take her rented Yukon. We each had a single bag which we tossed in the back. We dropped the Duster off in long-term parking at the Phoenix airport. As the reddish-orange glow pushed at the dark desert horizon, we bought coffees and drove south. I glanced over at her.

I could see a Glock .40 tucked into the space between her seat and the console. I did the same on my side. She pushed a Robert Earl Keen CD into the player. "...*the road goes on forever*..." It seemed to. We drove for two hours, saying little. It was boring until I heard her say, "We've got company."

I looked back. The pavement stretched out behind us. The yellow stripe plowed down the middle, and the road met it like an arrow at the horizon. An Arizona State Patrol cruiser was a half-mile back. It approached quickly. The overhead lights pulsed and kicked red and blue shadows against the sweaty distant haze. There were more lights in the grille, wigwags they're called, and a red light clipped to the visitor side visor. The cruiser had at least half a dozen antennae.

"Gotta stop," I said.

She summed it up. "Fuck."

Well said.

She pulled the Yukon into the dust at the side of the road. The door opened. A man stepped out, racked a shotgun, and fired it at the Yukon. He wasn't an Arizona State Trooper. He was a scar of a man—tall, lean, bald; his arm was a roadmap of veins and tattoos. He wore a sleeveless biker vest. I heard buckshot crash into the quarter panels and lodge in the tinted rear windows. With each step, he racked the shotgun, and fired.

"Out," I hissed at Brooke and opened my door. She opened hers. I pulled the Sig free and fell against the door and out of the Yukon. I scrambled towards the back of the vehicle. I could see the man's silver-studded boots underneath the SUV. Brooke followed. The man fired again. And again. He pumped buckshot in our direction.

I kept moving towards the rear, but Brooke had cleared the door and moved towards the front of the vehicle. Smart. She could use the large engine block for cover.

The man had no plan. No tactics. He began to combat load the shotgun. I peeked high and low around the corner of the vehicle. He continued to fire. I moved slightly from behind the SUV, around the high planks of the red plastic taillights to get a shot. I saw the ridges of the sights and focused on the front sight. The rear sights blurred in my open eye. I squeezed. I hit the man in the neck. He turned with a look on his face I didn't expect. Annoyance. Nothing more. Or less.

He spun back towards me and racked the shotgun. I ducked behind the Yukon. He fired. Shot bore into metal and glass. The rear window was shattered, held in place by the now spider-webbed tint film. I peeked back around the corner and fired again. I hit him in the shoulder. He was holding the shotgun western style, at his waist. I fired again and hit him in the opposite shoulder. The man was still standing. Meth or PCP, I thought. Totally geeked. Feeling no pain.

I ducked back behind the Yukon's metal. Isn't Brooke going to get in this fight? I thought. I moved deeper behind the Yukon, expecting the man to fire another round of buckshot. I heard a shot. It was from her Glock. Then another. And another. She was firing at a fast clip. I peeked around the corner. The man was still facing me. With as much face as he had left. She'd hit him three times in the side of the head. He staggered, fell onto one knee, then the other and slumped onto his chest. Blood gushed and mixed with the sandy dirt that dusted across the pavement. I kept my Sig trained on him as I reached down and took the shotgun.

SHE WALKED TOWARDS me. I turned and took a hard look at the police cruiser. I could see the blue carpet of sky fill the Ford's wide front window. Red lights danced against the glass. I blinked, fighting the sun. I stared at the car until a shape emerged from the glare. A man, seated in the passenger seat. I saw the reflection of mirrored aviator sunglasses. As I got closer, I could see he was strapped into the seatbelt. The reflection shifted as I walked, clicking between the man and the blue canvas of the cloudless desert sky. I trained my gun on the car. There was no movement. He remained perfectly still. I walked to the passenger door and opened it.

The man wearing mirrored sunglasses was a dead Arizona State Trooper. There were ligature marks around his neck. A pair of leather gloves rested on the console. I picked them up and slipped them on. I inched the sunglasses down. His eyes had bulged. Slightly. They'd swelled in their sockets. I pushed the sunglasses back up on the Trooper's face with my index finger. I'd heard about similar desert murders of lone Troopers on the long arid highways that cut through the sand, prairie dogs, coyotes, and horned frogs of the Grand Canyon state. It had all the markings of an OMG prospect making his bones to become a full patch member.

I reached in and snatched the microphone resting in a clip to the right of the radio. I picked it up, keyed the mic and then released. What to say? Keep it short, I thought. Simple. Atlanta PD doesn't use the common ten codes. I didn't know them. I keyed the mic again and used plain speak.

"Citizen to state police dispatch, emergency transmission,"

"Go ahead," a female voice responded. The voice had no inflection, no accent. No surprise. Metallic.

"Officer down," I said. I gave our location as best I could. It didn't matter; units would respond from both directions and inevitably meet at the cruiser. I dropped the mic on the seat. I turned back around.

Brooke stood over her kill, her stare blank, but her eyes calculating. She was asking the same thing I was, but she said it aloud.

"How did they find us?"

I was about to attempt an answer when I saw the blood on her arm. She saw my expression and followed my eyes.

"I'm hit," she said simply, looking at her arm.

The blood seeped from somewhere above her elbow, where her arm disappeared into her T-shirt. I walked back to the cruiser and grabbed the first aid kit from the trunk. I didn't know how much time we had. I couldn't hear any sirens. I set the plastic box on the Yukon's hood, realized it was still hot, and moved the kit down onto the bumper. I opened it. I pulled gauze from the kit and reached for her arm.

"Don't," she said suddenly, taking the gauze from my hand. It was clear she didn't want me to touch her. Odd. I handed her the kit. She took it in her empty hand and walked around to the other side of the Yukon. We got in. As I pulled away, I heard the first sirens.

She dressed her wound as we drove in silence. The edgy wail of sirens grew louder. Police cars flew past in the opposite lanes, their tires barely touching the pavement in a dry hydroplane. We drove until we needed gas.

WE STOPPED. I slid the pump into the Yukon's tank and walked inside. I poured two fountain drinks and grabbed a bottle of low-shelf bourbon in a squat plastic bottle and paid the man. I took a right out of the filling station. Ten miles later I saw a sign: EAGLE PASS, TX – 114 Miles. It didn't lie. Ninety miles later the outskirts of Eagle Pass rose from the cracked sand in the distance.

Brooke was tired, not hungry; she just wanted to sleep. I was restless. We checked into a motel. I sat in a chair near the window, and she stood at the opposite side of the room looking in the mirror. Pulling her T-shirt off, she examined the bandage on her arm, before fiddling with the clasp behind her back with her good arm. It wouldn't release, so she walked towards me in a faux pout. Standing before me in old jeans and a new bra. Pink. Lace, she spun around. I undid the clasp and let the bra drop to the floor.

Brooke walked to the small dresser where her bag laid and unzipped it, pulling on a fresh T-shirt, before heading over to the bed and pulling the covers back.

She turned towards me and looked into my eyes. Her smile was playful, even seductive, but her eyes were sad. Brooke stopped smiling suddenly, sat down, kicked her boots off, wiggled out of her jeans and slipped into bed, seeming to sink into sleep as soon as her eyes closed. I grabbed my motel key attached to a green plastic fob and walked out of the room. I didn't let the door slam and made sure it locked behind me.

MACK B'S WAS a saloon. There were two more people inside than motorcycles outside and a rail-thin waitress with a smoke-charred voice and varicose veins that rose from sunburned skin like brail. The building was barnlike, with a crumbling balcony, two dusty pool tables, a jukebox, and a gigantic antelope head over the mirrors behind the long bar. I drank a whiskey and chased it with a beer that had been plowed through dirty lines.

I sat down, ordered, and felt the stares cast at any stranger in a bar like this. The whiskey burned, and the skunked beer left a rancid taste in my mouth. A large fan overhead rotated at a slow clip. This might have been a bad idea, I thought.

But it wasn't. For once. It was just a night in a bar. I kept the race going with the beer chasing the whiskey and marveled at the good taste of whoever was feeding the jukebox. I was drunk when I left the bar. But I sobered up quickly.

Brooke's door was open when I returned to the motel. She was gone.

33.

THE JAMAICAN STIRRED awake when the pilot dropped the landing gear. His fingernails were painted black. He wore sleek glasses with green lenses. He wore a silk pinstripe suit, a dark, midnight-blue shirt, and a crisp white tie that matched an equally crisp white pocket square. The watch was a Chopard; his hair in dreadlocks.

The Jamaican carried a small metal attaché case as he walked up the ramp into the terminal. He walked past baggage claim to the row of rental car counters and talked to the woman behind the Hertz one. He pulled a reservation slip and Colorado driver's license from a long alligator skin wallet and paid cash. He took a shuttle to the Hertz lot and slipped behind the wheel of a 2007 black Dodge Charger.

He set the metal briefcase on the passenger seat, entered the coordinates of an address in the GPS from memory, started the engine, pulled to the edge of the lot, waited for the metal arm to rise, and drove off into the night. A woman's voice spoke to him until he got to the motel. He checked in and went to sleep. He didn't need a wake-up call. His eyes blinked open at five. Always.

He left the motel in the dark. He entered a new set of coordinates in the GPS unit, again from memory, and pulled out of the motel parking lot onto the road. The woman began talking to him again. It felt good to be in the car. He found the reggae station on the satellite radio. He didn't hum along, but the music felt good as it washed over him. He set the cruise control five miles over the speed limit and settled in for a long drive.

34.

A LIGHT ON the dashboard began to glow. The Yukon was low on gas. Again. You'd think the thing had a huge tank. A phone rang. Private number. The large tires glided across the cracked asphalt and parked between two long rows of pumps. I answered.

I didn't recognize the voice. It had a sharp echo but sounded almost disinterested. Like a vacant stare.

"Mr Stock? Is this Dan Stock?"

It wasn't my phone. It was Brooke's.

I didn't tell him what he already knew

"Who is this?"

There was no sense in lying. He wasn't fishing in the dark. He knew I had the phone.

"This is Mitchell Blood."

He'd called her cell phone. She told me she hadn't talked to him in years. It was unlisted; there was no indication he ever knew her real name. And now he had her. Why would he snatch her? After all this time? Revenge? Some kind of twisted love? Like a Möbius strip. No beginning for her. No end for him. It was possible. I'd seen stranger shit.

I pulled the picture clipped to the visor down and looked at. The picture of four men in front of a tank that I had tucked into my leather jacket back in Browning's car at the truck stop. It seemed like a lifetime ago; for some, it was. The picture was getting a little worse from wear as it had been folded into several different shapes to stuff into different pockets and clipped to the visor in a couple of different rides. This had to be the third friend. It dawned on me. Mitchell Blood. *Sangre*, Spanish for blood.

"Something tells me our paths will meet in the near future," he said in a tone that should have spewed from a forked tongue.

"She wants to say hello," he said after a brief pause where he was gauging me, trying to see if I'd make some hollow threat about how we *would* meet again and what I would do to him when we did, or something equally as futile. When dealing with a demented reprobate like Sangre, a man orbiting in the outer rings of evil and psychosis, there was no reason to puff. Or threaten. Or attempt a menacing voice. So, I didn't. I waited.

Then, I heard the muffles of a gagged hostage trying to speak. "But she can't," he said and hung up.

He had her. I unfolded a map of North America and looked to the south. I pumped the gas and pulled out onto the two-lane road. Towards Mexico. I had found where I would cross. He was right, and he was wrong. Our paths would meet. But it would be in the *very* near future. There were now two reasons to find the elusive Sangre: Bust up his operation, and rescue Brooke.

Part III

MEXICO

35.

THERE WERE FOUR lanes open and a fifth blocked with orange cones. I was in the lane furthest to the left. An overhead sign read *Nada que Declarar* – Nothing to Declare. As I waited, I saw a wooden sign for a dentist. Billboards were propped up over the single-story clapboard buildings, and a man in a straw hat walked by. I pulled through and drove into town.

I parked and got out. The street was busy. I needed information, and that meant hookers, taxi drivers, bail bondsmen, or cops. I didn't need a cab or know any bail bondsmen south of the border. Mexican cops were sure as hell out. Hookers it was.

I walked down the main drag until I saw a stroll. For now, I'd go with the working girls that paraded back and forth in front of a three-story building with a large Corona beer sign with the word *Billares* and a stick drawing of a ball dropping in a pool pocket.

There was a small metal cart hot dog style cart parked against the sidewalk. A red cooler sat next to the cart, and a plastic tarp hung down to block out the sun. A man in a green shirt sat in a folding chair, took money, and gave change. I walked past the cart and cut onto the sidewalk past two payphones and a blue and white taxi.

The *Dulceria "El Eden"* was larger inside than it had looked from the street. It was a bar. Pool tables were arranged in a square pattern in the back. Two dusty-looking men played pool. They talked but didn't laugh. One tapped the other with his pool cue and the man, who had slouched over the table to break a new game, stood, and looked in my direction. I looked away and seconds later I heard the cue ball slam against the others. There was a silent jukebox. It reminded me of The Rust Club, back in the Delta.

I watched the women stroll by. Some were young and looked lost. Some were older and looked tired. Most wore bright dresses and high-heel shoes. I went up to the counter and ordered a beer in Spanish. The woman slid it towards me with a smile. It was ice cold. I took a swig before pulling the wad of bills from my pocket, handing her a twenty and waving for her to keep the change. I wouldn't have to wait long.

I sat down. The woman behind the counter nodded at one of the girls as she walked by the open door. I took another swig of beer. She walked in, came over, and sat down. She wasn't the youngest of the girls. Or the oldest. She had long eyelashes and dark skin.

She was direct. Transactional. I didn't mind. I was past the point where I partook the delusion that they really liked me for me. I handed her money for another round. She walked back to the counter, paid the woman, took the drink, and walked back across the room. She handed me the beer and then took me by the hand. Her nails were long and red. Behind the jukebox was a staircase I hadn't seen. We walked to it. She led me upstairs to a large room with a two small beds. I sat on one and she knelt. I pulled the wad of cash out of my pocket. She reached for my belt. I redirected her hand, helped her stand, and sat her on the other bed.

Ten minutes later I walked back down the stairwell and out around the jukebox none the wiser. She told me nothing, but I still paid her. She couldn't walk down the stairs without any money. Nobody she was paying up the line would believe there was some guy who went upstairs, turned down head and just wanted to talk. Working sources isn't a linear series of interviews. In Atlanta, with known entities and players, it was like a scavenger hunt; in Mexico it was like a scavenger hunt without the clues.

I glanced in the back and the men were gone. I walked out into the bright sunlight. It reflected off the shiny metal cart and into my eyes. I slipped on a pair of sunglasses and walked down the street. A gaggle of half-dressed kids danced in the discharge of a fire hydrant that spit gusts of water into the muddy road and overwhelmed the inadequate gutters. Another group of them lit off loud firecrackers left over from Cinco de Mayo. I kept walking

THE PIPE HIT my leg just above the knee as I passed an alley. I buckled and felt the barrel of a snub-nosed revolver against my temple and a hand on my collar. It pulled me into the alley. The pain was searing. The gun would have been enough. The hand released my collar. I collapsed to the dirt and gripped at my knee. I looked at them in the sickly light. It was the pool players from the bar. The one without the gun flipped out a badge.

Thank God, the police, I thought. I glanced down the alley and saw the rear doors of a white van. No license plate. He flipped the badge closed and stuffed it in the pocket of his washed-out jeans. He hit me again, this time with the butt of the revolver. The muted light of the alley went black.

I WOKE UP in the back of the van. My leg throbbed. I opened my eyes but didn't move. My left wrist was handcuffed to a metal ring bolted to the floorboard. I felt my pocket. The wad of money was gone. I slid my hand down the right leg of my jeans into the stolen boot. Shitty cops. Search people much? I folded my hand around the molded grip of the K-frame Smith & Wesson I should have gotten rid of long ago. I pulled it free and held it against the side of my calf.

The men were speaking in Spanish. I was conversational not fluent, but I grasped enough. Sangre had put a bounty on my head they wanted to collect. Like so many things in life it was just timing. Freak timing that they were playing pool when I walked in. They recognized me. I'd never find out if they were real cops or just perps with a badge. Either way, at least one of them was a perp with a badge. They began talking more rapidly, bordering on arguing, in Spanish about football, not the kind I watched. They placed too much faith in the metal ring attached to the van's floor. Far too much. It was simply a ring screwed into the floor's metal. The handcuffs were tight, the screw was loose. I was able to unscrew it. Silently.

I pulled the shrouded hammer back with the flat part of my right thumb. I heard a sharp click. The man with the badge was driving. At first, I couldn't tell if the passenger heard the chamber roll.

36.

HE DID. I saw a vein in his neck twitch, and he turned his head. I raised the gun and fired. The hollow point round plowed through the man's right eye. Half his forehead and shards of skull splattered across the windscreen and side window. Blood poured. The driver screamed. Some type of profane prayer.

I crouched on my good knee behind the driver's seat. The man had the seatbelt strapped across him. 'Safety first,' I thought. It wouldn't help him. I pulled the seatbelt to his left side down with my left hand, one handcuff still clipped to my wrist, the other dangled. The gun was in my right, and I wrapped my arm around the seat and stuck it to his temple.

"Stop the van," I said in a low voice, in Spanish. He mashed the brake pedal down violently, no doubt hoping I would lose my balance. I gripped at the seatbelt strap harder and leaned my left shoulder against the seat to hold my balance. I shoved my chin against the headrest. The van jolted to a stop on a surprisingly quiet side street.

"Put it in park," I said.

The driver shoved the van into park with an upward jerk of his arm. I pulled the trigger. The shot echoed, then street was quiet again. Half his forehead and shards of skull splattered onto the other half of the windscreen and his side window. There was a green gym bag containing a lighter, motel key, a leather cigar case with two cigars, and a thick envelope. I folded the envelope and put it in my pocket. There was a ratty-looking white towel in the back of the van.

I tore it in half, wrapped half around my knee for some stability and shoved the other half into the van's gas tank.

I lit the cloth with the lighter and left the men entombed in the van. I was two blocks away when the van exploded. I covered two more blocks at a slow, wounded pace. I heard what sounded like gunshots. It wasn't. It was the van's tires exploding. The tank must have been almost full. I looked at the motel key. I walked back to my car. A thin man with a light complexion and pencil-thin mustache looked up as I approached.

"The Bay Breeze Motel?" I asked.

He frowned. I handed him fifty dollars. He raised an eyebrow.

"That way. Twenty minutes."

I pulled the Yukon from the curb. Sure enough, after sixteen minutes, it appeared in the distance. There was a diner on the near side of the motel. I pulled into the lot and parked. I glanced at the key fob. Room Eleven.

THERE WAS NO bay. There was no breeze. I walked into the diner and sat down near the window facing the motel. The coffee wasn't bad. I ordered huevos motuleños to go with it and skipped the water. The waitress—a Mexican woman in her mid-thirties with big hair, bright red fingernails, and an ample ass—brought the food and smiled. I gulped it down in five bites.

I glanced over my shoulder, saw her watching me, and waved for a refill on the coffee, watching the motel as I drank it. Doors on the near side opened and closed as men came and went. The motel was a long, T-shaped single-story building with a rusty, overworked air conditioner sagging from each window. There was an ice machine, and the word MOTEL in large letters perched on an overhang between two of the buildings leading to the check-in area. Must be the same in English and Spanish, I thought.

There were two payphones just outside the glass doors of the lobby and an old Chevy station wagon was parked underneath the overhang right near them. Metal folding chairs were arranged in a semi-circle behind the Chevy. No people in sight.

As I walked back to the Yukon, I checked my cell phone. Two texts and one call. I'd check the call later; I recognized the area code, not the number. Both texts were from Paul. Checking in. I texted back and told him where I was.

"BEEN TO MATAMOROS. WHERE?"

I texted him my location.

"BAD PLACE B CAREFUL, STAY SAFE – CHECK IN."

"FIND YOUR DAUGHTER YET?"

"NOT YET."

I turned back to the motel. It certainly looked like a bad place. Dark and ominous, even in the late afternoon sunlight. The only thing I had was the motel key. One of the two men that had taken me had been on the job in Mexico. Or on the take. Probably both. But I had only seen one badge. I assumed it was authentic. Not that it mattered much in Mexico.

I pulled a short-stock shotgun with a combat strap, some shells, and the Sig out of the black duffel bag. I stepped back out of the Yukon and walked around the back of the diner, past a gas tank and a metal dumpster filled to the brim with garbage bags. A ratty mutt with shredded ears and patches of missing fur limped across the lot. Pregnant. Everyone was getting laid in this motel, I thought. She glanced at me and barked meekly.

I crouched near the corner of the building and watched. A blue Corvette Z06 was parked at a hasty angle in front of the fifth room down.

I saw a dark sedan backed into a spot on the far side of the motel. The windshield was tinted, and I couldn't see if there was anyone behind the wheel. I didn't worry about the sedan.

I passed rooms seven, eight and nine. They looked empty. I paused at room ten and reached across to the next door to insert the key. The curtains on room eleven were drawn. I turned the key, pushed the door open, and racked the shotgun as I stepped into the doorway. There were two women and one man. He was wearing a loud purple suit with a bolo tie. Like most of the guys I'd seen here, he too had a pencil-thin mustache.

I had a clear shot at the man. He was sitting up. There were two double beds, and he was on the far one. Neither of the women was in my way. They were working together on him, alternating. I trained the shotgun on the man. He raised his hands. He looked annoyed, not scared. I couldn't tell if it was having the shotgun trained on him, or that the women hadn't been able to finish. It wasn't his first time for either, it appeared.

The women fell out of the way. One in her thirties, the other in her twenties. Both half-dressed.

"Comprende ingles?" I asked to no one in particular.

The older woman shook her head. No. The younger woman nodded.

"Yes."

The man shook his head too. Another no.

"Get dressed," I said.

The woman scampered up and began dressing. Quickly.

"Manos ariba," I said to the man, jerking the shotgun towards him in short upward thrusts. He raised them higher.

The women scuttled towards the door. The younger woman glanced at me as they left.

"Hermanas?" I asked.

"Is my stepsister, mi hermanastra," she said, and they walked out. Sick.

"Sit down," I said, and he did. "Cover yourself." He took a pillow and covered up his disappointed junk. Didn't speak English my ass. He realized it too.

"What do you want?" he asked.

"Sangre. Where is he?"

"I tell you that, I'm dead," he said.

"You don't, and you're just as dead," I said.

"You'll kill me nicer, gringo," he said.

"Don't bet on it," I said. His eyes got wider for a second and he looked like he was about to duck.

"Maybe just nicer than he thinks I will." The voice from behind me was even, with a gruff accent from a dusty throat. "Turn around slow and drop that gun."

I dropped the shotgun on the bed and turned slowly with my elbows bent, palms open about shoulder height. I stepped to my left, so he'd have a clear shot at the man on the bed with his hands still raised higher than mine. If he was loyal to the man with the mustache, I'd be dead already. He'd have shot me in the back.

"Who are you?" he asked.

"Me?" I asked, but it was clear who he meant.

The man's mouth caught a quick smile and then released it. "Yes, you, cowboy. I already know who he is."

I gave him my real name and took a closer look at him. American. Tall. Sunburned, with a slight paunch. His jeans were frayed where they met a pair of snakeskin boots. Looked like python. He wore an empty leather holster slung low. It was empty because it usually held the glistening .357 Smith & Wesson that was currently in his left hand. His hair was black with gray streaks and slicked back. His face was pockmarked and sported three days of stubble. It looked like a roadmap of a trip that would have killed lesser men.

"What brings you to Mexico, Mr Stock?"

"Looking for someone, who has someone, who's wrapped up in something I want to stop."

"And him?" He jerked the big revolver towards the man on the bed.

"Means to an end," I said. "He either works for the someone I'm looking for, or he might know where he is. Just following a trail."

"But you're not sure it's the right trail, huh, cowboy?"

"Not yet."

"Well, this sumbitch," he spit tobacco down towards a small metal trashcan near his boot. Would have been cool, except he missed, and the juice bounced on the cheap carpet. "...is named Cesar Molina-Avila. Jumped bail in California. I'm here to bring him back."

"What'd he do?"

"I only care what he's worth, not what he did. But, busted for rape in Whittier, up in LA County."

Bail on a rape charge, I thought? Same shit, everywhere. The system sucked.

He started to walk past me towards the man I now knew as Cesar. As he passed, I saw a pair of handcuffs hanging from his belt near the small of his back. He took out the cuffs and handed them to the man. Then he put the oversized pistol against the man's temple.

"Put 'em on," he said. The man clicked the cuffs around one wrist, then the other. I never cuffed perps in front. The bounty hunter didn't seem concerned. "Don't stand up."

He didn't turn his head back towards me. "You can pick up the shotgun," the big man said, reading my mind.

"Trusting soul," I said, picking it up.

"Trusting my ass," the man said, squeezing the cuffs tighter against the silent man's wrists. "I'm sure you have another one on you anyway," he said. He grabbed the center of the handcuffs in the palm of his right hand and pushed the pillow away from the man's groin with the barrel of the gun. The pillow fell to the floor. The bounty hunter pushed the gun's tip into the man's tip.

Cesar's eyes grew wide. Eight out of ten perps would have already pissed themselves. He was a hard con, though not now and not as hard as when I'd burst in. I almost felt bad for him. Almost.

"You won't do it; I'm worth more alive…"

The big man pushed the gun further into the man's groin. The man gasped.

"Than dead?"

The man nodded.

"Probably," I said from behind him. "But I can make up the difference, whatever it is."

"And I only care about the money," the bounty hunter said. "Just tell him, Cesar."

And he did. He talked about a place Sangre called "The Cell." A bad place. An evil place. An oasis of depravity in the desert. In other words, my next stop. He wasn't chatty, but he spoke long enough to start putting the bounty hunter behind schedule. He finally broke in.

"Pull up your pants," the bounty hunter said. The man pulled his pants up gracelessly. The bounty hunter frisked him quickly. Pro move. Given how he found the guy, he might think there is no chance he has a weapon; never assume. Worst thing you can do is miss a gun. Missing some dope stuck up a bodily orifice after checking a guy into jail was one thing. Unless you were an asshole most corrections officers would get word to you without telling the brass. You stop back by; they hand it off to you on a smoke break outside a side door. No fuss; doesn't even hit the paperwork. Chain of evidence be damned. Passing a perp off through the sallyport with a gun. Nobody was going to cover you on that. You just delivered the ultimate whirlwind of shit into their world, even though they'll catch it during intake. It cannot happen.

"Dinero," he said simply.

The man stretched his cuffed hands across his waist so he could fish the money out of the right-hand pocket of the pants. The bounty hunter tossed a wad of rolled bills with a rubber band around them to me with a single word: "Half."

I nodded and counted the money. "Six twenty, American," I said, peeling eleven twenties and two fives from the stack.

He pulled the man to his feet by the collar of his not-so-understated suit and walked him towards the door. I handed him the money as he passed.

"You good if I ask him one more question?" I asked the bounty hunter.

"Make it quick" he replied.

"How do the cops fit into this place?" I asked Cesar. I had an idea, but I couldn't quite figure out why a couple of fake cops, or rogue cops, had a key to this raunchy pad.

From what the man said, low rent prostitution wasn't their most profitable endeavor, but they had a couple of rooms in different shoddy motels around town they ran girls out of. It was a slow day apparently so Cesar—the cops' most recent pimp while on the lam—was sampling the product.

"No surprises on that one," the bounty hunter said pulling Cesar out the door. I agreed. The oldest occupation isn't usually much of a puzzle. Debauchery is time-tested and, usually, predictable.

We walked out of the motel towards the man's sedan. The mutt loped back across the lot, going the other way. The bounty hunter opened the door and pushed the man into the back seat behind the passenger seat, before holstering his gun, walking around the back of the car, and opening the rear driver's side door.

He reached in, unlocked the cuff around the fugitive's left wrist, and clipped and tightened it around a metal ring bolted underneath where the armrest used to be.

"Keys?"

The man reached into his pants pocket and handed them over. The bounty hunter closed the door and opened the one in front of it. He gave a small salute and tossed me the keys. I caught them.

"Good luck, cowboy. Vette's all yours. Hope it helps you find who you're looking for. Both know this piece of shit is probably lying."

"Don't you want to know who I am?" I asked him. I'd find out more about him later.

"You're a cop. Or something like a cop. Or you used to be."

I nodded. That obvious? He fired the engine and drove away. I searched the Vette. Nothing. I wanted to take it, but it wasn't practical. Damn. I walked back to the Yukon. I turned out onto the highway. As I passed, I could see the stepsisters sitting in the diner under the yellow light, talking. I U-turned, parked near the door and walked in.

I ordered a cup of coffee to go. The women were looking down at the counter. I realized there was a stool between them. They had stopped talking. The waitress handed me the coffee. I pulled the wad of cash from the motel room out of my pocket, pulled the rubber band from it, and separated a ten and a twenty. I handed them to the waitress. I wrapped the rubber band around the bills in my hand.

"Gracias, Señor," she said. Her eyes were wide, and she looked scared.

I walked down towards the women and saw a baby in a rocker resting on the stool between them. Wrapped in a pink blanket. Stepsisters; a daughter. Hopefully destined for something better; something more. I handed the roll of bills to one of the women and the keys to the Corvette to the other.

"Sell it quick," I said. She nodded. Then I walked out. I climbed back into the Yukon. I took a sip of coffee, expecting it to be from the same pot as before and cold. It was hot, fresh, strong, and surprisingly good. I added two fingers of whiskey and stashed the bottle back in the console. I steered through the parking lot and almost hit that same pregnant mutt.

The desert sun was setting. A coyote sunset. The sky to the west was red. The sky behind me was blue. I pulled out onto the two-lane road and drove back towards the town. I found a motel. I slept, but not well.

37.

A NOISE WOKE me. I reached underneath the other pillow and wrapped my hand around the molded grip of my Sig. The noise grew louder. It wasn't a creep—somebody was at the door.

"Abra la puerta," a loud but flat voice said from outside. I stood and tucked the Sig into the back waistband of my jeans.

"Momento," I said. I half-expected them to either kick it in or use a key. I'm sure the manager would hand it over without hesitation or interest. I pulled a Cuban shirt from the back of the chair and slipped it on, before peeking through the curtains. Two black Ford Explorers and some kind of military Jeep. Green with a star on the front bumper. I was buttoning the shirt when I pulled the chain and opened the door. I squinted in the sunlight.

Two men, one Black, one white, one tall, one medium, stood backlit in the doorway in front of three Mexican cops in and a dark-skinned Mexican with sunglasses and a grey pinstriped suit. A man sat in the front seat of the Jeep. Green uniform. Stars on his collar. Mirrored shades. A close-cropped mustache. A serious look on his face.

A soldier with taut posture sat in the passenger seat with his hands still gripped to the wheel. The man with the shades and mustache reminded me of Colonel Toro in the pre-credit scene in *Octopusssy*.

The two men directly in front of me wore beige cargo vests over black T-shirts. The Black guy was the tall one, and he was as broad and muscular as he was tall. Shaved head with a neck wrapped in veins and muscle, like an oak wrapped in moss. The shorter white man was thinner and rangier. Fibbies would be in dark suits. These guys had to be Marshals or DEA. Maybe ATF. This was Mexico—DEA, I guessed.

"Can we come in?" the white agent said.

"Got creds?" I asked. They looked the part, but, as I said, this was Mexico. Even if they were legit, they could be a couple of rogue cops working for Sangre. The Black guy would be out of place, but Sangre was American, and the guy could do some damage.

I guessed right. They flashed a couple of DEA creds in my face. I saw the gold shield with the eagle perched at the top. They knew I knew they could be fakes anyway. Credentials were for TV, getting into federal buildings and scaring civilians.

I stepped back. They stepped in and left the door open a crack. The others stayed outside.

"Gun," the white guy said, without doubt as to whether I had one. I reached back, pulled it out of my waistband, kept it pointed at the floor, and tossed it on the bed.

"I was having a good night's sleep," I lied. "What do you want?"

"An ex-cop on the run in a Mexican rattrap motel, yeah, I'm sure you were sleeping like a baby," the white man said. The Black guy stood stiff. They knew I wasn't scared. Not really. I'd dealt with DEA in Atlanta. Good guys. Most of them ex-street cops. Not like the FBI, a lot of whom were accountants and lawyers straight away. Secret Service were squared away and disciplined with good suits and better sunglasses. DEA were the street cops of the feds, like Marshal fugitive ops or ATF

"He talk?" I asked the white agent.

"He doesn't have to do much talking." The white agent glanced around at the bottles on the nightstand and the black gym bag on the floor next to the bed. They might have already searched the Yukon.

"I'm starting to sober up here agent...?"

"Hamby," he said. "Yeah, me too. We're looking for Brooke."

What a coincidence, I thought. "One of your very own," I said.

"She was," the Black man said.

"So, you just miss her?" I asked.

The white guy took back over. "Yeah, we miss her. Brooke was a hell of an undercover. Gutsy. Border and street all at the same time."

"But...?" I asked.

"But she gave notice out of the blue and stole almost a hundred thousand dollars from anevidence holding room. She signed it out in her own name. We haven't seen her, or the money, since."

"I haven't either," I said. They knew I was lying, but I wanted to see if they'd throw it back at me. Tell me about the meeting. Our ride south. Show me some surveillance photos. I was trying to figure out how they found me. I never did. But the government has many ways of finding people. Some we know about. Most we don't. Technology meant to free us has done anything but. I certainly didn't advocate his methods, but the Unabomber had some valid points in that manifesto.

I repeated the lie. "I haven't seen her."

I didn't know these guys. I could tell them that she'd been snatched. They could probably help me find her. Or they could be the working for whoever who had her. Maybe someone standing outside the door. They could be fishing to see if I had the money or knew where it was.

"Why would she run?" I asked. See if I could do some fishing of my own.

"Didn't you hear the part about the hundred grand?" he asked.

"So, it's just money. Obvious like that—just sign it out under her own name and walk away, sure to be chased?" I asked.

"It wasn't just money." He looked like he was going to say something else. He paused, and then said it. "We're worried about her."

I looked at him. Waiting for more. I raised my eyebrows. He didn't speak. Instead, he handed me a folder. I opened it. It was a stapled stack of photocopies of prescription records in the name of Erin Dean.

"Erin Dean. Who's that?" I asked.

"An old cover name she used on a prescription fraud case a few years back in Philadelphia. Six months under with an online pharmacy operation that was half legit, half not so much. We checked the file. She turned in most of her fake ID's and docs. Some other stuff she said was lost. At the time, it didn't really matter."

I flipped through the pages. Photocopies of prescriptions and drug labels. Some of the names I recognized. Others I didn't. A few of them were for depression. One was for high blood pressure. Pain meds. On the third page, two caught my eye. Atripla. Truvada. My knowledge of pharmacology was more street than prescription but if my memory served me: Brooke was HIV positive.

"We could be the least of her problems," the Black guy cut in.

"What could be the most?" I asked, thinking he meant AIDS.

"Jamaicans."

Nothing interesting happened after that until the men left. I listened as the sounds from their vehicles faded. I picked up the gun and tucked it into my belt.

Talking in riddles made me hungry. And thirsty. I went to a diner and ate machaca con huevos. I got a cup to go and opened another mini bottle of bourbon. I walked back to the motel and loaded my equipment into the SUV.

I knew finding Sangre wouldn't be the toughest part. Like all crime bosses, some visibility was necessary. For fear, respect, whatever.

38.

THE MAN ON his way back to the Los Angeles County jail from the motel had given me what I needed. He told me about a place at the base of the mountains with an abandoned Spanish mission perched just above it. I could watch from the mission. I drove south. And then east.

The man had told the story sequentially. Chronologically. I ticked through the sequence of events he had described. They found the girls in the poorest of Mexican villages. They liked girls with sisters, especially younger sisters, which I already knew. Occasionally, they'd just snatch the girls but usually the parents agreed, thinking the girls were going to work in restaurants or other business in the North.

The girls were collected and taken in groups to a place Sangre called *"The Cell."* That's where I was headed—the place I could watch from the mission. After spending a couple of months at the Cell, the girls were taken across the border in smaller groups, in a variety of ways. Almost always at night.

Once in the U.S., they were taken to stash houses in a large city. Sangre kept them moving. First, they'd be taken to a large city in the southeast. Houston. San Diego. Phoenix. Stash houses weren't where they serviced clients. There was always a family with kids that lived in the stash house, and to outsiders, it looked normal. The family's guests weren't there by invitation.

They'd stay for a day or two at a time either before or between being sent out. Being sent out meant either a brothel or being driven directly to a client's house. The client paid more for a personal visit, than having to come to the brothel. The shifts were long, and the girls would stay a few hours at a client's house or a few days at the brothel.

Sangre always had at least one person living at the brothel to watch over the groups of girls as they came and went. The girls were always raped by Sangre or one of his top handlers, usually on their first night at The Cell, always by their second. The girls were threatened. They were told that their families would be killed if they didn't behave, or ran away, or killed themselves. The girls with younger sisters were given extra incentive to submit.

Sangre's operation was expansive, the man knew that. And he didn't. He didn't know it stretched all the way to small towns across the American South. And he didn't know about the friends. Sangre had always had the help of three old friends: three now-dead friends.

I didn't know if Sangre knew they were dead. I promised myself that I'd tell him before he was dead too. Scratch that, before I killed him. But first, I'd cut his operation off at the head. And find Brooke. And maybe even figure out what in the hell she was up to. I kept driving.

39.

THE ROADS LAY flat and straight on the desert, like chalk on a baseball diamond and stretched for miles. And miles. And miles. I needed more information and more guns. And maybe a grenade or two. Like always, I'd make calls into a web of contacts that crisscrossed like red alarm beams in a museum of priceless art. The web was made up of an endless assortment of contacts.

Well represented in this assortment were bookies and bail bondsmen, former CI's and reporters, probationers and parolees, desk clerks, and prosecutors. But mostly cops. City cops in uniform, haggard detectives in tired suits, feds in better suits, state narcotics investigators working in shops so underfunded they drove their own cars, Highway Patrol, sheriffs' deputies working on both sides of the bars.

You never knew who you could trust, and almost everybody lied. At best, if you could figure out the people you couldn't trust, you were ahead of the game. It was shades of gray and a world of charcoal shadows. There was a day I would have called Paul. This wasn't that day.

I called an unlikely ally—a defense attorney. Cherry had softened my view of the profession, but only slightly. Phil Killmer was a criminal defense attorney in Maricopa County. He had been a federal public defender in Atlanta before he married an Episcopal priest and moved to Phoenix, where she took over a progressive Episcopal parish. I knew two men married to Episcopal priests. One was saltof-the-earth. The other had been. I thought about Browning for a moment.

Killmer answered on the third ring. I pictured him leaning back and palming his long grey ponytail that hung over the leather of his office chair.

"Dan Stock, one of the good guys. What's going on brother? Long time."

"Too long," I said.

We caught up for a few minutes, but he knew I hadn't called to chat. He brought it to a close.

"So, what's really going on? You okay?" I filled him in on most of what was going on. I said I was in Mexico and told him what I needed. He told me what he knew, promised he would find out whatever he could about what he didn't. I reminded him information was only part of it. I told him what else I needed.

"I know a guy," he said. "Jack A. Lope. Better known as Tarot." I liked it. A man with a colorful alias who still went by a nickname.

"Trust me, amigo," he said in a voice that seemed to brighten a little. "His name is the least colorful thing about him, and…" He paused.

"And…?" I asked cautiously.

"And, you might have to get a tattoo," he said.

Not my first, I thought.

40.

THE OLD MAN bought the place, fought through the cobwebs, and set up a tattoo parlor. Or something like that. He seemed to have come from nowhere. He hung a decrepit sign featuring a dinosaur, circa-1950's drive-in movie; a T-Rex with a pink Cadillac in his mouth; a young blonde couple seated in the front seat. Even with the car inverted in mid-air, the woman's blonde hair didn't budge. Under the sign, in painted black brushstrokes, the words "T-Rex Tattoos" loomed dark and unlit.

Nobody was sure where the tattoo artist came from. He had two vehicles, a seriously old and beat-up Chevy Impala he'd picked up at an Oklahoma sheriff's sale, and a new, glistening-chrome Harley Davidson Fat Boy, with a back tire almost as wide as the Chevy's. The Impala sat parked in the dust of the unpaved lot. The hog was somewhere out of sight. The name on the door was Jack A. Lope. In Mexico and everywhere else, he was known only as Tarot. He had been in town for less than two years, give or take a month. Nobody in this part of Mexico bothered to keep track.

He'd bought two old barber's chairs and bolted them to the floor. I walked in and sat down in the one furthest from the front door. The man and the chairs were old; the tattooing equipment was sterile, shiny, and organized.

The back of both of Tarot's hands sported red flaming number 8 tattoos. He raked his fingers through a thick, graying beard twisting it at the bottom between his thumb and index finger.

The windows of the place still sported the pawn-shop-issue security bars. Tarot had welded steel plates across the window at odd angles. He could see out, but nobody could see in. That's how Tarot liked it.

I told him who I was.

"Yeah, Killmer called."

He was in a gruff mood. According to Killmer, he was usually in gruff mood.

"What's up?" I asked, thinking it would bring minimal response. I was wrong. He ranted on about the government and spit out every stereotype under the sun about almost every type of person under the sun.

I'd heard this rant from many others and let Tarot's long list of bitches, and people to hate and blame, trickle out. I scanned the walls, waiting for Tarot to run out of steam and venom. A confederate flag covered an entire wall, some old Blitzkrieg concert posters, a couple of passages from *Mein Kampf* stenciled on the wall on top of a spray-painted "88." "H" was the eighth letter in the alphabet and 88 had become a subtle "Heil Hitler" for the younger set of skinheads and hate-mongers.

Tarot's tired rant finally fizzled out, and he returned to the barber's chair. He asked me what kind of tattoo I wanted. I chose. Tarot seemed disappointed in the racial neutrality of the design.

"What the hell," he said, as he began to stencil on my arm. The old man in a ratty sleeveless Harley shirt and urban camouflage pants, frayed at the bottom, several inches above commando-style black boots, looked like a run-of-the-mill roughneck, but when it came to tattooing, he didn't mess around. When the stencil was done, we made a few careful changes; the artist and his patron. Tarot washed his hands and forearms in a shiny metal sink and pulled a starchy towel from the rack to dry. He pulled a sterile cloth mask across his face and tied it in the back before putting on disposable gloves. He held his hands in the air away from his body, like Hawkeye walking into the E.R.

The tattoo took almost three hours. Tarot was silent during the outline; he began to talk when it was time to fill in the color. The needle hummed and dug into my bicep. I grimaced a few times, but it wasn't my first tattoo.

I glanced towards the floor. I saw the shiny silver hinge and could make out the faint outline of a trapdoor under a cheap oriental rug. Tarot's private arsenal of assault weapons, sniper rifles, grenades, munitions. Most likely military issue from the U.S., a few pieces bought from KGB-turned Russian Mafia after the fall of the Soviet Union. Some for sale. Others for a private, paranoid race-war Tarot had fought and won over and over in his frantic mind.

I told him what I needed, and he said he had it, even the stuff I wasn't sure he'd have: the demolition equipment. He could help. He said he would. He asked who it was for. I told him.

"Yeah, I've heard of that sick twitch," Tarot said. "Maggot's got napalm burns all over his face and hands. Wears one glove all the time."

"Like Michael Jackson?" I asked.

"Nah. Sangre ain't that sick," he said.

We laughed for a second. I told him what I knew. He told me what he knew. We were done talking. Tarot said he was getting to the hard part and had to concentrate. We fell into silence. I thought about how demented someone had to be for Tarot to call him a 'sick twitch.'

I watched his furled brow and focused eyes critically scan the piece. The rhythmic hum of the needle was therapeutic. The talk done, Tarot quickly bored of the silence and reached back to a grey plastic, circa 1985 single-cassette boom box. He pushed at one of the large black buttons, which clicked down into place. Tarot snarled along to the searing punk guitar and mouthed the vengeful lyrics in unison.

When he finished the tattoo, I studied the reflection in the full mirror. Tarot pulled off the rubber gloves and threw the needle into the autoclave. He'd kept the twisted part of himself under control for a couple of hours, but Killmer was right... Tarot was talented.

"Coffee for the road?" Tarot asked, taking a tall travel mug from a shelf next to a miniature pewter lawn jockey.

"Yeah, hit me with at least half—long trip." When I said "half" I didn't mean the amount of coffee.

"Half it is." Tarot said reading my mind.

He grabbed a bottle of Jack Daniels Green Label from the same shelf and poured it into the cup, topped it off with coffee and grabbed two Confederate flag shot glasses. He poured two tall shots of whiskey. We clicked the glasses in a silent toast and killed the whiskey in single gulps. I chased it with a couple of sips of the spiked coffee.

While I sipped with my other arm, Tarot put a large piece of gauze loosely across the fresh tattoo and then taped it at each corner.

"Thanks for the art," I said. "Best shit that's ever been scratched on me."

"You're welcome," he said.

He palmed the sides of my neck. "Be careful, brother. Stay loose on this one. Sangre ain't some perp on domestic beef or possession-weight dope. This thing's got teeth. Who knows who's involved? Jamaicans? Russians? OMG gangs for sure. For all we know, some of my friends are in this mix. Psycho militia—those crazy, zombie, Nazi bastards out of Little Rock—maybe the Aryan Brotherhood, inside or out. Maybe both. Bikers, Hell's Angels, Mongols, Banditos, Mexican Mafia. Who knows? Maybe you should just walk away."

I gave a noncommittal shrug.

"Personal, huh," Tarot snorted.

"Personal enough," I said.

"Personal gets you killed, and you know it," Tarot replied.

"I'll watch my ass," I looked into Tarot's intense, almost fearful eyes.

Tarot squeezed my neck.

"I'll say a prayer for you on this one. I just met you, but if Killmer says you're okay, you are. It just seems like you're chasing ghosts. Ghosts that are going to get you killed brother-man. Let me get you what you need."

He did. It took two trips for us to load the artillery. He went back inside. I walked across the pockmarked gravel to my car. I looked back to see that Tarot had already shut the door.

41.

I PARKED THE Yukon under a decaying tree, stepped out, and pissed against the scorched, tired tree bark. I reached back into the SUV and dropped a couple of mini bottles of Jack Daniels I'd stashed in the console into the deep side pocket of my BDU pants. I ducked my head under the long strap of the black duffel.

The sky was clear, the moon full. I cast a wide arc of focused light around the outer shell of the abandoned Mission. It was square with a portico entrance and a tall, rounded dark wood door. A series of shallow columns flanked the door and the sides of an upstairs window, leading to a line of etched triangles pointing towards a short steeple topped with a bronze cross. A floor above the cross, to the right, was a stout, boxy bell tower. No bell. The large wood door was heavy but unlocked.

I pulled the handle and felt its weight move against the rusted hinges. It opened enough for me to slip through. I stepped into a thick mess of cobwebs and made my way through a sanctuary to a back stairwell. Climbing the stairs, I stepped out onto the flat walkway running along the base of the bell tower. The lights from The Cell were over to the west, the glowing outline of the place in the distance cast in a constant shadow by a shy moon and the occasional pierce of headlights throwing light at odd angles as cars came and went. Even at a distance, I could feel its rancid energy— the bustling marketplace of a perverted type of empty-calorie existence.

I sat down against the wall, pulled out a Partagas Black cigar, cutter, and butane lighter from a leather case in the same pocket with the mini bottles of bourbon. I lit it. I drank and smoked and waited for the sun.

IT DIDN'T DISAPPOINT, and came up on time, piercing my eyes. I pulled a small backpack from the large black duffel. It was filled with water bottles, pemmican bars, and a jar of peanut butter. I pulled a desert boonie hat from the backpack and a pair of Oakley's tucked into a vertical pocket. I pulled the sunglasses from the soft pouch and wiped the steam off the lenses, before pushing them onto the bridge of my nose and tightening the strap against the nape of my neck. I watched and dozed. And drank bourbon. And smoked cigars. I thought about a past life and an October evening years before.

A friend's younger brother was graduating from the academy that night. I didn't have anything better to do, so I went. The first time I saw her was when a Deputy Chief I admired handed her a shiny detective's badge at the ceremony on the top floor of city hall. The same room where my graduation took place when I finished the academy. She was assigned to Vice, one of the first stops for many detectives, especially women. A couple of months later, I was in a takedown team for a prostitution detail they were working on Stewart Avenue. She was assigned to the same team. She stood on a corner with a couple of other female cops dressed in cat-suits, fishnet stockings and high, fake leather boots. The johns must have known they were cops, and not the crack whores that usually worked that stroll. The girls weren't malnourished, their fingernails weren't black, and they carried big purses with their guns, badges, and radios inside. They wanted to believe that a good-looking brunette or a natural blonde—white girls at that—could be had for five bucks or a piece of rock.

For about a month, my team assisted with the takedowns for the detail. We kept in touch after it ended. There was never any question of where it was going. The only mystery was where it would end. Even now. It seemed like yesterday. And it seemed like forever ago.

Sometimes the cold feeling in the ether of my memory, that inner twinge of unexplainable perception at the hazy edges of destiny, was that I'd moved to Atlanta to meet her, not for the job. That I'd blocked fate with fear and cynicism towards love, like a man watching a magician, second-guessing the tricks instead of enjoying the magic.

But that was then. And the filter of those past decisions would always allow the trickle of my life to unfold through it. For now, if time was in a bottle, it was in the mini bottles of Jack Daniels because I was getting bored. Nothing happened at the compound. Until it did.

A MAN OPENED the door of a half-exposed RV tucked under a parched, green tin overhang. He pulled on a baseball cap and reached over his shoulder to hook the strap of his overalls. The gate was unlocked and cast aside. The man fired up a cracked yellow school bus parked to the side of the gate and pulled it halfway across the space left between the gate and the heavy iron gatepost.

I moved the scope of my rifle to focus on the school bus. It was fortified with flat plates of steel across the roof and in the spaces where the windows had been. I could see turret holes in several of the plates, equidistant from one another, running the length of the bus. The man walked to a small office that looked like a construction trailer and probably had been. He stepped inside. Twenty minutes later, he came back out with a mug of what I guessed was coffee and began to unlock the silver rolling garage door of each bin. He unlocked eight doors with the same key and pushed them until they rolled up and over the rails on their own. Then he sat in a metal folding chair. He knew what he was waiting for. I didn't. We waited, together, almost a mile apart.

42.

THE FIRST VAN pulled through a gap to the left of the school bus an hour after the sun peaked in the sky; the second fifteen minutes later. They backed in underneath the same tin overhang as the RV. A tall Latino stepped from the first van. A squat, dark-skinned Latino stepped from the second. Each van's side door was opened and girls of the same complexion as their drivers stepped out. Four from the first van; three from the second.

The man with the coffee must have expected one more girl. The drivers herded the girls to the various storage units and closed the doors behind them. The tin roofs of the storage units baked in a sun that seemed to gather strength as it rolled to the western horizon.

The first car, a two-toned silver and black Cadillac Seville with the sloped back and the angled spare tire, pulled to the side of the outside gate and parked with its right tire slightly dipped into an arid ditch. A man with pasty skin, a glimmering belt buckle, and a black cowboy hat with a blue feather walked through the gate around the grille of the school bus.

The man in the folding chair stood and walked to greet him, and they shook hands. Cowboy Hat reached into his pocket and handed something to the folding chair guy. Then they strolled around the gravel lot to the open door of each storage bin. Cowboy stopped at the first and pushed his hat to the crown of his receding hairline. When he paused at the remaining seven bins, he looked in, but left his hat alone.

Cowboy pointed a few times and spoke to his tour guide out of the corner of his clenched jaw beside a Joker's smile. He backtracked to the bin second from the left and stepped in. The man rolled the door down and returned to his chair and his coffee to await the next customer.

Like the Cadillac, every car that came parked outside, and the men walked in through the gate past the school bus. They came and went. Each stayed in their chosen bin for fifteen or twenty minutes and then walked out the single door tucked to the right of the garage. Each time a man emerged, the guy in the chair would rise, shake hands with the departing customer, and walk to the bin and roll the door back up for the next round of depraved window shopping.

I watched the rest of the day. No sign of Sangre. No sign of Brooke. I continued to watch until the sun dipped past a row of cacti at the horizon and disappeared completely. The bartering didn't subside after traditional business hours. It picked up. The men began to form jagged, impromptu lines, waiting their turn. Two more guys joined the one in the chair to act as salesmen.

I watched the action through the green lines and shadows of a pair of Night Optik night-sight goggles. I knew the pattern wouldn't change; at most it would vary only slightly as the blue and black skyline morphed into an ink-black desert cover, the only cracks being the still, bright stars.

They were sick and depraved men. They didn't deserve the dry air they breathed. I would have loved to execute them like ducks in a pond. But I'd wait.

I WATCHED THE following day, and pulled away from the Spanish mission that night, after the vans drove out through the gates and accelerated down the two-lane road, their taillights disappearing just above a cluster of stars in the distance. I could have saved seven girls that day. Saving them now could cost their families their lives. Their little sisters. Parents. And it wouldn't help me find Brooke. Or Sangre.

The desert was too flat to follow the vans, even at night. I'd have to find the stash house or houses, Brooke, and Sangre before I made my move. Tipping my hand early could mean a death sentence for the girls and Brooke, which I couldn't let happen. Tipping my hand early could also mean that Sangre would survive, which, I sure as hell couldn't let happen either. I repacked the gear, stood up and pissed off the side of the mission.

The Willie Nelson and Ray Charles duet, *Seven Spanish Angels,* echoed in my head as I retreated to ground level and out to the Yukon. I opened the hatch and dropped the duffel bag into the storage area behind the back seat. Then, I left the mission and drove to a motel. I slept, but not well.

I woke up early. I cleaned the weapons on a wrought iron table next to a sludge-filled pool in the light of a pasty fluorescent security light. I watched the moon set and the sun rise. I heard a coyote. At least I thought it was, what the hell did I know?

43.

THE YUKON PITCHED to the left when the tire exploded. It almost rolled, but I caught it at the last second, accelerated hard, pushed the pedal to the floor, and then released it before braking so that the vehicle would stop on its tires without rolling. What we called threshold braking at the police academy. The van had been parked behind a lone roadside billboard between the motel and the nearest intersection to the east.

The flat left tire made it easier to open the door, and it fell when I released the latch. I felt for my Sig. The van approached. I opened the door and reached into the black duffel, pulling the short-stock shotgun free and moving it to the end of the seat. I reached further into the bag with my free hand and pulled a grenade from deep inside, slipping it into the side pocket of my cargo pants. I tucked the Sig into my belt and racked a shell into the shotgun. The van continued to approach. It was coming straight ahead. It wasn't surgical. It was blunt, and predictable. And too easy.

The window to my right exploded. I could feel glass graze my neck. I turned. A tensile jackrabbit of a man holding a twelve-gauge was almost on top of me. Where did he come from? I'd gotten sloppy. What we had always warned rookies about: getting blinders on. Focus was good; too much could be fatal.

He fired again, buckshot crashed into the side of my Kevlar vest and into the metal of the vehicle's shell. More glass exploded. Something stung my neck. I wasn't sure if it was buckshot or glass.

The man was armed to the teeth, but not smart. He had the shotgun, the reach. He got too close. He was almost an albino.

He racked the shotgun for a kill shot. He didn't know I had the Sig in the front of my belt. The barrel of the shotgun was close, almost against my chest, and still he came. He wasn't ready to kill me. He wanted to scare me with the hollow rake of the sound as he racked the shotgun. He wanted information. To keep me alive to tell him what Sangre wanted to know. I could imagine what that was. At least I thought I could.

He was almost to the bottom of the rack, his hand almost back to the trigger guard when I stepped forward, raised a knee. The man fell back as the shotgun hit him in the chest. His finger was inside the trigger guard, the gun exploded again, this time into the air over my right shoulder. The shot arced and fell harmlessly to the sand on the other side of the SUV.

Without thinking, the Sig was in my hand. Muscle memory. My first shot tore through the man's knee. Information flowed both ways and keeping him alive could lead me to the stash houses, Brooke, even Sangre. I could hear the van behind me.

Screw it, I thought. No time. I double-tapped him to the head. Blood flowed into the sand. I turned back towards the van. It was thirty or forty yards away, flattening sand and kicking up dust. I could see the forms of a driver and a man in the passenger seat and I had no idea how many might be in the back. I was alone.

I dropped my hand down to the pocket of my cargo pants and gripped the grenade. I pulled the pin out, dragged my arm back to my ear and began to release. It was a risk. Another layer of goons could be in the back. But so could the girls. In a split-second I corrected myself. It was a hell of a risk. The van was ten yards away.

The grenade arrived at an angle and landed near the van's front-left tire. It exploded. The van pitched to the left. The driver apparently hadn't had a threshold braking class. The van rolled several times, righted itself, and bounced on its tires to a stop. I pulled the shotgun from the bag. I reached up and touched my left hand to my neck. I pulled the glove back across my sightline, clicked my eyes away from my focus on the van for a moment. There were several drops of blood against the glove leather.

I reached the van. The men in the front were propped up in their seatbelts. The van was either pre-airbag, or they hadn't worked. The men looked dead, but I wasn't sure. The passenger window was closest to me, and it was open. I walked closer to the van and looked into the back over the short-back seats. I couldn't see anyone else in there. I pumped three shells into the van through the open window. Now, I was sure. I walked around the van and opened the rear doors.

There was a large plastic tarp strewn across the rear seat. First, I saw feet. Painted toenails. A silver ring around the pinkie toe of her left foot and a butterfly flying above some Asian lettering on her right ankle. The tarp was nondescript. Uninteresting. The naked female body underneath the tarp was more interesting. She was young and blonde, late teens, early twenties. She was bound with electric tape at the wrists. One thing was clear, she'd been dead before I spun the van.

There was a trash bag underneath her head. I opened it. A Michigan sweatshirt, jeans, brown Ugg boots, socks, a bra wrapped up in a red T-shirt, and a wallet. It was clear she wasn't taken from anywhere this close to the Equator. The Michigan sweatshirt was a hint. No panties. She wasn't wearing any jewelry. I opened the wallet. I glanced at her driver's license. It was consistent with the sweatshirt. The address was in Port Huron, a middle-class suburb outside Detroit. The first name, Kelly, didn't mean anything to me. Her last name did, and it would mean a call I didn't want to make for more than one reason. What I would have to say. And what I feared I would find out. I wrapped the tarp back around the body.

I still had some questions about why they snatched her in the first place, but not why they killer her. Because they were killers.

I walked back to the SUV and changed the tire. Not easy to do in sand. I drove to the van, removed the body, and then backtracked to the Spanish mission. I carried her inside and tucked her into a corner. She would be safe enough here until I'd made that call. I walked back outside and drove to a cantina and then a motel.

I opened the envelope that I'd lifted from the crooked Mexican cops. A thick stack of Western Union receipts. I studied them for a moment. I put them back in the envelope and lay down. I slept, but not well.

44.

THE WESTERN UNION slips had all listed the same recipient. I found the store's address and parked at the far side of the parking lot. There was a food truck parked between the Yukon and the Mexican bodega with the Western Union neon light in the corner of the front window. Berto's Taqueria was painted above the wide windshield. A man and a woman stood inside, serving. I waited in a short line, ordered two burritos and a Mexican Coke that was a little sweeter than the recipe used to the north, paid the woman, took the food from the man, and walked back to the SUV. I washed the meal down with the Coke splashed with bourbon with only a couple of shards of ice floating in it. When I finished, I walked towards the bodega.

I stepped inside accompanied by the sound of a bell, took another can of Coke from a tall cooler and walked to the counter. A yellow and black Western Union sign hung above the counter. I paid the young girl behind the counter. We smiled at each other as I reached to tuck a small transmitter underneath the counter. My hand hit a large bolt before I found a flat piece of wood to attach it to. It stuck. We were still smiling at each other, and her hand lingered in mine for a split second as she dropped the change into it.

"Gracias," she said.

"De nada," I said. I asked her if she was working late in Spanish: "Trabajo tarde?"

"Not too late," she replied, in English. That would make things easier I thought.

I crossed the lot past the food truck and got back into the SUV. The transmitter's range was less than a half-mile. I turned it on, and heard the cashier speak, a customer reply, and then the cashier again. I could hear the register and the sounds of the coins brushing against one another as she made change. She was polite.

I listened and scanned the Western Union receipts. There was a pickup almost every day, usually in the early afternoon. I'd have hope that the address was spoken out loud. But that was unlikely unless it was different people who came in every day. The cashier would know a regular collector on sight if they came in to get a pickup for the same recipient every day, and there would be little reason to say anything. I'd watch for a while, see if it got me anywhere, and, if not, go to plan B. Plan B was riskier, but would be more pleasant than spending days in the parking lot, waiting to detect a pattern. Plan B also had a nice smile. Although, for all I knew, she could also be in on it.

Patterns weren't easy to come by. Numerous men and women, alone and in groups entered the bodega multiple times while I watched. It wasn't just a Western Union stop. All kinds of people came and went more than once. I thought of the places I stopped for coffee or food or liquor daily, sometimes more than once. Hell, if someone was watching the food truck over the past three days I'd fit into an undeniable pattern. I was running out of time, and patience. Time for Plan B.

45.

PLAN B LEFT work a few minutes after five. I followed her from the bodega to a cantina three miles away in a similar strip mall. I waited a half-hour and walked in. She was seated at the bar, second stool to the end, smoking a cigarette and drinking a beer. I hadn't seen her legs or feet behind the counter in the bodega, and they didn't disappoint now. Long and smooth and brown. Like her lipstick, her toenails were painted bright red. Her stilettoes were high, the straps thin. As I walked towards her, she crossed her legs, fluttered her feet beneath her, and banged them lightly against the metal ring at the base of her stool.

"Hola," I said. She turned towards me and smiled, but I could tell she had already seen me in the mirror behind the bar.

"Hola," she watched me glance at legs that were clearly on display.

"Habla ingles?"

"Que?" she smiled a Cheshire smile. "I'm kidding, I do. But you already knew that."

I hadn't forgotten.

"Spent time in the states?" I asked.

"Some" she said.

The waitress placed two frosty longnecks in front of us and walked away. I pulled a stack of bills from my pocket, peeled a five, and tucked it underneath an ashtray.

We traded names. Hers was Aracely.

The waitress came and went six more times, each time leaving a frosty beer for each of us. I continued to tuck bills under the ashtray. On the last three trips, she also brought shots of low-shelf tequila that we hadn't asked for. She didn't seem to know Aracely well. But she knew her.

For a few minutes, I forgot about the hunt. And about the young blonde girl in the trash bag in the back of a van nineteen hundred miles from home. And about a faded snapshot of four war buddies. Three were dead; the other would be soon. Now they all caught up with me. My glazed eyes had strayed from hers for a few seconds. She reached up and lightly pinched my chin and tilted my head so our eyes met again. I refocused. The beer and tequila lubricated the conversation. We talked and laughed.

I had no idea whether I could trust Aracely At this point, given her legs and the booze, I barely trusted myself. I decided on a strategy I rarely employed. The truth. I pulled one of the Western Union invoices from a pocket and unfolded it. I flattened it on the bar with my palm, she sipped her beer and glanced at the paper.

She recognized the account number immediately. She looked away for a second and then picked up her beer and took a long sip.

"Sangre." She said and paused. "I wish you were asking about anyone else," she said.

"But why you're scared to tell me is why I'm asking…."

Her head nodded behind the neck of her beer. The place wasn't busy. The waitress leaned against the beer cooler, splaying her fingers, looking at an engagement ring with an unimpressive diamond. I nodded to her. It knocked her out of her trance, and she fetched two more beers and set them down. She hummed to herself as she filled our shot glasses with tequila.

"One for you," I said to her.

Aracely seemed to break from her own trance. She looked at the waitress.

"Uno para ti, Maria."

The waitress smiled and shrugged, plucked another shot glass from the shelf behind her, and filled it. She raised her glass; we did the same and clicked them together.

"Gracias. Por que?" she asked, setting her shot glass on the bar.

"For your engagement," I said. "Para su compromise," I added. I was nearing the outer limits of my Spanish proficiency.

"Gracias." The waitress refilled all three glasses. "En mi," she said, handing them out. The place was starting to fill up. She waited until we clicked our glasses together before serving three rough-looking Mexicans who had laid their construction helmets on the bar next to them.

"That was nice of her," Aracely said, glancing at the waitress as she served the roughnecks.

I was about to ask her again about the Western Union invoice still resting on the bar when she spoke without looking up.

"Where are you staying?" she asked in a voice less scared than her eyes had shown. I named the motel. I was half-lit. Why would I tell some random waitress where I was staying? Maybe in the haze I was hoping she would stop by for one last fling before entering marital bliss. Later, I couldn't remember. Either way, it was tactically unsound. Downright stupid, really. I re-folded the invoice as we stood to leave. The waitress had come back to our side of the bar. She picked up the money as we turned away.

"Gracias," she said, collecting the glasses and bottles and wiping the bar down with a limp rag. I glanced back and saw her pick up the phone.

We walked from the cantina. She answered my unspoken invitation to the motel. We got into the Yukon and drove to the motel. I figured I would ask her about the invoice again later.

46.

THE MOTEL SAT in a shallow parking lot. It was painted a pinkish orange. Stucco. Concrete stairs led to a second floor. We took a room on the ground level. We made love, or something like it, in the fog of the tequila buzz.

She rolled on top, slowed the pace, and arched her back, running her hands over her body and looking down at me with an edgier smile than I'd seen before. I had trouble focusing on her. We finished and fell asleep. Or passed out. She slept hard; I dozed in a restless state between the scratchy motel sheets. My restlessness frustrated me. I snapped my bouncing eyes open definitively, rolled out from under her arm and stood up.

In the bathroom, I splashed water on my face before crossing the motel room and unzipping the duffel bag. I took out a paper bag with two mini-bottles of Jack Daniels inside. I pulled them out, crumpled the bag and dropped it in the trashcan. I wasn't in the mood for shots; I'd seen a vending machine on the far side of the building through the hallway at the base of the stairwell. I slipped on a pair of jeans, stepped into socks and boots and a thread bear Hooter's T-shirt I'd picked up in DC's Chinatown on a trip to the Capital for an Emerald Society parade. I used to wear it under my Kevlar vest when I was in uniform.

I slipped the motel key and my money clip into my pocket and tucked the Sig into my jeans, with the T-shirt pulled down over it. With a glance at her still, sleeping form under the sheet, I opened the door and walked around the corner.

I set the mini bottles on a plastic trash can next to the vending machine. Coins rattled as they dropped, followed by the hollow, clanking sound of the bottle making its way through the machine, followed by a boot against a wooden door.

I pulled the Sig from my waistband and moved to the corner leading back to the room, peeking high, then low. I could just make out the back of a man's head. The rest of him was already in the room. A shot rang out. I stayed close to the wall and moved quickly towards my room. A scream followed by another shot.

The man took another step, his head disappeared. I turned silently through the doorway. He was less than a foot in front of me. Another shot—this one from my gun, and he slumped to the floor, blood gushing onto the carpet. As I glanced over to confirm the bodega clerk's inevitable condition, a boot punched me square in the small of my back, almost knocking me onto the man's prone body directly in front of me.

I stepped wide with my right foot and caught myself as my left knee almost sunk into him. I rolled onto my right knee and dropped my shoulder. I didn't fight the momentum the goon had provided. I began to rise to my feet. The goon's gun kicked, and a round sailed over my right shoulder, barely missing. It crashed into the bathroom mirror behind me. The mirror splintered into large shards that crashed onto the countertop below.

I raised the Sig and fired. The bullet hit him in the shoulder. At least I thought it did. He jerked to his left and went down on his left knee. He lifted his arm up to fire again. I dove to my right behind the bed. It wasn't great cover. From the mirror propped over a dresser I could see his back. He had turned and was running out the door. I stood and moved around the bed. I got to the door and he was still running. He ripped open the door to a powder-blue convertible and fell in behind the wheel. The tires screeched as he rounded the curb.

I turned around. Aracely would work the bodega cash register no more. I grabbed the duffel bag, collected a few loose items from the floor and shoved them inside and then slung it over my shoulder. I was on my way to the Yukon when I remembered. I walked back to the vending machine. The mini bottles were still there. I reached into the machine and retrieved the bottle of Coke. I twisted off the cap, drank a swig, and emptied the mini bottles into it. I walked back to the SUV and drove around the same curbs as the convertible and pulled out onto the same road. I could only think of one person who could have told Sangre's men which motel I was staying in. Maria, the recently engaged waitress. But I wasn't one-hundred percent sure.

UNTIL I GOT back to the restaurant. Parked directly in front of the door was the powder-blue convertible. I backed into a spot between a green dumpster and a red Volkswagen and raised a pair of binoculars to look through the large sliding glass doors that led into the cantina from the patio. The man was sitting on the stool Aracely had occupied. The waitress was leaning over the bar in front of him, and they held hands across the bar top. How sweet. I'd get to meet the fiancée. I doubted I'd buy him a shot of tequila; but then, he already had one.

47.

AFTER ANOTHER SHOT of tequila, the man walked out and got into the convertible. He backed out of the space, and the car lurched forward. I waited a few seconds and pulled out behind him. He drove fast and turned back out onto the highway without a signal, cutting off a utility van.

We caught green lights down the highway and turned onto a side street in a low-rent neighborhood of brick ranches and split-level houses with cracked aluminum siding. Some of the houses had sagging above-ground pools; others had trampolines. A few had both. Most had satellite dishes.

After a series of four-way stops there were two cars between my vehicle and the fiancé's. He pulled into a driveway of one of the houses on the corner of the street and a cul-de-sac. I pulled to the side behind a landscaping truck. The fiancé got out of his convertible and walked up an unkempt sidewalk leading to stone steps. He was carrying a paper grocery bag and a smaller plastic bag that could have been from a pharmacy.

Without knocking, he walked inside. I waited. Ten minutes later, the fiancé and a fat man with no neck and a gut escaping from the bottom of a ribbed white tank top, walked out. Both were holding bottles of beer. The fat man was eating something from a folded piece of aluminum foil. The fiancé smoked a cigar slowly, pausing to look towards the heavens before letting the smoke escape upward. When the fat man finally finished eating, he balled up the aluminum foil and shoved it into his pocket. A few minutes later the fiancé finished his cigar, dropped the stub to the ground and stamped it with his boot. They shook hands. The fat man went back inside. The fiancé drove away. I followed.

People have five senses; cops have six. They're street psychics, of sorts. So, one guy smoked a cigar, one ate, and two shook hands. Not the crime of the century. But I could usually tell when I was watching the innocent acts of guilty people.

The streets in this part of town were almost empty. Most likely, the fiancé wasn't splitting any atoms in his spare time, but even he would pick up my tail before too many more intersections. I took a side street to the right and looked over my left shoulder to see the fiancé pull through another stop sign and out of sight.

I DROVE TO a liquor store and then back to the bodega parking lot. I bought a Mexican Coke and a burrito from the food truck. I killed an hour listening to 80's hair bands on satellite radio, eating and drinking the cola and whiskey. The volume of the glam anthems rose with my buzz. I sang along to a few of the better ones. I drove back to the cantina. I guessed the lovebirds couldn't stay away from each other too long. I backed into the same spot. I was out of Coke, so I sipped whiskey straight from the bottle.

I was right, love carried the day. After forty-five minutes, the convertible glided across the lot and dove into the same parking spot as before. I screwed the cap back on the bottle and stepped onto the pavement. The Sig was in a paddle holster tucked into my jeans. I walked across the lot. The convertible top was down, and the man was combing his hair in the rearview mirror. I opened the passenger-side door and sat down next to him just as he had started to get out of the car. I crooked my elbow against my thigh and pointed the Sig at him.

"Sit," I said.

He sat.

"Habla ingles?" I asked.

He shook his head. No. Hard to believe after he understood "sit", but I didn't have time to argue.

"Walk and remember who is inside," I said in Spanish.

I stepped out of the car; he did the same. I guided us towards my SUV, glancing around. Nobody. I opened the front passenger door and nodded. He got in. I kept the gun trained on him, opened the passenger door behind him, and slid in. I hit him in the base of the neck with the butt of the gun. He slumped. I strapped the seatbelt across him, took a pair of handcuffs and a roll of duct tape from the duffel bag and cuffed the man's left wrist to a metal post supporting the SUV's large front seats.

I wrapped the tape around the man's mouth, ripped it, and tossed the roll into the backseat. I took a picture of the man with my cell phone and looked at it, before setting the empty bottle of whiskey on the seat between his legs and propping the cowboy hat on his forehead and down over his face. Siesta.

I closed the door and walked across the lot, past the convertible, across the patio and through the door. I sat in the same seat as the day before. The waitress hid her surprise well. She quickly replaced her confused look with a smile and walked over.

"Beer and bourbon," she said, raising an eyebrow before pulling a beer from a cooler and reaching for a bottle of whiskey.

I nodded. She set the beer down and poured the shot. I took a sip from the can as she slid the shot glass across the bar towards me. She set the bourbon bottle on the bar.

"Take a look at this," I said, sliding the cell phone across the bar to her.

I drained the shot glass as she focused on the cell phone's small screen. Her eyes widened, and she picked it up, as if taking a closer look would change the image. I sipped at the beer as she digested the photo. She placed the phone on the bar, turned and plucked another shot glass from the shelf behind her, set it next to my now empty shot glass and filled them both. We tossed them back.

There was only one question to ask. I was almost sure she had told Sangre where I was staying. If she hadn't, I had a different problem.

"What do you want," she asked as she refilled both glasses. After we each drank another shot, I finished another beer and then another. Then, I asked a single question. Predictably, she said "No" but even a rookie detective would have known she was lying. It didn't matter. She had no choice. I didn't live in her world. I'd never understand.

She knew I knew.

"Let's go," I said. She couldn't stay.

We walked out the door and across the patio.

"Wait here," I said, as we neared the convertible. I turned back to her, reached into my pocket, and pulled out the folded wad of hundreds. I peeled off ten and handed them to her. "You might want to start over."

I walked to the SUV, opened the door, and unlocked the cuff around the fiancé's wrist, released the seatbelt, and pulled the cowboy hat off his face. I put it on my own head. He was beginning to stir. I slapped him a couple of times before his eyes opened. He looked over, eyes wide, and gave muted screams into the tape.

"Get out," I said. "She can get the tape off."

I pointed the Sig at his head. He got out and I reached across to pull the door shut. In the rearview mirror as I drove away, I saw the waitress hurrying towards her fiancé, who had slumped down onto the pavement.

48.

I HAD MY lead. And it was time to make the call I didn't want to make. I didn't like the idea of a fellow cop, even a fed, selling me out. Blue betrayal hurt but I understood: red family blood trumps even blue blood, and, for the life of their child, who wouldn't a parent sell out? But I wanted to hold onto hope as long as I could. Anyone in the game for any length of time knows there are bad people on both sides of the badge.

The call I didn't want to make was about the blonde with the silver ring on her pinky toe and the butterfly flying on her ankle. The girl whose dead body was rotting in an abandoned Spanish mission. The girl whose name I recognized, whose father I thought was my friend. I couldn't use my cell, must have been a dead zone. I found a payphone at the far end of another large lot near another bodega.

He answered on the fourth ring. He was drunk. Edgy. The thin line between panic and despair. He murmured a somewhat incoherent greeting.

"Paul," I said, in an even voice. No response. "Paul?" I said louder.

"Yeah," his voice was tired. So was mine.

"I need some answers," I said.

"Yeah," he said again, louder but no more focused. I could tell he wasn't surprised to hear from me.

"I found her, Paul," I said.

"Who?"

Was he serious with this? "Who do you think? Your daughter."

"Where?" he asked.

"In Mexico, in the desert," I said. "In Sangre's town."

"She's dead?" he asked. He already knew.

"If she was alive, I'd have had her call."

"How'd she go?"

"Does it matter?" I asked. "She's gone."

"They take advantage of her?" he asked.

I lied to him about the way I found her. Blonde, blue-eyed, female hostage they were going to kill anyway. Hell yes, they took advantage of her, a number of different men, a number of different times, a number of different ways. He knew I was lying as sure as he knew what they'd done to her. At least I didn't insult him by telling him she didn't suffer.

"So, can I assume that Sangre's Kreskin-like abilities are fueled by your betrayal?"

"Something like that. It's a little more complicated," he said.

"Simplify it for me," I said. "I assume you were on board with me until she went missing."

"Yeah, the first couple of calls were that she hadn't come home. You know, she's seventeen, I figured it would turn out to be no big deal. The call at the Mexican restaurant, when we met Brooke, that's when they called me and told me they had her."

I thought back to the ashen face, the sweating. I thought the panic was because she was missing, figured she'd never even missed curfew before.

His voice cut into my thoughts. "The way I've got it figured, against everyone's advice, now-Father Santos reconnected with Dana Lee Moon when he heard that she'd gotten mixed up in Meth. He thought he was doing right by her. Like always. He assumed she'd do right by him. Faith can be a bitch, ya'know? So, he mentioned me. I'd dealt with her some when they were both in WITSEC. She gave both of us up. I didn't know they were onto me until I had left to meet you. I got the first call when I was on a layover in Cincinnati and then another after we'd met up."

I thought back to the call Paul took while he walked around the motel parking lot outside the restaurant when we first met Brooke.

"Like I said, I didn't think too much of it. She's seventeen. At the time, I thought, worst scenario, she's doing half of what girls were doing with me when I was seventeen. Now, I wish like hell she had been doing that."

I listened. It was hard for me to muster much sympathy. But he was right. Dana Lee Moon gave up both Santos and Paul; they killed Santos and turned Paul by snatching his daughter. Sangre knew I was in town.

"What are you going to do?" Paul asked.

"Finish this," I said. I couldn't think of anything else to say even if it sounded like a line from a vapid movie. Paul had his reasons, but we had reached the end of our road.

"Anything else?" I asked.

"I'm sorry," he said and then he solved one of the mysteries, something Brooke had asked several times. *How did they keep finding us?* "GPS. Maybe the waitress told him where I was staying, but she apparently didn't need to. Check your tactical bag. Backup ammo pouch, taped to one of your extra magazines."

I remembered seeing Paul from the Mexican restaurant's window digging into the trunk and the way the bags were rearranged. It was a good placement; Paul knew that no matter how many times I switched cars I'd never leave that bag behind, but I'd have little reason to inspect empty backup magazines until I had the ammo to load them.

A logging truck whizzed by on the road. A couple of kids doubled up on a cheap bicycle were too close to the road, and the driver growled the truck's air horn at them. As the horn faded with the taillights of the truck, I heard a noise on the other end of the phone.

"Paul?" I said.

He didn't respond. The line didn't clear, but I assumed he'd hung up. I did the same. I checked the tactical bag. As expected, electric-taped to one of the spare magazines was a small but powerful GPS tracker.

49.

I WALKED OUT of another motel carrying the duffel bag over my shoulder. I drove to the parking lot and headed to the food truck. The wide-faced man with a bright western shirt and mesh John Deere hat smiled with recognition and handed me breakfast wrapped in aluminum foil, and a large plastic cup filled with piping-hot coffee. He'd left room for cream, or in my case, whiskey.

Back in the SUV, I topped the coffee off with Jim Beam, and drove back to the stash house. A half-hour later, as the sun peeked up over the row of houses to the east, the vans drove past me and pulled to the curb in front of the house. Within five minutes, eight girls emerged and climbed into the vans, four in each. The drivers didn't get out. The vans drove away.

I sipped at the coffee. The food was long gone. I'd have gone in strong, but I wasn't sure what I would find in the stash house. For all I knew, the people living there with the girls were also being held against their will. The way I'd approach these storage units and wherever the hell I'd finally track down Sangre had to be different— this stash house was one of the few places I might actually leave a few witnesses. But, if I had my way, the only guy who would want to ask any questions wouldn't be around to ask them.

I thought back to my nights on patrol, all the cold, wasted cups of coffee. Wasting coffee was one thing; wasting whiskey was another. I sipped at the cup. Slowly. I listened to the satellite radio. Ten minutes of national news and Chicago blues.

On minute eight, a man and a woman walked out the front door. The man was lifting a stroller down the stairs. The woman followed, carrying a baby. The woman placed the baby in the stroller after the man unfolded it. They turned right and walked away. I waited until they were out of sight. The house was empty. Hopefully.

I reached down and lifted the short-stock shotgun onto the passenger seat. I shifted gear and pulled around the landscaping truck and into the driveway. I entered through the front door with the shotgun flush against my waist. There were several small cameras attached to the exterior of the house at various angles, tucked up under the gutters, almost invisible to an untrained eye. Luckily, my eyes were trained. I couldn't see a red power light on any of them. I took a closer look at one of the cameras. I could tell from the lack of wiring and the fact that the brick and plastic of the gutters was undisturbed that they were fakes. Fugazi. Only for show. I'd assume if one was fake, they were all fake. Assuming was never a good policy but neither was a white guy standing around outside a house in this neighborhood in broad daylight trying to conceal a shotgun. My cover was intact, and I'd save time not having to look for a recording receptacle inside. Once I could forget about the cameras my mind turned back to the house. I hoped again that it house was empty. I'd seen the couple leave and, if my hunch was right, the other occupants of the house were up and out early. I didn't need surprises. Sooner or later, something had to be easy. Right? I'd have to take my chances.

The greasy Mexican fare mixed with the bourbon and carbonation sent razor slivers of acid against the walls of my gut. The furnishings were sparse. I walked through a living room and turned down a narrow hallway. There were three bedrooms. Two on the right, one on the left. The last door on the left was a bathroom. I scanned the bedrooms. Each had one large bed and two bunkbeds. Clothes and other items were strewn on the floor. I walked into the bathroom. It would have been typical, except for the two shoeboxes at the end of the long counter. One was filled with condoms, the other with different lubricants in jars and vials. I opened the medicine cabinet. Plastic pill bottles with prescription labels were arranged neatly on the shelves behind the mirror. Several different names were listed on the labels. Amoxicillin and nitrofurantoin—antibiotics commonly used for urinary tract infections. Assorted other pills. I closed the medicine cabinet. I thought about torching the place, but then there'd be a baby in a stroller without a roof.

Back in the Chevy, I wedged the shotgun back under the seat and pulled away from the curb. As I slowed to a stop at the third stop sign from the house, I saw the man and the woman walking back. The man was pushing the stroller. As I passed, I saw the woman walking backwards in front of the stroller so she could make faces at the baby. The couple looked like as if they were feigning happiness. I'd guess they were the rightful owners of a home that had been invaded and lived under constant threat so the house would appear somewhat normal and not draw attention. I couldn't see the baby. A kid who wouldn't likely have a chance.

50.

I DROVE BACK to the storage-unit-bordello. The Cell. I approached from the rear and parked the SUV flush against the concrete wall. I stepped out. I slung the short-stock shotgun over my shoulder and grabbed a small green nylon bag from inside the larger duffel bag. It had an adjustable shoulder strap, which I pulled to give it slack and slung it over the other shoulder.

A series of metal ladder rungs had been pushed into the concrete to give access for repairs to the gears and motors that retracted the largest of the storage-stall doors. I followed the rungs to the top of the rear wall. The top of the wall was two feet wide. I looked down. A set of identical rungs were embedded into the concrete inside the compound between two storage units.

I swung my leg over the top and rested on the wall above the enclosed compound below. The yellow school bus was pulled across the gate. The man sat in the same folding chair drinking from the same mug. I stepped onto the second rung and descended into a four-foot gap between the storage bins. I crouched. Through the short alleyway, I could see the front of two of the storage units. The wide metal doors were raised. I couldn't see a girl in either bin, but I knew they were there.

I moved to the edge. The man stood. I thought a customer had arrived, but he walked to the makeshift office and stepped inside. Less than a minute later, he stepped back out, sipping at a mug of coffee. He sat back down. It was a wasted trip and would be a waste of a decent cup of coffee. I stepped out. His head was down. The

Sig had better range, but the shotgun was more of a statement. The man looked up and fixed his eyes on me over the rim of the mug. His expression told me he really couldn't process what he was seeing. He held his mouth to the mug as his pupils grew wider, staring into the black hole that was the barrel of the shotgun. I racked the gun and pulled the trigger. He dropped the mug and died in a folding chair in the cruel heat of a Mexico morning.

The girls screamed. A few dove to the ground. Within seconds, all eight peeked out into the center of the compound where I stood holding a shotgun in the direction of a man not one of them would mourn. I wouldn't either. All eight emerged, at different paces, and walked towards one another, towards me. They stood in a wide circle, lingering, looking at one another and then at me. They had no idea if I had killed the man to help them or hurt them; was I friend or foe?

"Anybody speak English?" I asked the group. My Spanish was conversational, nowhere near fluent. Easier to speak English when I could. Only two of the girls nodded. Yes.

"What time will the vans come back?" I asked.

One of the nodding girls, the taller of the two, spoke up.

"Sometimes it is late in the afternoon, sometimes not until almost midnight. It is never the same. Sometimes they pick all of us up together, sometimes in groups. Never the same." She had large, dark, serious eyes and an intelligent face.

I nodded. I had at least a couple of hours until the vans returned, but a customer could show up at any time. The girls stayed in the semi-circle staring at me and each other.

I talked to the serious-looking girl. Three weeks shy of seventeen; she gave me a rundown of the facts of their abduction and their lives. They were all from the same village.

"Wait here, yell if anyone comes," I told her. She relayed the message to the girls who looked at her each time I spoke.

I set the green bag down on the ground and unzipped it. I ran the cord and set the timers. Before the police department, I'd given four years to the U.S. Army. Petroleum Supply Specialist MOS. I was far better with fuel quality, spillage, and fires than demolitions, but I knew the basics.

WE HEARD THE Cell explode from a half mile away in a deliberate sequence of destruction. I knew that what was left would look like a desert Stonehenge of twisted steel and crumbled brick. But I never saw it.

I drove the girls back into town. I took them to the food truck and bought them all something to eat and drink. Standing in the parking lot was a risk. But a calculated one, because risk in the context of this Mexican town was becoming something only to be judged in degrees, not absolutes.

"Is there anything any of you need from the house?" She shook her head. No.

"If I give you money, can you get them home?" She nodded. Yes. I could never be sure, but I hoped she would. I handed the serious girl a stack of hundred-dollar bills and got back into the SUV. I drove out of the parking lot. I saw the girls walking back towards the food truck.

51.

THE WAITRESS HAD told me about a barber shop which sat at the base of a hill in a congested part of the city. She was right. Power lines were strung between beaten wooden poles leading on either side of the street, forming a loose cat's cradle. Cars and pickup trucks were all parked facing the same direction. A food truck with a green and white canopy sat in an alley.

The barber shop was a burnt-orange building, bordering a vacant lot. I parked behind a silver pickup truck. I reached into the back and grabbed my backup revolver in the ankle holster and a lock pick set from the duffle bag. I strapped it on and put the lock pick set in a pocket. I got out and walked up the sidewalk away from the barber shop. Three doors up, a cantina with a porch faced the street. I sat on a stool where I could see the barber shop, ordered a shot of tequila and a beer from the waitress. I bought a cigar, cut it and lit it. I watched the barber shop. I didn't see anything for almost two hours and three more rounds. Not until Sangre got out of a black car and walked inside.

I recognized him from the picture. He was older, of course, but his lean features had stood the test of time. He was tall, at least six foot four and had a long goatee that was braided. Tight. I knew from the picture and the file, that he had sustained burns to the right side of his body in a tank fire. I kept watching. He reached for the door; his black glove gripped the door handle. There was no glove on his left hand. It was Sangre, alright.

I drained my beer, took two long pulls on the cigar, and stubbed it out in an ashtray. I stepped out through the cantina's arched door onto the sidewalk and walked in the direction of the barber shop. I thought about going back to the Yukon for the shotgun which was good for dusting an alley, for defense. Not great in crowds, not that I was too worried about hitting anyone standing around inside Sangre's barber shop. It was also not great in hostage situations; the other long guns would be as worthless. I palmed my Sig in its holster under my untucked burgundy Cuban shirt.

I GLANCED ABOVE the door, in a crack between the shade and the top of the window. I could see a cluster of small bells. I opened the door slowly, so the bells hardly made any sound. The front room of the barber shop was empty. The inside walls were exposed brick. Chairs with red plastic covers faced large mirrors. Combs floated in jars filled with some type of blue liquid. Scissors and clippers were lined up, and there was a small sink next to each workstation. Hairdryers hung from large hooks on the wall above each sink.

There was no hair on the floor. No trash in the trashcans. Not a barber in sight. I looked for cameras but didn't see any. A door led off from the main room. I opened it and stepped into a short hallway with a door on either side. The first was a bathroom. The second led to another, longer hallway. At the end, was a third door with a poster nailed to it. Tarot told me that Sangre had a somewhat demented sense of humor to accompany his demented character. My brief conversation with him did nothing to dispel Tarot's assessment. The poster was of an old Robert Hutton movie, *The Secret Door* showing a man in a yellow trench coat pointing a revolver in the air, with a perky, but concerned-looking blonde woman beside him. A hand worked a safe tumbler below the couple. Fortunately, the door in front of me didn't take a combination—not that I had one. Unfortunately, it was locked anyway. The lock was factory and cheap. Not a deadbolt, just the center lock. I pulled the lock pick set out. This still felt like a trap. The thin razors in my gut morphed to rusty, jagged nails. Instead of slicing, they were being hammered in with a mauler. I picked the lock and twisted the doorknob. As I closed the door behind me, I could see that it blended into the wall and was barely visible.

I walked into a small warehouse. The walls were metal, the roof flat. I scanned the exposed ductwork, pipes, and electric wires. I saw several cameras bolted to the metal catwalk above. Small dots of green light emitted from them. Several of them were fixed, others rotated at slow intervals. I studied their angles. None of the cameras appeared to be aimed directly at the door behind me. Most of them, and the sightline of the rotating cameras, were aimed at the shelves and the work areas beyond. They weren't for intruders; they were to watch the employees to see if anyone was stealing. Sangre knew that his best security was fear and reputation. Still, Sangre probably knew I was here. He knew I wanted Brooke. I had no idea what he wanted. It might be to avenge his friends personally, eye to eye. I didn't know what Brooke had told him; or them. How personal this was depended on how much Sangre knew.

I knew Sangre was into a lot of different types of contraband. A smuggler was a smuggler. The human trafficking, I was sure of. I'd heard whispers about guns and dope. I didn't know about the cars. Until now. The door I had walked through came out behind rows of car parts stacked onto shelves. I could hear the screech of metal being cut and the shrill sizzle of blowtorches. I could hear men talking. Music floated behind the sounds of dropped tools, hydraulic air jacks, and the hum of illicit activity.

I looked towards the warehouse's southern wall and saw a loading dock and several large retractable doors, next to which, in the corner, was a small door. It was open. I watched through gaps in the stacked parts. Men would take a break from stripping a vehicle and walk outside for a few minutes, then return. Smoke break.

I walked around the side of one of the shelves. Most of these guys probably weren't in on anything, just mechanics or guys looking to pick up some extra money. This still felt like a trap. I glanced at my watch. It was deep into the afternoon. I had no way of knowing if this was an all-night, three-shift system or if the place would clear out completely at some point.

I thought about my options, and patience won out. I backtracked through the barber shop, locking the door I had picked—I wouldn't be coming back in this way—and walked back out on the street. The nails in my gut continued. Food might help. Alcohol might hurt. Or they might balance one another out. I walked back to the cantina and ordered food, another round of drinks, and another cigar. I stayed for a while. It got dark.

I DROVE THE Yukon to a side street with a view of the loading bays. There was a ramp into the warehouse for vehicles. One of the bay doors was open with a truck backed up to the dock. A few men loitered around, smoking, and talking while others loaded the truck. I watched and waited. Best case, the truck was loaded at the end of each day, and the men would filter out after the truck was full. Sometimes, even I get lucky.

52.

I GOT LUCKY. A half-hour later, the truck's headlights came to life. A minute later, it rolled down the alley giving me a better view into the warehouse. Only a dozen or so men remained. I didn't see Sangre or Brooke. Workers continued to filter out, most smoking and drinking from cans of beer when they walked down the alley into the night.

I waited until only one man was in sight inside the warehouse, his face hidden behind a welding mask lit by the strobing glow of the torch. The loading door was still open. There could be another truck, another shift, I thought. For all I knew, Sangre wasn't even in the warehouse. I stepped out of the Yukon and walked to the short stairwell leading up to the loading bay. The man with the welding torch was facing away. I waited until the torch was silent. He seemed to be getting it ready to use again, adjusting the flame. I walked up behind him silently and hit him with a wrench at the base of his neck. He slumped and dropped the blowtorch. It was a shallow blow. I didn't want to kill him. Most likely, he was putting in some extra hours for his family to save money to move north. It didn't matter and I didn't care. He hadn't done anything to me or anybody I cared about. Unless that changes, I'd do my best not to kill him.

I reached down to his neck, near where the wrench had struck. He was unconscious. His pulse was strong. I stayed crouched behind trunk of the car he had been working on. I didn't see anybody else. There was a door in the corner. If Sangre was here, he was behind that door.

HE WAS THERE. The door was unlocked, so I opened it and walked into an office. In sharp contrast to the metal and concrete of the chop-shop, the office was all dark mahogany. The head of a gigantic boar hung on the wall behind a large desk, and a pool table with rich, green felt sat in the middle of the room. There was a large humidor on the desk and a well-stocked bar with three stools on the other side of the pool table. A huge plasma-screen TV took up one wall with two leather couches facing it. It was a classy room.

Except for one thing, Sangre himself, sitting behind that important-looking desk. I pointed the Sig at him.

"Where is she?"

"No introductions, Mr Stock?"

"Killing so many of your friends makes me feel like we already know each other, Mitchell."

His eyes were green. The burns on his face were more extensive than I had imagined. He still wore only one glove. He was looking at me, not the gun. Most people look at the gun.

"Where is she?" I cocked the hammer on the Sig. "I'm not exactly in a good mood, Mitchell, my gut is screaming, and if you didn't have her, I'd have already killed you. The only hesitation I have is that it would be selfish—there are probably so many people ahead of me in line who deserve the pleasure."

I moved my arm slightly upward and pulled the trigger. The hammer dropped, and the round plowed through one of the boar's tusks. Sangre barely flinched. I got the feeling he really didn't fear death. I knew he didn't value other lives. I was beginning to think he didn't value his own. I knew he didn't value mine. Or Brooke's.

THE DROOLING PIT bull was in full stride when it rounded the corner and plowed through the doorway. I fired and missed. The dog leapt. It caught me by my right wrist, just as it had been trained. It clamped down. The pain in my gut and a splitting headache were now the least of my problems. I saw the waitress's fiancé standing in the doorway. No good deed goes unpunished. Shouldn't have let him live.

I dropped the gun and fell to the ground. The dog swarmed me, I thrashed around with it. I couldn't get it off me. I banged my head against the dog's linear cranium. The dog clamped onto the side of my head. I could feel the puncture near my temple and the dog's teeth grind into my ear.

"Enough," Sangre said.

"Atajar!" the fiancé yelled.

The dog stopped. I couldn't focus. Blood poured and collected in the socket around my right eye. The eye that still hadn't finished healing from the beating I took in my barn in Mississippi. I looked up. The sheriff's words floated in my consciousness. When he told me how easy it was to lose an eye. Sangre was holding my Sig. He pointed it at me. My short run of good luck was apparently over.

"Mr Stock, have a seat." It wasn't really a request. The fiancé pulled me up into the chair. Sangre sat down. The fiancé leaned against the pool table. I could feel myself skate on the edge of consciousness. He opened the lid of the humidor and pulled out a cigar. A Churchill. He picked up a cutter, poked the end of the cigar into it and squeezed. The tip of the cigar dropped into a large, molded ashtray. He picked up a butane lighter, pushed the button and rolled the cigar in his fingers. The cigar lit and glowed evenly. I tried to focus on the orange glow. Everything went black.

THE BLACKNESS REMAINED, but the burn intensified. At first, I thought it was a cigar being burned into the flesh around my eyes. Then I hoped that's what it was. The burn was spreading like lava spitting from a volcano. I opened my eyes. The pain was so intense it was almost beyond the outer edges of nerve perception to detect. I closed my right eye. Through my left, I could see Sangre standing in front of me. In his hand was a small blue bottle with a black rubber top. Acid. The bottle was empty. The fiancé was nowhere to be seen.

"Let me tell you a story, Mr Stock. Can I call you Dan?"

He was one of those pricks who answered his own questions. At least he wasn't talking about himself in the third person.

"I think I will. Dan, let me tell you a story. But first, let me tell you why you're here. You must have figured out by now that I could have had you killed along the way, without blackmailing your partner or kidnapping his daughter. You aren't exactly subtle, Dan, more of a blunt edge. But I decided I wanted to kill you myself, here in Mexico. Far from your home. You and I are both vets but no flag-draped coffin for you. Or me, for that matter. No body for anyone to recover and identify. We know what it means to serve our country but only one of us will be buried there. And it won't be you. Your life becomes nothing. It evaporates like the proverbial dust in the wind. Here in the desert in a foreign land one minute, gone the next. Just a memory to a bunch of cops in Atlanta who can't figure out what the hell happened to you. Just Dead. Gone. And…." He paused for a minute "I wanted to kill you myself. Up close. As you know, in the Army I drove tanks. Yeah, I fired the artillery when some butter bar lieutenant told me to that likely killed dozens, even hundreds, and leveled villages upending generations from their home. Women. Children. But I never got to look them in the eye when I shot them. So, I put out the bounty to have you brought in but you're such an upstanding soul you saved me some money and came to me. And here you are. Me and my friends—friendship you could never understand—built something. And you tore it down, burned it down. I wanted to kill you myself. And very personal. But now that you're here, what's the rush? First, I owe you a story, isn't that right, Dan?"

"I can't wait," I muttered. The area around my eye was a zone of pain. I thought I could smell burnt flesh. This was turning into a hell of a bad day. I hoped the story was at least moderately interesting and that Brooke was still alive. He started to tell the story. As expected, it started with four friends and a tank. Everything went black again.

53.

WHEN LIGHT CREPT in between my eyelids, I opened my left eye. My right eye throbbed, and I couldn't open it more than a sliver. I was in a different chair, a chair with wheels that had been rolled near the trunk of the car the welder had been working on before I'd hit him with the wrench. I tried to move my hand to my eye. I felt the metal of the handcuff on my wrist, and it reminded me of Cherry. I lifted my leg up to my restrained wrist and felt for the revolver on my ankle. Predictably, it was gone.

"Dream on," the man I'd hit with the wrench said, holding something up. My vision was blurry, but I could see that it was my Smith & Wesson K-frame.

The next sound I heard was the same sound I had last heard from Brooke—the muffled sound of a gagged hostage. Sangre had lifted the trunk of the car. The man I hit with the wrench stood near the front, leaning with his hand pressed flat against the hood. I should have killed him earlier. Like the fiancé.

Sangre put on the welder's mask and picked up the torch. He slid the shield down. Brooke thrashed around in the trunk; her muted screams becoming more intense and desperate. I banged my wrist against the metal arm of the chair. The cuffs were clamped on tight.

"You sick twisted skell," I said to Sangre, as he lit the torch.

"Dan. How can you call me such things, now that we have so much in common?"

I thought for a second that he meant that we had Brooke in common, his mistaken belief that we had both been with her; later, I figured he meant the burnt skin. And the dead friends.

The torch sizzled as Sangre lit it. He stepped forward and looked down into the trunk of the car. I couldn't see Brooke but could hear her panic.

"See, Dan, that story I told you, about me, my friends, the Army. It's all about honor and loyalty. This little slut here…" He pointed down at her waving the lit torch. "She has neither."

"Maybe she had loyalty to her country," I said.

He turned back in my direction and smiled a viper's smile. He turned back to Brooke. He spoke without looking at me.

"That's possible. But to a man like me, a man without a country, it doesn't mean a hell of a lot. Now, you can watch while I melt the skin off this bitch like a molting snake. But, if you do, you'll probably burn up your one good eye. Not that it will matter much."

He turned back to the trunk, but I knew he was still smiling that wicked smile. I heard her scream as he lowered the torch towards her. Then I heard the shot. Sangre folded and collapsed, already dead. He dropped the torch; the flame receded as he lost his grip. Blood seeped from his chest.

The man I'd hit with the wrench charged towards me. He pointed my gun in my direction and fired. Once. Twice. He was ten feet away. He fired a third time. He hadn't hit me. At least I didn't think that he had. You never knew right away. Not for sure, and the pain in my eyes might have made me welcome a bullet anywhere else if it wasn't fatal. He wasn't much of a shot, and it wasn't an easy gun to hit anything with at any distance.

I reached into the pocket of my pants and worked my fingers into the lock pick set. I pulled out the largest of the sharp tools. He kept charging. He was only a couple of feet from me. He pointed the gun at my head and pulled the trigger. The gun clicked. Empty. He almost fell into me as he looked at the gun. I plunged the sharp metal tool into the man's gut. I thrust my foot into the man's knee. He buckled.

I swept his cracked leg out from under him, grabbed his head and twisted the chair so that I could thrust the tool into his throat within the slack given by the handcuff chain. He gurgled and collapsed. He wasn't dead. Yet.

I heard a noise to my left. I turned and looked over my shoulder. Footsteps. I could just barely make out the ever-growing shadow of a large man walking towards us.

54.

THE RIFLE WAS slung over his shoulder. He wore a suit. He calmly walked towards the car, reached it, and looked down into the trunk. He ignored me. The Jamaican looked around the tool bench for a moment and picked up a pair of large bolt cutters. I could barely see the man's hands work as the cutters disappear into the trunk for a few seconds and I heard metal popping.

The Jamaican put the cutters back on the bench and reached down into the trunk. Tape ripped, Brooke gasped and then I heard her voice. He picked her up and set her on her feet. She was battered but unbeaten. She rubbed at her wrists.

"Him?" the Jamaican asked Brooke, nodding towards me. Scenarios ran through my mind.

"Him," she repeated. "What can I say about him?"

The sight in my good eye was beginning to focus. Then she smiled "Take the cuffs off," she said.

The Jamaican picked up the bolt cutters again and snipped through the handcuff attaching me to the chair. My eye throbbed. The pain wasn't as sharp, but only because the damage was more severe. Nerve-endings had died. The eye was likely lost. Permanently.

Brooke walked to me and hugged me as I stood. She looked at my eye and stated the obvious.

"We've got to get you to a hospital."

The Jamaican spoke more than a single word for the first time. "First, we have business."

"We do," Brooke said. "And it's good we are in an auto garage."

I must have looked confused because she smiled again. She asked me where the Yukon was parked, and I told her. I fished the key from my pocket and handed it to the Jamaican. He walked out the smoke break door to get the car. He drove it up the ramp into the garage and onto the lift. The man obviously knew something about cars. He lifted the Yukon and began to disassemble what looked like the SUV's large gas tank. It was. He unbolted it sufficiently to detach part of it.

As he separated the compartment from the main tank, I was almost sure that he would be doused in gasoline. Instead, he reached in and began to retrieve stacks of money bound tight and wrapped in plastic. No wonder the damn thing had to be filled up so many times, I thought. I stood beside Brooke and watched him reassemble the tank. I picked up my Sig. The Jamaican got the Yukon down off the lift and walked back across the room, returning with a duffel bag he'd obviously brought with him. It appeared he'd come through the barber shop, like I had. Most likely, he'd seen me use the entrance earlier. He unzipped the bag, carefully arranged the money inside, nodded, and walked away without a word. He smiled at Brooke, but only for a second.

I walked over towards Sangre. His blood had seeped out onto the floor and traveled through spontaneous tributaries towards a nearby drain.

"Be careful," Brooke said.

"I think he's pretty harmless," I said. I was pretty sure he was dead.

"No, not that, the blood," she said.

I looked up at her. We were both past the point where we were bothered by blood. I thought about the HIV medicine she had picked up using her undercover alias, but I let it pass. For now. There was no doubt he was dead. Four for four, I thought. The Jamaican was a pro. The shot went through his heart. He was D.R.T. or 'dead right there.' There was some doubt about my friend the welder, but I hedged my bets when took my Sig from Sangre's pocket. I put an insurance shot in his temple and wrangled my backup revolver from the welder's hand.

I holstered both guns and looked at Brooke. She was staring at Sangre. Brooke backed the Yukon out of the garage and drove away. I could barely see. For someone who had been gagged for several days, she wasn't chatty. But she was a thief. And the Jamaicans whose money she stole were in on it. Somehow.

I hoped she would fill in the blanks, and that she had a good reason for stealing dope money and breaking one of the cardinal sins of narcotics work. Several miles of silence later, she filled in the blanks. She had a good reason.

55.

VERY GOOD REASONS: survival. Or at least hope. We got back in the Yukon. My eyes had started to crust over. I had to get to a hospital. I knew she had HIV. I remembered the prescription bottles, and her panic when I almost touched her when she was bleeding after the shootout in Nevada. In a strange way, my ego was restored. She didn't volunteer any information about her condition, and I only had one or two questions. I didn't need the full story, and I knew she didn't want to tell it.

"You were worried about Sangre's blood because he's the one who gave you HIV?"

"Yes," she nodded slowly.

"That's why the undercover operation ended before it bore all the fruit you hoped?"

I was still looking at her. She didn't even offer a quiet answer this time, just nodded again slowly. I saw a tear fall from her eye down the ridge of her nose and sit on top of her lip for a moment before streaming away when another one hit it. If she'd gotten involved with an undercover target willingly, I doubted she'd have gotten on with DEA when she left Border Patrol, so I figured we were talking rape. She confirmed.

"He drugged me," she said.

I had other questions, but they could wait, or never be asked at all. It wasn't my money, and I had the gist. If she wanted to tell me, she would...

Her voice cut into my thoughts.

"...the money is for a holistic clinic in Brazil. A very expensive holistic clinic in Brazil. I knew I couldn't take the money and go anywhere in the Western Hemisphere without them finding me. Jamaican gangs have reach, you know that." She wiped her eye.

"Shower Posse," I asked.

"Yeah," she said. The "Shower Posse" was a brutal gang, deeply rooted in Jamaican politics. They'd been the most ruthless cocaine peddlers up and down the East coast until *Operation Rum Punch*, a federal law enforcement sting. Almost like the Shower Posse's gang's equivalent to the mafia's Apalachin in '57. Still, she was right, they would have found her. She must have known that her DEA friends would look for her, about as hard as police worked to find out who killed Tupac and Notorious B.I.G.

Even my visit from the DEA was more out of concern for her than to recover stolen dope money. Not a bad plan, if the Jamaicans were honest gangsters and they didn't change their mind and come back for the other half of their money. It reminded me that I hadn't told her about my visit from the DEA. I told her. She smiled.

"How sweet," was all she said.

"So, what now?" I asked.

"Now, we get you to a hospital, and I drive south."

"A Mexican hospital?" I asked.

"God, no, that would probably cost you both eyes," she said.

"What were you doing in San Diego when we called?" I asked.

"That was the last specialist I saw before I was sure I would head to Mexico."

I nodded.

She eased the accelerator down; we picked up speed. I closed my eyes, really just one eye, and leaned my head against the window. I texted Chy and told her where I was. It looked like it went through, but I wouldn't be sure or see her answer until later. Brooke turned the radio on. She made a call. I knew where we were going. Where I was going wasn't a bad idea unless I couldn't get back out. I'd have to take that chance. If I ran now, I'd lose the eye and maybe more.

She took a cut-off path just before a billboard and drove another three miles. We came to a clearing with sparse trees on each side of a patchwork barbed-wire fence drooping between rusty posts. She parked the Yukon and turned the volume up on an old Gordon Lightfoot song. We were a long way from the gloomy November skies up in the Great Lakes. It was a long song. It was just easing into silence when a U.S. Border Patrol Chevy Tahoe pulled up on the American side of the border.

A female agent stepped out. Green jumpsuit with duty rig, exterior green tactical vest with U.S. Border Patrol in blocky gold letters on the right-side, a radio tucked into a center pocket, her badge was over her left breast, the microphone clipped to an epaulette on her left shoulder, hanging slightly down towards her chin. Her hair was in a messy ponytail behind a headband. Her skin was fresh. She wasn't wearing any jewelry. She smiled at Brooke and gave a slight wave. Brooke smiled back and offered the same hesitant wave.

"Friend," I asked.

"Used to be. I was her field training officer when she first got out of the academy. She's a few years younger." I got the feeling they'd had a falling out. I sensed in her the pain of regret.

"Obviously," I said. I couldn't resist. She smiled.

"You're such an asshole. Don't screw her."

"I'm flattered, that you even think I could. Hot younger woman. My eye all chewed up."

"Don't be flattered. It's not you, just her lack of options out here. Even you might look good to her even though you never did to me." She smiled.

"I'll try to behave," I said and started to walk towards the gate in the fence. Brooke's former protégé hadn't moved.

"Dan," Brooke said in a softer voice. I stopped and turned.

"Good luck..." she said. She paused. "In case I don't see you again." She climbed out of the car, reached into her pocket, and pulled an envelope out. She held it towards me. "Give her this," she handed me the envelope.

"I will."

"Thanks," she said.

"Do me a favor. Get rid of this?" I handed her the Smith & Wesson .38. "Dump it somewhere in Mexico."

She glanced at it as I handed it to her butt first.

"I will," she echoed. "Just what I always wanted. What a sweet parting gift."

There was an awkward moment and then we hugged. She stood on her tiptoes and kissed me on the cheek. As she pulled away, her eyes were sad, and tears welled in them. She turned and walked away.

I walked towards the Border Patrol vehicle and handed the envelope to Brooke's protégé. Her last name, Griffith, was stitched above her breast on the opposite side of her badge. Her eyes grew curious. I could tell she wanted to open it, but she slipped it into her pocket. She pulled a pair of handcuffs from a pouch on her hip.

"Gotta cuff you if I'm going to take you in," she said, holding them out towards me. Her voice was soft.

"Thought we'd wait for that kind of stuff," I said. She smiled. Her teeth were perfect. She glanced at the eye quickly and then politely acted as if she didn't notice it.

"You'll be waiting a long time," she said. I held my hands out and she clicked the cuffs around them.

"I'll settle for your first name," I said.

"You'll have to settle a lot more than that," she said. "But it's Reese. I can only imagine what Brooke told you about me."

I let it pass. She opened the door. I slipped into the back seat. There was a Plexiglas divider in front of me. My patrol car in Atlanta had an old-school wire cage that let the perps spit on you. It was the first time I'd ridden like a perp. She got in and blasted the AC. The frosty air reached the back. It felt good on my eye which had been in an ember-slow burn since the acid was thrown in my face. She drove fast, like cops do and took me straight to a hospital. We walked inside, she checked me in for in-custody medical treatment. An hour later, a doctor looked at my eye.

"What happened," he asked.

"Long story," I said. But he never heard it.

56.

A WEEK LATER, I left the hospital. Reese picked me up. She still drove fast. The Border Patrol substation was a squat, single-story sandstone building with a red Spanish-style roof. A large radio tower loomed over it. We pulled up to an intake entrance in the back. She did some paperwork.

"Good luck," she said, as she escorted me down a short hall to a row of holding cells.

"Hey, I had fun too," I said. She smiled. "The letter from Brooke was good?"

"Yeah," Reese said. "I talked to her last night. We caught up."

We walked to the end of the row, to a vacant cell. She opened the door. I stepped in. She pulled the door closed. It clicked. She looked at me.

"I've got some leave time. I might take a quick trip to Brazil. It was good to talk to her," she said. "Very good," she gave me a final smile before she started to walk away. She turned back.

"Brooke told me something else," she started. There was no way in hell this was good news.

"Paul Silva shot himself. They found him in his house. Gunshot wound to the head. His cell phone was lying next to him. No note. I'm sorry," she said, and walked away. I thought back to my last conversation with Paul. I thought the sound was him hanging up. I guess I was wrong. I was in a cell for three days.

MY MIND TICKED through the different combination of charges that could be in the various databases. Border Patrol had no interest in me. I was born in the U.S., a citizen. I couldn't be deported. They'd transfer me over to another agency, most likely the FBI It was the Bureau's kind of case. The warrants were in NCIC, they'd come up with some interstate nexus to give them jurisdiction, I was already in custody. More press releases than sweat.

I stood up in the holding cell when I heard a man approaching. He was a squat Hispanic, with a wide chiseled forehead. His uniform was crisp. The leather of his duty belt was worn smooth, the leather cracked in places. Not his first day on the job. The creases around his dark eyes made me think of the endless desert roads he'd patrolled, the bullets fired and the fistfights in dirt and sand, streaked with blood in a type of wild west the public didn't comprehend. He pushed numbers into an electronic keypad, and the door opened with a click. He pulled it to the side and waved me out.

"I'm free?" I asked.

"Far as the Border Patrol is concerned. We got a call from Mississippi Bureau of Investigation with new information. NCIC shows everything voided. For now, anyway, according to MBI at least."

He walked me around three corners into the same booking area I entered through. He handed me an envelope with my personal effects. My name was written in Sharpie across the front. I looked through the bulletproof glass. Jamie stood in the far corner on her cell phone. I could see her gold sheriff's star on a chain around her neck. I watched her until the squat man interrupted me.

"Sangre was an unhinged wretch," the agent said. "Everyone's better off without him, Mexicans, gringos, everyone. Who knows, maybe you even saved some of these young girls from something. Maybe even made a difference. Who knows?" It was clear he thought I killed him.

"Still got hope, huh?" I asked.

"Well, you know what the *Dirt Band* said, if you're ever going to see a rainbow, you got to stand a little rain." He smiled.

"You're in the desert. Ain't no rain" I said.

"Oh yeah," he said, still smiling. "I keep forgetting that. I read some background on you. You're a long way from your own deserts, the concrete kind. Atlanta. City too busy to hate, huh?"

"Well, people always seemed to fit it into their busy schedules. Maybe I'm just on vacation. Retired."

"Running's more like it."

"Think I'm running to something or from something?"

"Seems like from, and only you know what." He paused, and his drawl rolled a bit more. "But, amigo, I know one thing, whatever you've been running from, you ought to run to that." He nodded in Jamie's direction.

He opened the door. I shook his hand and walked into a waiting area with a row of pay phones, instructional signs in English and Spanish tacked to bulletin boards, molded plastic seats and a cluster of vending machines. Jamie looked up and folded the phone shut. We nodded a wordless hello. We both wanted to get the hell out of there. We walked out of the lobby and got in her car.

"The warrants…" I asked.

"Some were stalled; others voided. Some never filed. I reached out to a few friends," she said.

I didn't ask how many there had been, or which agencies had filed them. It had been a whirlwind of possibilities in the "most wanted" sense. Now I was thinking of other possibilities. There were two cups of coffee in the cup holders between us. I picked one up. It was still warm. I wasn't sure where she got the coffee but, as always, I was grateful. I took a sip.

"You were pretty confident it wouldn't take long to get me out," I said.

"I had a feeling," she said, picking up the other cup. I watched as she held it to her lips, sipped and then pulled it away. I could see the imprint of lipstick as she set it down.

"Who called from MBI, Chy?"

"One of the friends," she said, and I could tell by her tone that it was someone important from her past. Likely someone she hadn't wanted to call for a favor. I knew the feeling. I had a her; she had a him. Everyone has a past, I thought.

We drove and drank coffee until the Border Patrol station was a half-hour of desert nothingness behind us. I thought about one word the agent had said. Maybe. Maybe I had made a difference. Nice to think about rainbows in the desert, but I knew I hadn't changed a thing. Nothing. Dope, guns, chop shops, sex, whatever. There's a market, there's a supply. There's an endless market and an endless supply. With each arrest, you just knock out some other perps' competition. Expand his area. Give him more corners to pimp girls or sell dope. Whatever. Enough of this ghetto Keynesian shit, I thought.

I put the brakes on my rambling thoughts, broke the silence, and told her that I had a call to make. I glanced at my cell. No service. They were becoming increasingly rare, but we found a phone booth on the side of a small store with a faded RC Cola sign.

I dialed Brett King's office number.

"King," he answered like cops do.

"It's Stock," I said.

"Dan, I figured you'd be calling. About that gun?"

"Yeah, you talk to ATF again?"

"I didn't. She did. Told him that she pulled the file, and the match must be a mistake. That she had a destroy receipt from that gun going back a couple of years. Incinerated. Told him it wouldn't look too good if a gun that APD destroyed several years back showed up in a federal murder case now. She asked him for a favor."

"So, she lied," I said.

"Beckett got the hint. Said he'd run the numbers again. Doubted there'd be a match this time. Even if it was a second match, they'd attribute it to theft from the Atlanta weapon incinerator pool. Either way, the paperwork clearly says that you surrendered that gun after the thing with the off duty shoot and the East Point cop."

"Big favor," I said.

"As favors go, but she can be pretty convincing. There's also some kind of history there. She helped him out on some fraud thing or something involving his cousin a few years back."

"Thanks Brett," I hung up. I thought about her for a second. There was just enough love between us for one last lie. But that was all. I looked through the cracked glass of the phone booth. Jamie was leaning on her car, wearing sunglasses.

She drove to a motel with a scarred pool and a half-lit vacancy sign. I glanced over at her. It was time to get past even. We got a room. I slept well.

ACKNOWLEDGMENTS

I wrote *Out of the Blue* when I lived in North Mississippi and completed the manuscript in early 2008 before I moved to Northern Virginia. It has been a long journey to publishing and I offer my sincere thanks to Sean and everyone at Red Dog Press for their faith in my writing, for helping to make this dream a reality, and for inviting me to be a proud member of "The Kennel."

I have been blessed to have a great family and fantastic and loyal friends made at every stage of my personal and professional lives. As such, there are FAR too many people to thank generally so I will restrict these acknowledgments to only this project.

To Ace Atkins for his writing advice over the past two decades but even more for his friendship. Hopefully, I will get to Oxford soon for a Partagas Black cigar & Eagle Rare bourbon on a porch somewhere.

To the following for background information and encouragement specific to this project: Jeff Wenk, Aaron Joyce, Ron Rychlak, Michael Gorman, Dan and Janet Argiro and Jim and Rachel Waide.

To Natalie Gallagher-Gorman for muddling through a rough version of the manuscript and for her careful editing and excellent suggestions.

To you, the reader. I hope you enjoy *Out of the Blue* and look forward to the Dan Stock series. Please leave me a review on Amazon and Goodreads if you are willing. It means more than you know, especially to a debut author.

As an aside, I need to note that the *Red Dog Unit* was a real unit within the Atlanta Police Department (I was not just currying favor with my publisher).

Finally, and most importantly, to Sarah, my wife, and Diego, my stepson. I love you both and cannot imagine taking life's journey without you.

ABOUT THE AUTHOR

M.M. Harrold is a DC-based attorney for a federal agency. He has served as a TV and radio crime and trial analyst on major national and international networks including CNN, CNN HLN, FOX News and Court TV. He is a former Ole Miss law professor, George Mason University adjunct professor and City of Atlanta Police Officer.

Born in Huntington, West Virginia, he was raised in Mt. Lebanon, outside Pittsburgh, Pennsylvania, and then spent almost two decades living throughout the South in South Carolina, Georgia, Mississippi, and Tennessee.

His short stories have appeared in *Punk Noir Magazine* and *Close to the Bone.*

He lives in Northern Virginia with his family where he is working on the next Dan Stock thriller.

Lightning Source UK Ltd.
Milton Keynes UK
UKHW010207070223
416581UK00021B/762/J